The Chemical Garden Trilogy

Book

Two

F

Also by Lauren DeStefano

Wither

LAUREN
DESTEFANO

EVER

SIMON & SCHUSTER BFYR

New York London
Toronto Sydney New Delhi

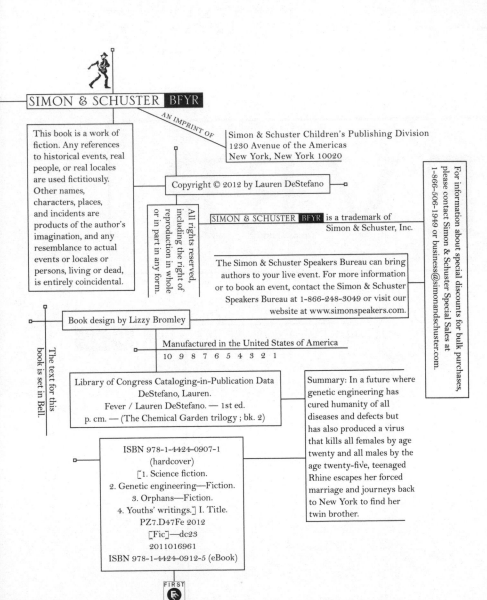

SIMON & SCHUSTER BFYR

AN IMPRINT OF

Simon & Schuster Children's Publishing Division
1230 Avenue of the Americas
New York, New York 10020

SIMON & SCHUSTER BFYR is a trademark of Simon & Schuster, Inc.

The Simon & Schuster Speakers Bureau can bring authors to your live event. For more information or to book an event, contact the Simon & Schuster Speakers Bureau at 1-866-248-3049 or visit our website at www.simonspeakers.com.

For information about special discounts for bulk purchases, please contact Simon & Schuster Special Sales at 1-866-506-1949 or business@simonandschuster.com.

Book design by Lizzy Bromley

The text for this book is set in Bell.

Manufactured in the United States of America
10 9 8 7 6 5 4 3 2 1

Library of Congress Cataloging-in-Publication Data
DeStefano, Lauren.
Fever / Lauren DeStefano. — 1st ed.
p. cm. — (The Chemical Garden trilogy ; bk. 2)

ISBN 978-1-4424-0907-1 (hardcover)
[1. Science fiction. 2. Genetic engineering—Fiction. 3. Orphans—Fiction. 4. Youths' writings.] I. Title.
PZ7.D47Fe 2012
[Fic]—dc23
2011016961
ISBN 978-1-4424-0912-5 (eBook)

Summary: In a future where genetic engineering has cured humanity of all diseases and defects but has also produced a virus that kills all females by age twenty and all males by the age twenty-five, teenaged Rhine escapes her forced marriage and journeys back to New York to find her twin brother.

FIRST EDITION

FOR AMANDA L-C,

WHO BRAVELY

LOSES HERSELF

IN THE RAIN

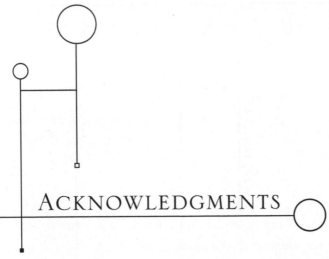

ACKNOWLEDGMENTS

I once again find myself with the impossible task of using this portion of my book to thank a group of people too astounding and too brilliant for words. My words are all that I have, however, so here goes . . .

Thanks to my family, who passed this story amongst one another, calling and texting me at every turn. And to my dad, who isn't here, but whose image is superimposed over every good thing that's happened in this process.

Thanks to Harry Lam, for not letting me take the easy way out of plot conundrums. To Allison Shaw, for hearing this story over steering wheels and across restaurant tables and through phone lines. To Amanda Ludwig-Chambers, who cried on my pages. To Andrew O'Donnell, who knew a thing or two about tarot cards. Thanks to the small crowd of you who willingly endured my moments of "please please please read this and tell me what you think" and offered honest critiques. Thanks to my former professors at Albertus Magnus College, who continue to cheer me on even now.

Thanks in triplicate to my editor, Alexandra Cooper, for understanding my very erratic language and for making every page of this story stronger. To Lizzy Bromley, whose covers for this series are an enchanted magnifying glass to what's inside. Thanks to the entire crew at Simon & Schuster Books for Young Readers for being so passionate and for believing in Rhine's story. Thanks again and always and eternally to my agent, Barbara Poelle, who opened all the doors and cleared all the paths so that I could step into this world to share my stories.

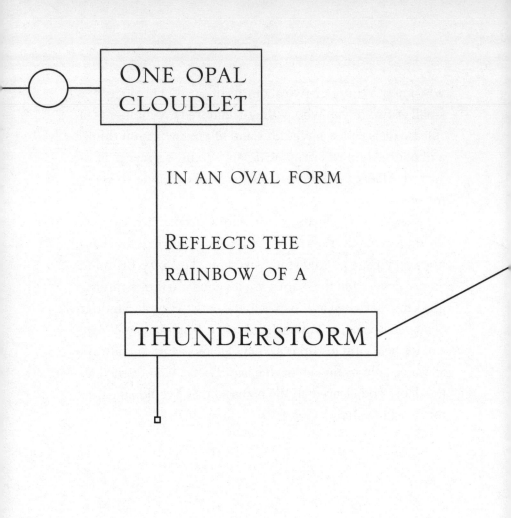

ONE OPAL
CLOUDLET

IN AN OVAL FORM

REFLECTS THE
RAINBOW OF A

THUNDERSTORM

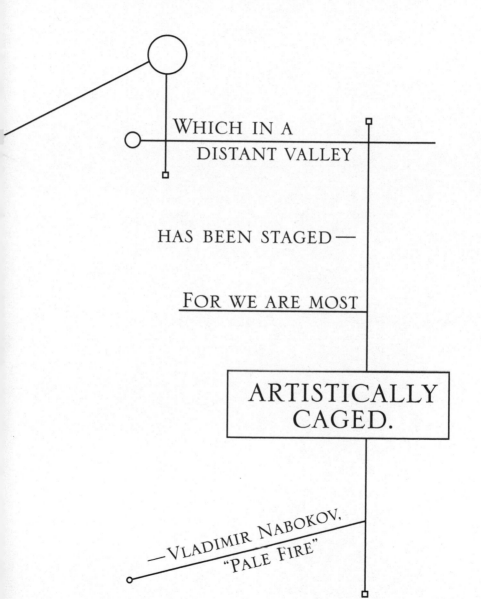

WHICH IN A
DISTANT VALLEY

HAS BEEN STAGED —

FOR WE ARE MOST

ARTISTICALLY
CAGED.

—VLADIMIR NABOKOV,
"PALE FIRE"

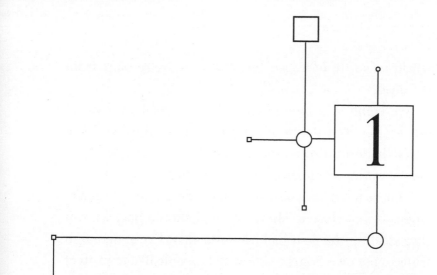

WE RUN, with water in our shoes and the smell of the ocean clinging to our frozen skin.

I laugh, and Gabriel looks at me like I'm crazy, and we're both out of breath, but I'm able to say, "We made it," over the sound of distant sirens. Seagulls circle over us impassively. The sun is melting down into the horizon, setting it ablaze. I look back once, long enough to see men pulling our escape boat to shore. They'll be expecting passengers, but all they'll find are the empty wrappers from the packaged sweets we ate from the boat owner's stash. We abandoned ship before we reached the shore, and we felt for each other in the water and held our breath and hurried away from the commotion.

Our footprints emerge from the ocean, like ghosts are roaming the beach. I like that. We are the ghosts of sunken countries. We were once explorers when the world was full, in a past life, and now we're back from the dead.

We come to a mound of rocks that forms a natural barrier between the beach and the city, and we collapse in its shadows. From where we're huddled we can hear men shouting commands to one another.

"There must have been a sensor that tripped the alarm when we got close to shore," I say. I should have known that stealing the boat had been too easy. I've set enough traps in my own home to know that people like to protect what's theirs.

"What happens if they catch us?" Gabriel says.

"They don't care about us," I say. "Someone paid a lot of money to make sure that boat is returned to them, I bet."

My parents used to tell me stories about people who wore uniforms and kept order in the world. I barely believed those stories. How can a few uniforms possibly keep a whole world in order? Now there are only the private detectives who are employed by the wealthy to locate stolen property, and security guards who keep the wives trapped at luxurious parties. And the Gatherers, of course, who patrol the streets for girls to sell.

I collapse against the sand, faceup. Gabriel takes my shivering hand in both of his. "You're bleeding," he says.

"Look." I cant my head skyward. "You can already see the stars coming through."

He looks; the setting sun lights up his face, making his eyes brighter than I've ever seen, but he still looks

worried. Growing up in the mansion has left him permanently burdened. "It's okay," I tell him, and pull him down beside me. "Just lie with me and look at the sky for a while."

"You're bleeding," he insists. His bottom lip is trembling.

"I'll live."

He holds up my hand, enclosed in both of his. Blood is dripping down our wrists in bizarre little river lines. I must have sliced my palm on a rock as we crawled to shore. I roll up my sleeve so that the blood doesn't ruin the white cabled sweater that Deirdre knitted for me. The yarn is inlaid with diamonds and pearls—the very last of my housewife riches.

Well, those and my wedding ring.

A breeze rolls up from the water, and I realize at once how numb the cold air and wet clothes have made me. We should find someplace to stay, but where? I sit up and take in our surroundings. There's sand and rocks for several more yards, but beyond that I can see the shadows of buildings. A lone freight truck lumbers down a faraway road, and I think soon it'll be dark enough for Gatherer vans to start patrolling the area with their lights off. This would be the perfect place for them to hunt; there don't appear to be any streetlights, and the alleyways between those buildings could be full of scarlet district girls.

Gabriel, of course, is more concerned about the blood. He's trying to wrap my palm with a piece of seaweed, and the salt is burning the wound. I just need a minute to take this all in, and then I'll worry about the cut. This time yesterday I was a House Governor's bride. I had sister wives. At the end of my life, my body would have ended up with the wives who'd died before me, on a rolling cart in my father-in-law's basement, for him to do only he knows what.

But now there's the smell of salt, sound of the ocean. There's a hermit crab making its way up a sand dune. And something else, too. My brother, Rowan, is somewhere out here. And there's nothing stopping me from getting home to him.

I thought the freedom would excite me, and it does, but there's terror, too. A steady march of what-ifs making their way through all of my deliciously attainable hopes.

What if he's not there?

What if something goes wrong?

What if Vaughn finds you?

What if . . .

"What are those lights?" Gabriel asks. I look where he's pointing and see it too, a giant wheel of lights spinning lazily in the distance.

"I've never seen anything like it," I say.

"Well, someone must be over there. Come on."

He pulls me to my feet and tugs my bleeding hand, but I stop him. "We can't just go wandering off into lights. You don't know what's over there."

"What's the plan, then?" he asks.

The plan? The plan was only to escape. Accomplished. And now the plan is to reach my brother, a thought I romanticized over the sullen months of my marriage. He became almost a figment of my imagination, a fantasy, and the thought that I'll be reunited with him soon makes me light-headed with joy.

I had thought we could at least make it to land dry, and during the daylight, but we ran out of fuel. And we're losing daylight by the second; it's not any safer here than anywhere else, and at least there are lights over there, eerie as they may be, spinning like that. "Okay," I say. "We'll check it out."

The impromptu seaweed wrap seems to have staunched the bleeding. It's so carefully tied that it's amusing, and Gabriel asks what I'm smiling about as we walk. He is dripping wet and plastered with sand. His normally neat brown hair is in tangles. Yet he still seems to be searching for order, some logical course of action. "It's going to be okay, you know," I tell him.

He squeezes my good hand.

The January air is in a fury, kicking up sand and howling through my drenched hair. The streets are full of trash, something rustling in a mound of it, and a single flickering streetlight has come on. Gabriel wraps his arm around me, and I'm not sure which of us he means to comfort, but my stomach is churning with the early comings of fear.

What if a gray van comes lumbering down that dark road?

There are no houses nearby—just a brick building that was maybe once a fire department half a century ago, with broken and boarded windows. And a few other crumbling things that are too dark for me to make out. I could swear that things are moving in the alleys.

"Everything looks so abandoned," Gabriel says.

"Funny, isn't it?" I say. "Scientists were so determined to fix us, and when we all started dying, they just left us here to rot, and the world around us too."

Gabriel makes a face that could be perceived as disdain or pity. He has spent most of his life in a mansion, where he may have been a servant, but at least things were well-constructed, clean, and reasonably safe. If you avoided the basement, that is. This dilapidated world must be a shock.

The circle of light in the distance is surrounded by bizarre music, something hollow and brassy masquerading as cheerful. "Maybe we should go back," Gabriel says when we get to the chain-link fence surrounding it. Beyond the fence I can see tents illuminated by candlelight.

"Go back to what?" I say. I'm shivering so hard, I can barely get the words out.

Gabriel opens his mouth to speak, but the words are lost by my own scream, because someone is grabbing my arm and pulling me through an opening in the fence.

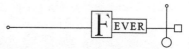

All I can think is, *Not again, not like this*, and then my wound is bleeding again and my fist is hurting because I've just hit someone. I'm still hitting when Gabriel pulls me away, and we try to run, but we're being overpowered. More figures are coming out of the tents and grabbing our arms, waists, legs, even my throat. I can feel the skin bunching under my nails, and someone's skull crashing against mine, and then I'm dizzy, but some otherworldly thing keeps me violently moving in my own defense. Gabriel is yelling my name, telling me to fight, but it doesn't do any good. We're being dragged toward that spinning circle of light, where an old woman is laughing, and the music doesn't stop.

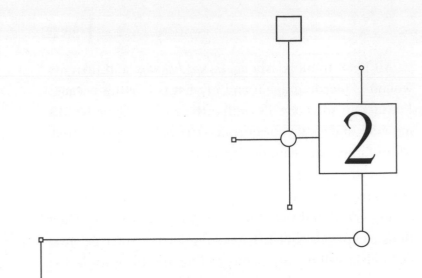

THE SICK SOUND OF bone hitting skin.

Gabriel lands a perfect punch that sends one of the men crashing backward onto the dirt, but then there are others grabbing his arms and kneeing him from all sides.

"Who do you work for?" The old woman's voice is calm. Smoke billows out of her mouth and from a stick held in her fingers. "Who sent you to spy on me?" She's a first generation, short and stocky, with gray hair arranged in a bun encrusted with gaudy glass rubies and emeralds. Rose, who over the years had been showered by our husband, Linden, with trinkets and gems, would laugh at this cheap jewelry— the oversize pearls hanging from the woman's chicken-skin neck; the silver bangles, rusted and peeling, that run up to her forearm; the ruby ring as big as an egg.

The men are holding Gabriel up by his arms, and he's struggling to stay on his feet, when another man hits him. A boy, really; he can't be any older than Cecily.

"Nobody sent us," Gabriel says. I can see in his eyes that he's not entirely here right now. He took the worst from our assailants, and I'm worried he might have a concussion. He takes another punch, this one to the ribs, and it sends him to his knees. My stomach lurches.

One of the men has got me by the throat, and two others by the arms, and all of them are smaller than me. It's so difficult to see them as boys, even though that's what they are.

Gabriel's eyes are closing and then jolting open; his breath escapes in fluttery astonished gasps. My heart is pounding in my ears; I want to go to him, but the only thing that reaches him is my frustrated whimper. This is all my fault. I was supposed to be able to protect him; this is my world. I should have had a plan. I mutter something indignant and snap, "He's telling the truth; we're not spies." Who would spy on a place like this?

Filthy girls are peeking out from a slit in the rainbow-striped tent, blinking like bugs. And I know immediately that this must be a scarlet district—a prostitution den of unwanted girls that Gatherers couldn't sell to House Governors, or who simply had nowhere else to go.

"You shut up," one of the men—boys—says into my ear. The old woman cackles and clatters with fake jewels that are like big glass insects and infectious boils on her fingers and wrists.

"Bring her into the light," the old woman says. They drag me into the rainbow-striped tent below a ceiling of swaying lanterns, and the bug-girls scatter. The old woman grabs my jaw and tilts my head for a better look. Then she hocks spit onto my cheek and smears it, clearing away some of the blood and sand. Her black, horrible eyes light up with joy, and she says, "Goldenrod. Yes, I think that's what I'll call you." The smoke makes my eyes water. I want to spit back at her.

The girls in the tent moan their protest, and one of them raises her head. "Madame," she says. Her eyes are languid and filmy. "It's after sunset. It's time."

The old woman backhands her, and in that same calm voice she says, as she examines her jeweled fingers, "You do not tell me. *I* tell *you*."

The girl sinks in with the others and disappears.

Gabriel spits a mouthful of blood. The boys tug him to his feet.

"Bring her into the red tent," the old woman says. It doesn't matter that I've slumped to a dead weight and refuse to move my legs; two of the boys have no trouble dragging me away.

This is it, I think. *Gabriel is going to die, and this old woman intends to make me one of her prostitutes.* I can only assume that's what those girls in the rainbow tent are. All that trouble to escape, all Jenna's efforts to help me, for less than one day of freedom before a new hell emerged.

The red tent is lit up by lanterns that hang from the low ceiling. One of the lanterns hits my head, and when

the boys let go of me, I drop to the cold earth. "Don't go anywhere," one of the boys, who is about a foot shorter than me, says. He pulls back his moth-eaten coat to show me a gun holstered in the waist of his pants. The other boy laughs, and they leave. I can see their silhouettes taking shape outside the zippered doorway, hear their sneering laughter.

I scan the tent for another opening I can wriggle through, but it's rooted into the ground, and much of it is bordered by furniture. Polished, ancient-looking bureaus and trunks with things like hissing dragons painted across the drawers, cherry blossoms, gazebos, black-haired women staring sullenly into the water.

Antiques from some Eastern country that's long gone. Rose would like these things. She would have stories for what's saddening the black-haired women, could chart a path among the cherry blossoms that would take her where she wanted to go. For a moment I think I see what she would—an infinite world.

"Now, then," the old woman says, appearing from nowhere and pulling me into one of two chairs on either side of a table. "Let's take a look at you."

Smoke ribbons up from a long cigarette held in the old woman's wrinkled fingers. She brings it to her lips for a breath, and smoke rolls through her mouth and nostrils when she speaks again. "You are not from this place. I would have noticed you." Her eyes, made up to match her jewels, are on mine. I look away.

"Those eyes," she says, leaning closer. "Are you malformed?"

"No," I say, forcing myself not to sound angry, because there's a boy with a gun outside, and Gabriel is still at this woman's mercy. "And we're not spies. I keep trying to tell you. We just took a wrong turn."

"This whole place is a wrong turn, Goldenrod," she says. "But tonight's your lucky night. If you're looking for a fancier district to do business in"—she flits her fingers dramatically, letting ashes fly—"you won't find any for miles. I'll take good care of you."

My stomach turns. I don't say a word, because if I open my mouth, I'm sure I'll vomit all over this beautiful antique table.

"I am Madame Soleski," the woman says. "But you call me Madame. Let me see that hand." She reaches across for my wrist and then slaps my bleeding left hand onto the table. The seaweed bandage is still holding on, though it's bunched from my fist and dripping with blood.

She raises my hand toward the lantern and gasps when she sees my wedding band. She's probably never seen real jewelry before. She sets her cigarette on the edge of the table and takes my hand in both of hers, examining the vines etched into my wedding band, the blossoms that Linden often copied along his building designs when he was thinking of me. They were fictional, he said. No such flower blooms in this world.

I clench my fist again, worried she'll try to steal the

ring. Even if that marriage was a sham, this small piece of it belongs to me.

Madame Soleski admires it for a moment longer, then lets go of my hand. She rummages through one of her drawers and returns with gauze that looks like it's been used, and a bottle of clear liquid. The liquid burns when she clears away the seaweed and pours it onto my wound. It bubbles and hisses angrily. She's watching me for a reaction, but I won't give her one. She dresses my palm with gauze expertly.

"You've messed up one of my boys," she says. "He'll have a black eye tomorrow."

Not good enough. I still lost the fight.

Madame Soleski fingers the sleeve of my sweater, and I resist, but she digs her fingers into my bandaged wound. I don't want her touching me. Not my wedding hand, and not this sweater. I think of Deirdre's small, capable hands making it for me; they were etched with bright blue veins—her soft skin the only indication of her youth. Those hands could turn bathwater to magic, or thread diamonds into her knitting. Precision was in everything she created. I think of her wide hazel eyes, the soft melody of her voice. I think of how I will never see her again.

"Leave the bandage put," she says, picking up her cigarette and tapping away some ash. "Wouldn't want to get an infection and lose that hand. You have such exquisite fingers."

I can no longer see the outlines of the boys standing guard outside, but I hear them talking. The gun was
much smaller than the shotgun my brother and I kept in
the basement, but if I could get my hands on it, I could
figure it out. But how quick would I be? Some of the others might have weapons too. And I can't leave without
Gabriel. It's my fault that he's even here.

"Don't speak unless spoken to, huh, Goldenrod? I like
that. This isn't exactly a talking business."

"I'm not a part of your business," I say.

"No?" The old woman raises her penciled eyebrows.
"You look as though you have been running from some
other kind of business. I can offer you protection. This is
my territory."

Protection? I could laugh. I have sore ribs and a
throbbing forehead that suggest otherwise right now.
What I say is, "We got a little lost, but we'll be on our
way if you'd let us go. We have family waiting for us in
North Carolina."

The woman laughs and takes a languid breath through
her cigarette, her bloodshot eyes never leaving mine.

"Nobody with a family finds their way here. Come,
let me show you the pièce de résistance." She says those
last words with a practiced accent. Her cigarette has run
out, and she stomps it with her high-heeled shoe, which
appears to be a size too small.

She leads me outside, and the boys standing guard
immediately stop their laughing as she passes. One of

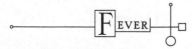

them tries to trip me with his foot, and I step around it.

"This is my kingdom, Goldenrod," Madame says. "My carnival of *amour*. You wouldn't know what *'amour'* is, of course."

"It's 'love,'" I answer, gratified when her eyebrows raise in surprise. Foreign languages are something of a lost art, but my brother and I had the rare advantage of parents who valued education. Even if we could never use it, even if we could never grow to be linguists or explorers, the knowledge filled our minds, brightened our daydreams. Sometimes we ran through the house, pretending we were parasailing high over the Aleutians, that later we'd sip green tea under the plum blossoms in Kyoto, and at night we squinted at the starry darkness and pretended we could see our neighboring planets. "Do you see Venus?" my brother said. "It's a woman's face, and her hair is on fire." We were crammed in the open window, and I answered, "Yes, yes, I see it! And Mars is crawling with worms."

Madame wraps her arm around my shoulders and squeezes. She smells like decay and smoke. "Ah, love. That's what the world has lost. There's no more love, only the illusion of it. And that's what draws the men to my girls. That's what it's all about."

"Which?" I say. "Love, or illusion?"

Madame chuckles, squeezes me again. I am reminded of the long walk I took with Vaughn through the golf course that one chilly afternoon, how his presence

seemed to erase all the good in the world, how it felt like an anaconda was coiling around my chest. And all the while, Madame brings me to her spinning circle of light. What is it with first generations and their collection of breathtaking things? I hate myself for being intrigued.

"You know your *français*," Madame says pertly. "But here is a word I bet you haven't heard." Her eyes widen with intensity. "Carnival."

I know the word. My father tried to describe carnivals to my brother and me. Celebrations for when there was nothing to celebrate, he'd say. I could understand, but Rowan couldn't, so the next day when we woke up, there were ribbons draped all over our bedroom, and a cake was waiting on our dresser with forks and cranberry seltzer, which was my favorite, but we almost never had any because it was so hard to find. And we didn't go to school that day. My father played strange music on the piano, and we spent the day celebrating nothing at all, except maybe that we were all alive.

"This is what carnivals were all about," Madame says. "They called it a Ferris wheel."

Ferris wheel. The only thing in this whole wasteland of abandoned rides that isn't rotting or rusted.

Now that I'm close enough to really look at it, I can see that the wheel is full of seats, and there's a little staircase leading up to the lowest point. The chipped paint reads: ENTER HERE.

"It didn't work when I found it, of course," Madame

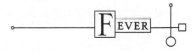

goes on. "But my Jared is something of a genius with electrical things."

I say nothing, but tilt my head to watch the seats spinning against the night sky. The wheel makes a rusted creaking groan as it goes, and for just a moment, I hear laughter in that eerie brass music.

My parents have looked up at Ferris wheels. They were a part of this lost world.

One of the boys is leaning on the railing surrounding the thing, and he eyes me warily. "Madame?" he says.

"Bring it to a stop," she says.

A cold breeze swirls around me, and it's ripe with antique melodies and the smell of rust and all of Madame's strange foreign perfumes. An empty seat comes to a stop before the staircase where I stand. Madame's bracelets clack and clatter as she lays her hand on my spine and presses me forward, saying, "Go on, go on."

I don't think I can stop myself. I climb the stairs, and the metal shudders beneath my feet and sends tremors up my legs. The seat rocks a little as I settle into it. Madame sits beside me and pulls the overhead bar down so that it locks us in. We start to move, and I'm breathless for an instant as we ascend forward and into the sky.

The earth gets farther and farther away. The tents look like bright round candies. The girls move about them, shadows.

I can't help myself; I lean forward, astounded. This wheel is five, ten, fifteen times taller than the lighthouse

I climbed in the hurricane. Higher even than the fence that kept me trapped as Linden's bride.

"This is the tallest place in the world," Madame says. "Taller than spy towers."

I've never heard of a spy tower, but I doubt they're taller than the factories and skyscrapers in Manhattan. Even this wheel couldn't claim as much. Maybe, though, it's the tallest place in Madame's world. I could believe that.

And as we make our way toward stars that feel frighteningly attainable, I feel myself missing my twin. He was never one for whimsical things. Since our parents' death, he's stopped believing in things more fantastic than bricks and mortar, less horrific than ominous alleyways where girls become soulless and men pay for five minutes with their bodies. His every moment is consumed with survival—his and mine. But even my brother, who is all practicality, would have his breath taken away by this height, these lights, the clarity of this night sky.

Rowan. Even his name feels far away from me now.

"Look, look." Madame points eagerly. Her girls are milling below in their dingy, exotic clothes. One of them twirls, and her skirt fills up with air, and her laughter echoes like hiccups. A man grabs her pale arm, and still she laughs, tripping and flailing as he drags her into a tent.

"You've never seen girls as beautiful as mine," Madame says. But she's wrong—I have. There was Jenna, with her gray eyes that always caught the light, her grace;

she would swirl and hum through the hallways, her nose buried in a romance novel the whole time. The attendants blushed and averted their eyes, she so intimidated them with her confidence, her coy smiles. In a place like this she would have been a queen.

"They want a better life. They run away, come here to me. I deliver their babies, I cure their sniffles, I feed them, keep them clean, give them nice things for their hair. They come to this place asking for me." She grins. "Maybe you've heard of me too. You've come here for my help." She takes my left hand with a force that rocks our car. I tense, thinking we'll capsize, but we don't. We've stopped ascending now; we're at the top. I look out over the side. There's no way down, and the fear starts to set in. Madame controls this thing. If I wasn't completely at her mercy before, I am now.

I force myself to stay calm. I won't let her have the satisfaction of my panicking; it would only empower her.

My heart is thudding in my ears.

"That boy you came here with—he is not the one who gave you this beautiful wedding ring, is he." It's not a question. She tries to slide the ring from my finger, but I make a fist and draw away.

"Both of you show up like drowned rats," she says. Her laughter creaks like the rusty gears that hold our car together. "But under that you are all sparkles and pearls. *Real* pearls." She's looking at my sweater. "And he is made up like a lowly attendant."

I can't deny any of this. She's managed to sum up the last several months of my life perfectly.

"Running off with your attendant, Goldenrod, behind the back of the man who made you his wife? Did your husband force himself on you? Or maybe he couldn't satisfy you, and so you met with that boy of yours in secret—in secret, late at night, rustling in your closet among your silk dresses like a pair of savages."

My cheeks burn, but it's not like the embarrassment I felt when my sister wives teased me about my lack of intimacy with Linden. This is sick and invasive. Wrong. And Madame's smoky stench is making it hard to breathe. The height is making me dizzy. I close my eyes.

"It isn't like that," I say through gritted teeth.

"It's nothing to be ashamed of," Madame says, wrapping her arm around my shoulders. I catch the whimper before it leaves my throat. "You're a woman, after all. Women are the fairer sex. And one as lovely as you— your husband must have turned into a beast around you. It's no wonder you found yourself a sweeter boy. And this one is sweeter, isn't he? I can see it in his eyes."

"His eyes?" I splutter, furious. When I open my eyes, I focus on one of Madame's gaudy hair gems so I don't have to look at her or the ground. "Before your henchmen beat him half to death?"

"That's another thing." Madame tenderly brushes the hair from my face. I jerk back, but she doesn't seem to

care. "*My* men know how to protect my girls. It's a rough world, Goldenrod. You need protection."

She grabs my chin, and her fingers press against my jawbone until it hurts. She stares at my eyes. "Or maybe," she sings, "your husband didn't want to pass this defect of yours on to his children. Maybe he threw you out with the trash."

Madame is a woman who loves to talk. And the more she says, the less accurate she becomes. I realize that she couldn't read me as easily as she thought. She's just probing through the options, hoping to get a rise out of me. I could lie to her and she wouldn't know.

"I'm not malformed," I say, feeling suddenly giddy about this small power I have over her. "My husband was."

This makes Madame beam with intrigue. She releases my face and leans close. "Oh?"

"He might have turned into a beast around me, but it didn't matter. Nine times out of ten, he couldn't do anything about it. And like you said, women have needs."

Madame bounces a little, rocking and creaking our car. It's clear she gets off on the idea of young lust. I hardly have to continue the lie; she's writing the rest of the story herself.

"And you were forced into the arms of your attendant."

"In my closet, like you said."

"Right under your husband's nose?"

"In the very next room."

She can have whatever deranged lie she wants. But

the truth, like my wedding band, is something of mine that she can't have.

The girls, hundreds of feet below, are a chorus of giggles. They all dance with the men for a while before disappearing into tents. And Madame's henchmen sometimes peel the opening in the tent for a glimpse.

"Oh, Goldenrod, you are a gem." She takes my face in her hands and kisses my cheek between the words. "A gem, a gem, an absolute gem! You and I will have great fun."

Great.

In a second we're orbiting backward. The music is louder the closer we come to the ground, and the girls sadder.

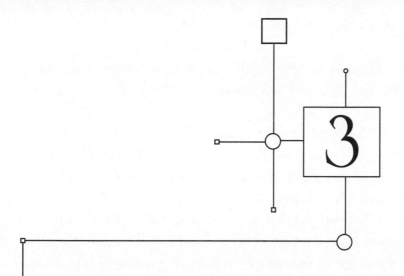

GABRIEL IS SLEEPING on the ground in the tent, curled up so closely to the wall of the tent that its green tinges his skin. There's a dingy blanket under him, and his shirt is gone.

Madame told me this is where I'll rest tonight, while she figures out what to do with me. There's a basin of water and some towels and soaps that look like they were hand-carved.

I wet a towel and dab at the red mark on Gabriel's cheek. Tomorrow it will be just one of many bruises. He mutters something, draws a breath.

"Did I hurt you?" I say.

He shakes his head, nuzzles his face against the ground.

"Gabriel?" I whisper. "Wake up." He doesn't answer me this time, even when I turn him onto his back and wring cold water over his face. My heart is pounding with fear. "Gabriel. Look at me."

He does, and his pupils are two small, startled dots in all that blue, and he's scaring me. "What did they do to you?" I say. "What happened?"

"The purple girl," he mumbles, smacking his lips and closing his eyes. "She had a . . . something." He moves his arm as though in indication. And then he's gone again. Shaking him does nothing.

"He'll be out for a few hours." One of the girls is standing at the tent's entrance, a blanket bunched in her arms. "He seemed like he was in a lot of pain. I just gave him a little something to help. Here." She offers me the blanket. "It's fresh off the laundry line."

She tries to help me cover him, but I shrug her away and snap, "You've helped enough, thanks. Whose fault is it that he was in pain to begin with?"

"Neither of you are from here," the girl nonchalantly says, wringing a towel out over the basin. "Madame is very paranoid about spies. If I didn't subdue him, she would have ordered the bodyguards to beat him unconscious. I was doing him a favor." There's no malice in the way she speaks. She hands me the wet towel, and she keeps a polite distance.

"What spies?" I ask, and gently rub away the sand and blood from Gabriel's face and arms. I don't like whatever is subduing him. He's all I have in this terrible place, and he's so far away.

"They don't exist," the girl says. "Most of what that woman says is nonsense. The opiates make her so paranoid."

What have we stumbled into? At least this girl is not as nightmarish as the rest. Under all that makeup I can see the sympathy in her eyes that are two small dark stars in a nebula of green eyeliner. Her skin is dark. Her short hair is curled into glossy ringlets. And she, like everything here, carries that musty-sweet scent that radiates from everything Madame has touched.

"Why did he call you 'the purple girl'?" I say.

"My name is Lilac," she says, and indicates the light purple flowers on her faded dress, the strap of which keeps falling off her shoulder. "Ask for me if you need anything else, okay? I have to get back to work."

She opens the tent flap, exposing the night sky and filling the tent with cold air and laughter, and the desperate grunts of men and the giggling of girls, and the steady rhythm of brass.

"This is my fault," I whisper. I trace the line between Gabriel's lips. "I'll get us out of here. I promise."

There's salt crusted in my hair, and I feel so grimy that it's tempting to climb into the basin to wash everything away. But whenever the bodyguards hear the water sloshing as I dip towels into it, they peer through the slit in the tent. Privacy is a lost practice in scarlet districts, I suppose. I settle for rolling up my sleeves and the legs of my jeans to wash as much as I can. Someone has laid out a silk dress for me—as green as this tent, with an orange dragon running up the side—but I don't wear it.

I curl up beside Gabriel, fitting my arm around him.

The soaps have left me with Madame's strange scent, but he still smells of the ocean. I feel his skin moving under my fingers as he breathes, his muscles in constant, steady motion over his ribs. I close my eyes, pretend his is an ordinary sleep and that saying his name would bring him right back to me.

Time passes. Girls come and go. I pretend I am asleep and strain to hear what they're whispering to each other. They say things I don't understand. Angel's blood. The new yellow. Dead greens. Men yell at them from a distance, and they go, their jewelry clattering like plastic shackles.

I feel myself falling asleep and try to fight it. But one minute I'm here, and the next I'm rocking on the glittering waves. One minute Gabriel is beside me, and then in the next, Linden is wrapping himself around me the way he did in sleep. He sobs in my ear and says his dead wife's name, and I open my eyes. The hard dirt and thin blanket is an unwelcome change from the fluffy white comforter I was just hallucinating, and for a moment Gabriel seems strange. His bright brown hair nothing like Linden's dark curls; his body thicker and less pale. I try rousing him again. No response.

I close my eyes, and this time I dream of snakes. Their hissing heads erupt from the dirt, and they coil around my ankles. They try to take off my shoes.

I wake in a panic. Lilac is kneeling at my feet, easing my socks off. "Didn't mean to scare you," she says. I feel

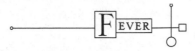

like hours have passed, but I can see through the slit in the tent that it's still nighttime.

"What are you doing?" My voice is hoarse. It's so cold in this tent that I can see my own breath. I don't know how these girls haven't frozen to death in their flimsy dresses.

"These are soaked. You have to keep extremities warm, you know. You could get pneumonia."

She's right, I *am* freezing. She wraps my bare feet in towels. I watch her as she rummages through a small suitcase. Her curls are disheveled, her dress more rumpled. When she kneels by Gabriel this time, she's got an array of things in a black handkerchief. She mixes powder and water in a spoon and takes a lighter to it until it bubbles, then draws it up into a syringe. Then she starts tying a strip of cloth around Gabriel's arm above the elbow—which is something my parents used to do before administering emergency sedatives to hysterical lab patients—and that's when I push her away. "Don't."

"It's going to help him," she says. "Keep him calm, keep you both out of trouble."

I think of the warm toxins flowing through my blood after I was injured in the hurricane, how Vaughn threatened me and I couldn't even muster the strength to open my eyes. How helpless and numb and terrified I was. I would rather have suffered the pain of my injuries, the broken bones, sprained limbs, stitched skin, than have been paralyzed.

"I don't care," I say. "You're not giving him anything."

She frowns. "Then, it's going to be a rough night."

I could laugh. "It already is."

Lilac opens her mouth to say something else, but a noise at the tent's entrance makes her turn her head. There's a moment of fear in her eyes; maybe she thought it would be a man, but then she relaxes. "You know you're supposed to stay hidden," she says. "You want to piss Madame off?"

She's talking to the child who has just crawled into the tent, not through the guarded entrance but through a small opening along the ground. Dark, stringy hair is covering her face. She moves more into the light, tilts her head to me, and her eyes are like marbled glass, so light they're barely even the color blue—a startling contrast to her dark skin.

Lilac sets down the spoon and pushes the child back in the direction she came from, saying, "Hurry up. Get lost before we both get hell for it."

The child goes, but not before pushing back and huffing indignantly through her nose.

Gabriel stirs, and I snap to attention. Lilac offers up the syringe again, gnawing her lip. I ignore it. "Gabriel?" My voice is very soft. I brush some hair from his face, and I realize how damp and clammy his forehead is. His face is splotchy with fever. His eyelashes flutter, but it's like he can't quite raise them.

Out in the night someone yelps in pain or maybe just

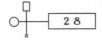

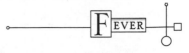

aggravation, and Madame's shrill voice cries, "Useless, filthy child!"

Lilac is on her feet the next instant, but she has left the syringe on the ground for me. "He'll want it," she tells me as she hurries for the exit. "He'll need it."

"Rhine?" Gabriel whispers. He's the only one in this broken carnival who knows my name. He screamed it in the gale, pieces of Vaughn's fake world whipping around us. He whispered it within the mansion's walls, leaning close to me. He's lured me from sleep that way, while my husband and sister wives slept before dawn. Always with such purpose, like it matters, like my name—like all of me—is a precious secret.

"Yes," I say. "I'm right here."

He doesn't answer, and I think he's lost consciousness again. I feel stranded, start to panic about him going back to that dark, unreachable place. But then he sucks in a hard breath and opens his eyes. His pupils are back to normal, no longer losing themselves in all that blue.

His teeth are chattering, and he's stuttering and slurring when he asks, "What is this place?"

Not *where*, but *what*. "It doesn't matter," I say, blotting some sweat from his face with my sleeve. "I'm going to get us out of here." We're both lost here, but of the two of us I have a better understanding of the outside world. Surely I can figure something out.

He stares at me for a long while, shuddering from the cold and the aftereffects of whatever was in that first syringe. And then he says, "The guards were trying to take you away."

"They took me," I say. "They took both of us."

I can see him fighting to stay awake. There's a dark bruise forming on his cheek; his mouth is chapped and bleeding; he's shaking so hard, I can feel it without touching him.

I wrap the blanket around him more snugly, trying to imitate the cocooning technique Cecily swaddled the baby with on a cold night. It was one of the few times she looked sure of what she was doing. "Rest," I whisper. "I'll be right here."

He watches me for a long time, his eyes darting up and down the length of my face. I think he's going to speak. I hope he will, even if it's just to say this is all my fault, that he told me the world was dangerous. I don't care. I just want him here with me. I want to hear his voice. But all he does is close his eyes, and then he's gone again.

I manage a fitful sleep beside him, shivering, covered with only a damp towel so Gabriel can have all the covers. I dream of crisp bed linens; of sparkling gold champagne that warms my throat and stomach as it goes down; of category-three winds rattling the edges, revealing bits of darkness behind a shiny perfect world.

I'm ripped from sleep by a gurgling, retching sound that at first makes me think I'm at my oldest sister wife's deathbed. But when I open my eyes, I see Gabriel doubled over in a far corner of our tent. The smell of vomit is not

quite as overwhelming as all the smoke and perfume that keeps this place in a perpetual smog.

I hurry to his side, all earnest, heart pounding. And now that I'm close to him, I can smell and see the coppery blood coming from a gash between his shoulder blades; the skin tears as he tenses his muscles. I don't remember there being any knives in the struggle, but we were ambushed so fast.

"Gabriel?" I touch his shoulder but can't bring myself to look at the stuff he's coughing up. When he's finished, I offer him a rag, and he takes it, slumping back on his heels.

It seems stupid to ask if he's all right, so I'm trying to get a good look at his eyes. Shades of purple are tiered under them, from dark to light. The cold is making clouds of his breath.

In the light of the swinging lantern, his own shadows dance behind his still form.

He says, "Where is this place?"

"We're in a scarlet district along the coastline. They gave you something; I think it's called angel's blood."

"It's a sedative," he says; his voice is slurred. He crawls back for the blanket and collapses facedown. "Housemaster Vaughn kept it in stock. Hospitals used to carry it, but they stopped because of the side effects."

He doesn't resist as I position him onto his side and draw the blanket over him. He's shivering. "Side effects?" I say.

"Hallucinations. Nightmares."

I think of the warmth that spread through my veins after the hurricane, think of being unable to move; Vaughn only kept me conscious long enough to threaten me. And though I don't remember it, Linden claimed I muttered horrible things while I dreamt.

"Can I do anything?" I say, tucking the blankets around his shoulders. "Are you thirsty?"

He reaches for me, and I let him draw me to his side. "I dreamt you'd drowned," he says. "Our boat was burning and there was no shore."

"Not possible," I say. His lips are chapped and bloody against my forehead. "I'm an excellent swimmer."

"It was dark," he says. "All I could see was your hair, going under. I dove after you and realized I was chasing a jellyfish. You were nowhere."

"I've been here," I say. "You're the one who's been nowhere. I couldn't wake you up."

He raises the blanket like a wing, wrapping me inside with him. It's warmer than I thought it would be, and I realize at once how much I've missed him while he's been under. I close my eyes, breathe deep. But the smell of the ocean is gone from his skin. He smells like blood and Madame's perfume, which lingers in the white soapy film that floats in all the water basins.

"Don't leave me again," I whisper. He doesn't answer. I reposition myself in his arms and draw back to look at his face. His eyes are closed. "Gabriel?" I say.

"You're dead," he mumbles sleepily. "I watched you

die"—his voice hitches with a yawn—"watched you die all those horrible deaths."

"Wake up," I tell him, and sit up, and pull the blankets away, hoping the sudden cold will shock him awake.

He opens his eyes, glossy like Jenna's when she was dying. "They were cutting your throat," he says. "You tried to scream, but you had no voice."

"It's not real," I say. My heart is pounding with fear. My blood is cold. "You're delirious. Look; I'm right here." My fingers brush his neck, which is flush and warm. I remember when we kissed, Linden's atlas between us; I remember the warm air of his little breaths on my tongue and chin and neck, the sudden draftiness when he drew back. Everything dissolved from around us in that moment, and I'd never felt so safe.

Now I worry that we'll never be safe again. If we ever were.

The rest of the night is miserable. Gabriel succumbs to an unreachable sleep, and I fight to stay awake so I can keep watch against the dangers that lurk beyond our green tent.

When I sleep, I dream of smoke. Curling, twisting, weaving paths that lead nowhere.

"—up!" someone is saying. "Rise and shine, little love-bird! *Réveille-toi!*"

An arm tightens around me. I snap to attention.

Madame is speaking in that phony accent again, her consonants flourishing like the smoke from her lips.

Daylight is a blinding force behind her, filling the silk outline of her scarves like rainbow lizard crests, making her face a shadow. And the whole tent is full of green, reflecting on my skin.

Sometime in the night Gabriel pulled me back into the blanket with him, and his arm is encircling my ribs. He buries his face in my hair, and I can feel the clamminess of his forehead. When I sit up, the movement doesn't rouse him. He doesn't regain consciousness at all.

The syringe. The syringe is no longer where Lilac left it.

Madame takes my hands and pulls me to my feet. She cups my face in her papery hands and smiles. "Even lovelier in the daylight, my Goldenrod."

I'm not her Goldenrod. I'm not her anything. But she seems to have claimed me as one of her possessions, her antiques, her plastic gems.

I will Gabriel not to mutter my name again. I don't want Madame to have it, rolling it off her tongue the way she fondled the flowers of my wedding band.

She pouts. "You do not want to wear the beautiful dress I laid out for you?" It hangs over her arm now like a deflated corpse, like the bloodless body of the girl who wore it last.

"Your sweater is so beautiful. How can you stand to wear it while it's filthy?" she says sadly. I think her frown

could melt right off her face. "One of the little ones will wash it for you." Her accent has morphed to something else now. All of her *THs* come out like *Zs*, and her *Ws* like *Vs*. *One of ze little ones vill vash it for you.*

She thrusts the dress at me, and unwinds a fur stole from her shoulders and drapes it around my neck. "Change. I'll wait for you outside. It's a beautiful day!"

I'll vait for you.

When she's gone, I change quickly, figuring it's my only way out of this tent. And I admit that the silk feels nice against my skin, and the stole, despite the choking must, is so warm I could get lost in it. Wearing these things may be the only way Madame lets me out of the tent, but what about Gabriel? Gabriel, who is still trapped in a haze. I kneel beside him and touch his forehead. I'm expecting it to be feverish, but it's cold.

"I'll get us out of here," I say again. No matter that he can't hear me; the words aren't entirely for him.

Madame peels back the tent flap and tsk-tsks, snagging my wrist and tugging so hard, I think of the time my arm was dislocated and my brother had to snap it back into place. "Don't worry about him," she says. My bare feet are dragging, and I realize I'm not really trying to keep pace with her.

As we leave the tent, two small girls sweep past us and gather my rumpled clothes. Their heads are down, mouths tight. I only get a glimpse of them, but I think they're twins. I'm pulled out into the cold sunshine, and the sky is a light candied blue, like I'm looking up through a sheet of ice. Madame fusses with my hair, which smells like a combination of salt water and a scarlet district. It feels heavy and tangled; her expression is distant, maybe disapproving, and I'm sure she's going to criticize it, but she only says, "Don't you worry about the boy." She grins, and I swear I can see my outline repeated in each of her too-white teeth. "He'll wake up when he can learn to be reasonable about sharing you."

In the daylight, without the commotion or the light of the Ferris wheel, I can see what a wasteland this place is. Long stretches of just dirt, or a rusty piece of machinery erupting from the ground like it's growing from a seed. There's another ride off in the distance, and at first I think it's a smaller Ferris wheel turned onto its side, but as we get closer, I can see metal horses inside of it, impaled by poles, their legs poised as though they were trying to escape before they were immobilized. Madame catches me staring and tells me it's called a merry-go-round.

The black eyes of the horses fill me with pain. I want to break the spell on them, to animate the muscles in their legs and set them running free.

Madame brings me to the rainbow tent, the biggest and tallest of them all. Four of her boys are guarding it, their guns crossed at their chests like half an X. They don't bother to look at me as Madame ushers me past, ruffling one of their heads.

She opens the tent flap, and a gust of cool air rolls in, unsettling the girls inside like wind chimes. They mutter and stir. Most of them are sleeping, piled against and atop one another.

The girls are all the same, like I'm looking into a house of mirrors. Long, bony limbs hunched against each other, and lipstick-smeared mouths full of rotted teeth. And for some girls it's not lipstick—it's blood. Unlit lanterns hang over their heads. The sun through the tent lights them up in oranges and greens and reds.

And farther down is the entryway to another tent that is veiled off by silk scarves trailing sickly sweet perfume, and something else. Decay and sweat. When Rose was dying, she concealed herself in powders and blush, but Jenna didn't, and as I cared for Jenna during those final days, I could see her sallow skin beginning to bruise, and then the bruises would sink down to the bones and fester. It was a smell that haunted my dreams. My sister wife rotting from the inside out.

"I call this my greenhouse," Madame says. "The girls sleep all day, so they can be fresh as daisies in the evening. Lazy girls."

A few of the girls bother to look at me, blinking lazily and then returning to sleep.

She says she names the girls after colors, so she can keep track of them. Lilac is the only girl named for a color that is also a plant, because Jared, one of Madame's best bodyguards, first found her lying unconscious in the lilac shrubs that border the vegetable gardens. "Belly about to burst," Madame jokes, laughing maniacally. Lilac gave birth under a swinging lantern in the circus tent, surrounded by curious Reds and Blues. And the Greens, Jade and Celadon, who have since died of the virus.

"Nasty, useless little girl," Madame Soleski says, indicating the little girl from last night with the strange eyes, who has crept out from a shadow. "One look at that shriveled leg and I knew on the day she was born that I'd never be able to get a decent price for her when she was the right age. But she can't even be put to work! She scares the customers away. She bites them!"

Lilac, who is burrowed among the others, draws her daughter into her arms without opening her eyes. "Her name is Maddie," she mutters, her voice slurred.

"Mad is right," Madame Soleski says, nudging the child with her shoe. Maddie cants her head up at her with a violent stare. She snaps her little teeth at the old woman, venomous and defiant. "And she doesn't speak!" Madame goes on. "Malformed. Horrible, horrible girl. She should be put down. Did you know that a hundred years ago when an animal was useless, they used to have a chemical that would put it to sleep forever?"

The smell of so many girls in such a small space is making me dizzy, and so are Madame's words. One of the girls is twirling her hair, and it's falling out in her hands.

A guard stands in the entryway. When nobody else is looking, I watch him reach into his pocket and then hold

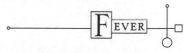

out a strawberry for Maddie. She pops it into her mouth, stem and all, a delicious secret she devours whole.

I hear a noise from the tent that's veiled off. I think it's a cough, or a groan. Either way, I don't want to know. Madame is unfazed, and tightens her arm around my shoulders. I fight to keep my breathing even, but I want to cry out. I'm furious—maybe as furious as I was when I climbed out of the Gatherers' van. I stood very still in a line with the other girls. I said nothing when I heard the first gunshot—the unwanted girls being murdered one at a time. There are so many of us, so many girls. The world wants us for our wombs or our bodies, or it doesn't want us at all. It steals us, destroys us, piles us like dying cattle in circus tents and leaves us lying in filth and perfume until we're wanted again.

I ran from that mansion because I wanted to be free. But there's no such thing as free. There are only different and more horrible ways to be enslaved.

And I feel something I've never felt before. Anger at my parents for bringing my brother and me into this world. For leaving us to fend for ourselves.

Maddie stares at me, her eyes glassy and bizarre. This is the first time I've really looked at her. She's obviously malformed—not just the strange, almost colorless blue of her eyes. In addition to her shriveled leg, one of her arms, the left, is shorter and much thinner than the other; her toes are almost nonexistent, as though something kept them from growing all the way out of her feet. But her face is angular and sharp, her expression all fearlessness and ire. It is the face of a girl who has seen the world, who realizes that it hates her, and who hates it in return.

Maybe that's why she doesn't speak. Why should she? What could she possibly have to say? She watches me, and then her eyes become distant, inaccessible, like she's diving into waters too deep for me to follow her into.

Madame mutters something unkind and kicks the child in the shoulder, then she steers me outside.

There are plenty of other children, with stronger bodies and normal features. They work, polishing Madame's fake jewels, doing laundry in metal basins and hanging it on wire that's strung between dilapidated fences.

"My girls produce like jackrabbits." Madame says the last word with malice. "Then they die and leave me to care for the mess they leave behind. But what can be done? The children make good workers at least." *Ze children.*

Long ago President Guiltree did away with birth control. He's of the pro-science mentality and thinks geneticists will fix the glitch in our DNA. In the meantime he feels it's our responsibility to keep the human race alive. There are doctors who know how to terminate pregnancies, though they charge more than most can afford.

I wonder if my parents ever did it. For all the time they spent monitoring pregnancies, I'm sure they knew how to terminate one.

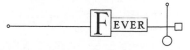

Abortions are supposed to be banned, but I've never heard of the president actually punishing anyone for disobeying one of his laws. I'm not entirely sure what the president even does. My brother says the presidency is a useless tradition that might have once served a purpose but has become nothing but formality—something to give us hope that order will be restored one day.

I hate President Guiltree, who has been in charge of this country longer than I've been alive. With his nine wives and fifteen children—all sons—he does not believe the end of humankind is near. He makes no move to stop the Gatherers from kidnapping brides, and encourages madmen like Vaughn to breed infants who will live their lives as experiments. Sometimes he's on television, promoting new buildings or attending parties, flashing smiles, toasting his champagne glass at the TV like he expects us all to be celebrating with him. Or maybe he's mocking us.

"He's kind of handsome," Cecily said once, when we were all watching TV and his face appeared in a commercial. Jenna said he looked like a child molester. We'd laughed about it then, but now that I'm in a scarlet district, Jenna's former home, I think she must have been serious. Living in a place like this, she must have learned how to see all the monsters that can hide in a person.

Madame shows me her gardens, which are mostly patches of weeds and buds, encased in low wire fences. The strawberries, though, are growing under a weatherproof

tarp. "You should see them in the spring sunshine," she says giddily. "Strawberries and tomatoes and blueberries so fat they explode between your teeth." I wonder where she gets the seeds. They're so hard to come by in the city, where all of our fruits and vegetables seem to have taken on the city's gray tinge.

She shows me the other tents, full of antique furniture, silk pillows piled on the dirt floors. Only the best for her customers, she says. The air in each of them is muggy with sweat. At the last tent, which is all pink, she turns to face me. She takes my hair from either side, in both hands, holding it out and watching the way it falls from her fingers. A strand gets caught on one of her rings, but I don't flinch as it's ripped from my scalp. "A girl like you is wasted as a bride." She says the word like *vasted*. "A girl like you should have dozens of lovers."

Her eyes are lost. She's staring through me suddenly, and wherever she's gone, it brings out the humanity in her. For the first time I can see her eyes under all that makeup, see that they're brown and sad. And oddly familiar, though I'm sure I've never seen anyone like this woman in my life. I never even dared to peek into the shadows of scarlet districts nestled in alleyways back home.

I was never even curious.

Her lips curl into a smile, and it's a kind smile. Her lipstick cracks, revealing a bleary pink underneath.

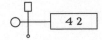

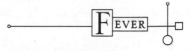

We're standing by a heap of rusted scrap metal that is humming mechanically and emitting a faint yellow glow. One of Jared's projects, I assume. Madame raves about his inventions. "Contraptions," she calls them. "This will be a warming device for the soil. My Jared thinks it will make it easier to plant crops in the winter," she tells me, patting one of the rusted pieces.

"So, what do you think of my carnival, *chérie?*" she asks. "The best in South Carolina."

It amazes me how Madame can speak without the cigarette ever falling from the corner of her mouth. Maybe I've been breathing in too much of her smoke second-hand, but I'm in awe of her. Things fill with color as she moves past them. Her gardens grow. She created a strange dreamland with only the ghost of a dead society and some bits of broken machines.

She also never seems to sleep. Her girls are napping now that it's daytime, and her bodyguards seem to alternate shifts, but she is forever weaving between tents, tilling, primping, barking orders. Even my dreams last night smelled of her.

"It's not like any other place I've seen," I admit, which is the truth. If Manhattan is reality, and the mansion a luxurious illusion, this place is a dilapidated, blurry line that divides the two places.

"You belong here," she says. "Not with a husband. Not with a servant." She wraps her arm around me, leading me through a patch of shriveled, snowy wildflowers.

"Lovers are weapons, but love is a wound. That boy of yours," she says, unaccented, "is a wound."

"I never said I love him," I say.

Madame smiles mischievously, her face flourishing with creases. It strikes me how the first generations are aging. Soon they'll be gone. And no one will be left to know what old age looks like. Twenty-six and beyond will be a mystery.

"I've had many lovers," she tells me. "But only one love. We had a child together. A beautiful little creature with hair that was every shade of yellow. Like yours."

"What happened to them?" I ask, feeling brave. Madame has prodded and scrutinized me from the moment I arrived, and now, at last, she's exposing her own weakness.

"Dead," she says, picking up her accent again. The humanity vanishes from her eyes, leaving them reproachful and cold. "Murdered. Dead."

She stops walking and tucks my hair behind my ears, tilts my chin, inspects my face. "And I am to blame for the pain. I should not have loved my daughter as I did. Not in this world in which nothing lives for long. You children are flies. You are roses. You multiply and die."

I open my mouth, but no words come. What she says is horrible and true.

And then I wonder, does my brother think of me this way? We entered this world together, one after the other, beats in a pulse. But I will be first to leave it. That's what

I've been promised. When we were children, did he dare to imagine an empty space beside him where I then stood giggling, blowing soap bubbles through my fingers?

When I die, will he be sorry that he loved me? Sorry that we were twins?

Maybe he already is.

The tip of Madame's cigarette flares red as she breathes deep. Lilac says the smoke makes her delusional, but I wonder how much of what Madame says is truth. "You are to be loved in moments. Illusions. That's what I provide to my customers," she says. "Your boy is greedy."

Gabriel. When I left him, his dry lips were muttering silently. I noticed the stubble growing on his chin; he'd been re-dressed in his attendant's shirt, which was ripped where the bodyguards had pulled at him. I was worried for the purple skin around his eyes, his raspy breaths.

"He loves you too much," Madame says. "He loves you even in sleep."

We walk through the strawberry patch, Madame prattling incessantly about the amazing Jared and his underground device that keeps the soil warm, simulating springtime so that her gardens can grow. "The most magical part," she says, "is that it keeps the ground warm for the girls and for my customers."

As she goes on, I think of what she said about Gabriel, about him loving me too much, but mostly about how he is a wound. Vaughn thought the same thing of Jenna;

she served him no purpose, bore him no grandchildren, showed his son no real love, and she died for it.

It's important to be useful in this world. The first generations seem to all agree about that.

"He's a strong worker," I say, interrupting her tangent about summer mosquitoes. "He can lift heavy things, and cook, and do just about anything."

"But I cannot trust him," Madame says. "What do I know about him? He was dropped at my feet as if from the sky."

"But you *are* trusting me," I say. "You're telling me all of these things."

She squeezes my shoulders, giggling like a bizarre and maniacal child. "I trust no one," she says. "I am not trusting you. I am preparing you."

"Preparing me?" I say.

As we walk, she rests her head on my shoulder, and her warm breath makes the hair on the back of my neck rise. The smoke from her cigarette is choking, and I suppress coughs.

"I do the best I can for my girls, but they are weary. Used up. You are perfect. I have been thinking, and I will not hand you over to my customers so they can reduce your value."

Reduce my value. My stomach twists.

"Rather," Madame says, "I think I could make more money off you if you remain pristine. We shall have to find a place for you. Dancing, maybe." I can feel her smile

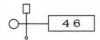

without seeing her face. "Letting them have a taste. Letting them be hypnotized."

I can't follow the dark path her thoughts have taken, and I blurt out, "What about the boy I came with, then? If I'm doing all of this for your business"—the word gets caught on my tongue—"then I need to know that he's okay. There needs to be a place for him."

"Very well," Madame says, suddenly bored. "It's a small enough request. If he proves to be a spy, I will have him killed. Be sure to tell him that."

By evening Madame sends me back to the green tent. I think it might have belonged to Jade and Celadon before the virus overtook them. She says one of her girls will be in to see me soon.

Gabriel is still out of it, and there's a child holding his head in her lap. One of the blond twins I saw earlier.

"Please don't be mad; I know I shouldn't be here," she says, not looking up. "He was making such awful noises. I didn't want him to be alone."

"What noises?" I ask, my voice gentle. I kneel beside him, and his skin is paler than before. There's a rash of red across his cheeks and throat, and the skin around his bruise is fiery orange.

"Sick-person noises," she whispers. Her hair is very blond. Her eyelashes are the same color, fluttering up and down like wisps of light. She's running her small hands through his hair and across his face. "Did he give

you that ring?" she asks me, nodding at my hand.

I don't answer. I dip a towel into the basin, wring it out, and dab at Gabriel's face with it. This feeling is horrible and familiar—watching someone I care for suffer, and having nothing but water to help them with.

"Someday I'll have a ring that's made of real gold too," the girl says. "Someday I'll be first wife. I know it. I have birthing hips."

I'd laugh under less dire circumstances. "I knew a girl who grew up wanting to be a bride too," I say.

She looks at me, and her green eyes are wide and intense. And for a second I think maybe this girl is right. She will grow up to be passionate and spirited; she will stand out in a line of dreary Gathered girls; a man will choose her, and come to her bed flushed with desire.

"Did she?" the girl asks. "Become a bride, I mean."

"She was my sister wife," I say. "And yes, she was given a gold ring too."

The girl smiles, revealing a missing front tooth. Pale brown freckles dot her nose and spill into her cheeks like a blush.

"I bet she was pretty," the girl says.

"She was. Is," I correct myself. Cecily is gone from me, but she's still alive. I can't believe I almost forgot. It seems like forever ago that I left her screaming my name in a snowbank. I ran, didn't look back, angrier with her than I'd ever been with anyone in my life.

The memory is a lifetime away from this smoky, dizzy-

ing place. I don't even feel angry anymore. I don't feel much of anything at all.

"How's the patient?" Lilac says from the doorway. The girl whips to attention, and her expression turns sheepish. She's been officially caught. She eases Gabriel's head from her lap and hurries off, muttering apologies, calling herself a stupid girl.

"It's her job to tend to the sickroom," Lilac says. "She can't resist a Prince Charming in distress."

In the daylight, without makeup, Lilac is still a creature of beauty. Her eyes are sultry and sad, her smile languid, her hair messy and stiff on one side. Her skin, as dark as her eyes, is cloaked in gauzy blue scarves. Snow is flurrying around behind her.

She says, "Don't worry. Your prince will be fine. Just a little sedated is all."

"What have you given him?" I say, not hiding my anger.

"It's just a little angel's blood. The same stuff we take to help us sleep."

"Sleep?" I growl. "He's comatose."

"Madame is wary of new boys," Lilac says, not without compassion. She kneels beside me and presses her fingers to Gabriel's throat. She's silent as she monitors his pulse. Then she says, "She thinks they're spies coming to take away her girls."

"Yet she lets anyone with money come in and have their way with them."

"Under strict supervision," Lilac says pointedly. "If anyone tries something funny—and sometimes they do . . ." She makes a gun shape with her hands, points at me, shoots. "There's a big incinerator behind the Ferris wheel where she burns the bodies. Jared rigged it from some old machinery."

It's not surprising. Cremation is the most popular way to dispose of bodies. We're dropping off so quickly, there's not even room to bury all of us, and there are some rumors that the virus contaminates the soil. And just as there are Gatherers to steal girls, there are cleaning crews who scoop up the discarded bodies from the side of the road and haul them to the city incinerators.

The thought makes me ache. I can feel Rowan, for just a moment actually feel him, looking for my body, worrying that I've already withered to ash. When the dust is heavy as he passes the incineration facilities, does he fear it's me he's breathing in? Bone or brain, or my eyes that are identical to his?

"You're looking a little pale," Lilac says. How can she tell? Everything in this tent is tinted green. "Don't worry; we won't be doing anything strenuous tonight."

I don't want to do anything but sit here with Gabriel, to protect him from another debilitating injection. But I know I have to play by the rules of Madame's world if I hope to escape it. I've done it all before, I tell myself, and I can do it again. Trust is the strongest weapon.

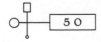

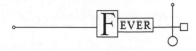

Lilac smiles at me. It is a tired, pretty smile. "We'll start with your hair, I think. It could stand to be washed. Then we'll figure out a color scheme for your makeup. Your face makes a nice canvas. Has anyone ever told you that? You should see the messes I've had to work with before. The noses on some of these girls."

I think of Deirdre, my little domestic, who called my face a canvas too. She was a wonder with colors; sometimes I would let her do my makeup if I was bored. Sensible earth tones for dinners with my husband; wild pinks and reds and whites when the roses were in bloom; blue and green and frosty silver when my hair was drenched with pool water and I sat in my bathrobe, reeking of chlorine.

"What is my makeup for?" I ask, though my stomach is twisting with dread.

"It's just practice for now," Lilac says. "We'll do a few trials, show them to Her Highness." She says the last two words without affection. "And whenever she approves a color scheme, we can begin training you."

"Training me?"

Lilac straightens her back, pushing out her chest and mock-primping her hair; it pools between her fingers like liquid chocolate. She mimics Madame's fake accent. "In the art of seduction, darling." *Ze art of zeduction.*

Madame wants me to be one of her girls. She still wants to sell me to her customers, even if it's not in the traditional sense.

I look at Gabriel. His lips have tightened. Can he hear what's happening? *Wake up!* I want him to rescue me, the way he did in the hurricane. I want him to carry us both away. But I know he can't. I've caused all of this, and now I'm on my own.

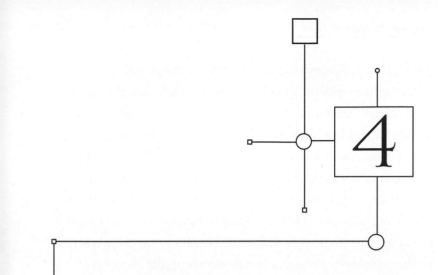

THIS TENT IS RED, like the strings of beads that droop down from the ceiling, so low our heads almost touch it as we stand before the mirror. The air is heavy with smoke; I've been exposed to it for so long now that my senses are not as offended. Lilac twists my hair into dozens of little braids and douses them with water, "to bring out the curls."

Outside, the brass music has begun. Maddie is sitting at the entrance, peeking out into the night. I follow her gaze and catch the smooth white of a thigh, wisp of a dress. There are desperate, shuddering grunts and gasps. Lilac giggles as she smears lipstick onto my mouth. "That's one of the Reds," she says, "probably Scarlet. She wants the whole world to know she's a whore." She straightens her back, yells the word "Whore!" out into the night; it flies over Maddie, who is stuffing her mouth full of semi-rotten strawberries and watching.

The girl outside yips and howls with laughter.

I want to ask why Lilac is okay with her daughter watching what's going on out there, but I remember the teasing I got from my sister wives. They would undress while I was in the room, run into the hallway in their underwear and ask to borrow each other's things. Late in her pregnancy Cecily didn't even bother with the buttons of her nightgown, and her stomach floated in front of her everywhere. I guess being raised in such close quarters with so many other girls leaves no room for shyness.

And here, I am supposed to blend in. I can't be shy. If Madame finds out that I lied about my torrid affairs, she won't believe anything else about me. And so I act unfazed as Lilac explains Madame's color-sorting system for her girls.

The Reds are Madame's favorites: Scarlet and Coral have been with her since they were babies, and she lets them borrow her costume jewels. She lets them take hot baths and gives them the ripest strawberries from another little garden she grows behind the tent, because their bright eyes and long hair fetch the highest prices.

The Blues are her mysterious ones: Iris and Indigo and Sapphire and Sky. They cling to one another when they sleep, and they giggle at the things they whisper among themselves. But their teeth are murky and mostly missing, and they only get chosen by the men unwilling to pay for more, and they're never in the back room for long. Men take them hurriedly, sometimes standing up,

against trees, or even in the tent with all the others there to see.

There are more girls. More colors that blend together into one muddy mess as Lilac talks about them, pausing to ask Maddie to hand her the peroxide. Maddie, fingers and mouth stained red with strawberry juice, crawls (she hardly walks, I've noticed) to the assortment of jars and bottles and vials. She finds the one that's labeled peroxide and offers it up.

"How did she know which bottle was the right one?" I say.

"She read it." Lilac tilts the bottle onto a cloth, wipes some of the blush from my cheeks. "She's very smart. 'Course, Her Highness"—again, said with malice—"likes to keep her hidden, thinks she's just a useless malfie."

"Malfie" is an unkind term for the genetically malformed. Sometimes women would give birth to malformed babies in the lab where my parents worked—children born blind, or deaf, or with any of an array of disfigurements. But more common were the children with strange eyes, who never spoke or reached the milestones the other children did, and whose behavior never synced with any genetic research. My mother once told me about a malformed boy who spent the nights wailing in terror over imaginary ghosts. And before my brother and I were born, our parents had a set of malformed twins; they had the same heterochromatic eyes—brown and blue—but they were blind, and they never spoke, and despite my parents' best efforts they didn't live past five years.

Malformed children are put to death in orphanages, because they're considered leeches with no hope of ever caring for themselves. That's if they don't die on their own. But in labs they're the perfect candidates for genetic analysis because nobody really knows what makes them tick.

"Madame said she bites the customers," I say.

Lilac, holding an eyeliner pencil close to my face, throws her head back and laughs. The laugh mingles with the grunts and the brass and Madame shouting an order to one of her boys.

"Good," she says.

In the distance Madame starts bellowing for Lilac, who rolls her eyes and grunts. "Drunk," she mumbles, and licks her thumb and uses it to smudge the eyeliner on my eyelids. "I'll be back. Don't go anywhere."

As if I could. I can hear the gun rattling in the guard's holster just outside the entrance.

"Lilac!" Madame's accented voice is slurred. "Where are you? Stupid girl."

Lilac hurries off, muttering obscenities. Maddie follows her out, taking the bucket of semi-rotted strawberries with her.

I lie back on the bubblegum pink sheet that's covering the ground and rest my head on one of the many throw pillows. This one is framed with orange beads. I think the smoke is to blame for my fatigue. I'm so tired here.

My arms and legs feel so heavy. The colors, though, are twice as bright. The music twice as loud. The giggling, moaning, gasping girls are a music of their own. And I think there's something magical about it all. Something that lures Madame's customers in like fishermen to a lighthouse gleam. But it's terrifying, too. Terrifying to be a girl in this place. Terrifying to be a girl in this world.

My eyes close. I wrap my arms around the pillow. I'm dressed in only a gold satin slip (gold has become Madame's official color for her Goldenrod), but despite the winds outside, it's warm in the tent. I suppose this is from the lingering smoke, and Jared's underground heating system, and all the candles in the lanterns. Madame has truly thought of everything. To have her girls bundled in winter gear would hardly make them appealing to customers.

I'm eerily comfortable in this warmth. A nap seems incredibly inviting.

Don't forget how you got here. Jenna's voice. *Don't forget.*

She and I are lying beside each other, surrounded by canopy netting. She's not dead. Not while she's tucked safely in my dreams.

Don't forget.

I squeeze my eyelids down tight. I don't want to think about the horrible way my oldest sister wife died. Her skin bruising and decaying. Her eyes glossing over. I just want to pretend she's okay—just for a little longer.

But I can't stave off the feeling that Jenna is trying to

warn me to not be so comfortable in this dangerous place. I can smell the medicine and the decay of her deathbed. It gets stronger the more I feel myself fading to sleep.

The curtain swishes, clattering the beads that frame the entrance, and I snap to attention.

Gabriel is here, clear-eyed and standing on solid feet, dressed in a heavy black turtleneck and jeans and knit socks. The type of clothes Madame's guards wear.

For a long moment we just stare at each other as if we've been apart for ages, which maybe we have. He has been beyond reach with angel's blood since our arrival, and I have been whisked away by Madame at her every free moment.

I ask, "How are you feeling?" at the same time he says, "You look—"

I sit up in the sea of throw pillows, and he sits beside me, and the lanterns show me the deep bags under his eyes. When I left him this morning, Madame gave Lilac strict instructions to stop the angel's blood, but he was sleeping, his mouth moving to make words I couldn't understand. Now, at least, there's color in his cheeks. His cheeks are flushed, actually. It's especially warm in this tent, with all the incense sticks Lilac ignited, and the hot, sugary-sweet smell of the candles in the lanterns.

"How are you feeling?" I ask again.

"All right," he says. "For a few minutes I was seeing strange things, but that's passed now." His hands are trembling slightly, and I put my hands over them.

His skin is a little clammy, but nothing like it was as he lay comatose and shivering beside me. Just the memory makes me cling to him.

"I'm so sorry," I whisper. "I haven't come up with a plan to get us out yet, but I've bought us some time, I think. Madame wants me to perform."

"Perform?" Gabriel says.

"I don't know—something about dancing, maybe. It could be worse."

He says nothing to that. We both know the type of performances the other girls put on.

"There has to be a way through the gate," Gabriel whispers. "Or—"

"Shh. I think I heard something outside."

We strain to listen for it, but the rustling I thought I heard doesn't repeat itself. It could be the wind, or any of Madame's girls flitting about.

Just in case, I move on to a safer topic. "How did you know I'd be here?"

"There was a little girl waiting for me to wake up. She handed me these clothes and told me to look for the red tent."

I can't help it. I wrap my arms around him and crush myself against him. "I was so worried."

The response is a soft kiss against the hollow of my neck, his hands sweeping the hair over my shoulders. It has been too much to lie beside him every night, feeling a rag doll's emptiness, to have the fragmented dreams of June Beans on silver trays and winding mansion hall-ways and hedge maze paths that took me no nearer to his presence.

Now I feel the full weight of him. And it's making me greedy, making me tilt my head so that his kisses to my neck reach my lips, and making me take him with me as I lean back into the pillows that clatter with beads. A gemstone button is pressing into my back.

The smoke of the incense is alive. It traces the length of us. The heady perfume of it makes my eyes water, and I feel strange. Weary and flushed.

"Wait," I say when Gabriel slides the strap of my slip down my shoulder. "Doesn't this feel weird to you?"

"Weird?" He kisses me.

I swear the smoke has doubled.

There's a rustling sound on the other side of the tent, and I bolt upright, startled. Gabriel blinks, his arm coiled around mine, sweat trickling from his damp-ened hair. Something has happened. Some kind of spell. Some supernatural pull. I'm certain this can be the only explanation. There's the feeling of returning from someplace far.

Then I hear Madame's unmistakable cackling. She pushes into the tent, clapping, her white smile floating in the smog. She's saying something in broken-sounding French as she stomps on the incense sticks to extinguish them. *"Merveilleux!"* she cries. "Lilac, how many was that?"

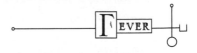

Lilac slips into the tent, sorting through a wad of dollar bills. "Ten, Madame," she says. "The rest complained they couldn't see through the slit."

Horrified, I hear male voices grumbling their disappointment on the other side of the tent. Amid a curtain of beads I can see a deliberate slit in the tent. I swallow a scream, cover myself by hugging a pink silk pillow to my chest.

Gabriel's jaw tenses, and I put my hand on his knee, hoping it will quiet him. Whatever Madame was planning, we must play along.

"Aphrodisiacs are quite potent, aren't they?" Madame says, reaching into a lantern and snuffing the flame with her finger and thumb. "Yes, you put on quite a show." She's looking at me when she adds, "Men will pay great money to see what they can't touch."

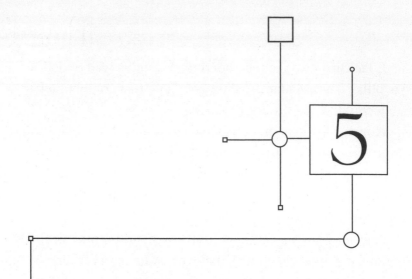

THE LOVEBIRDS, she calls us. LES TOURTEREAUX is painted in red cursive on a broken plank from an old fence. She is building a cage from bits of rusted wire and coat hangers. She has Gabriel bend the lengths of wire into curves and paint them with a coating I've spent the morning mixing from gold eye shadow, water, and paste. The girls are not happy to forfeit their gold makeup. They shove me as they pass; their lifeless eyes bore into me; they mutter words I can't hear, spitting on the ground.

"They're jealous," Lilac says, a pin in her lips as she sews ruffles onto a white shirt. "New blood and whatnot."

We're huddled in the red tent, and I'm dunking gray feathers onto a galvanized bucket of blue dye and then fastening them with clothespins to a makeshift clothesline to dry. I wonder what type of bird had to die for this cause. A pigeon or seagull, I'd guess.

The dye stains my fingers, lands in fat drops on the

threadbare oversize shirt that makes up my entire outfit. Madame will not have dye spilling onto her good clothes.

"No, no, no!" Madame cries, bursting into the tent and shaking all its walls. "You're making a mess of those feathers, girl."

"I told you I didn't know what I was doing," I mumble.

"No matter." Madame grabs my arm and pulls me to my feet. "I wanted to speak to you anyway. Lilac will finish your gown."

Lilac mutters something I can't hear, and Madame kicks a clod of dirt at her, making her cough onto the ruffled shirt.

"There's a washbasin and a dress laid out for you in the green tent," Madame says. "Make yourself presentable and meet me by the wheel."

With effort I'm able to scrub most of the dye from my fingers. Some of it is trapped along my cuticles, outlining my nails in blue, making my hands look like sketches of themselves.

When I meet up with Madame, the Ferris wheel is slowly turning. "The gears have to warm up in this chill," Madame says, wrapping a knitted shawl around my shoulders. "But we have things to discuss," she goes on. "Things that would be overheard on the ground."

Jared pulls a lever, and the wheel comes to a stop with a car waiting for us.

Madame ushers me ahead and then climbs in after me. The car rocks and creaks as we ascend.

"You have remarkable shoulder blades," Madame says. I can't tell what type of accent she's trying for today. "And your back shows just the right amount of spine. Not too knotted. Subtle."

"You were watching me change," I say. It's not a question.

She doesn't bother denying it. "I need to know what I'm selling."

"What *are* you selling?" I say, daring to look away from my clenched fist and at her smoke-shrouded face. Embers flit on the wind, and I feel their tiny pinches on my bare knee. Up high, away from the device Jared uses to warm the earth, it's blustery cold. My nose is starting to drip. I hug the shawl around my shoulders.

"I've told you," she says. "An illusion."

She smiles, her eyes dark and faraway as she traces her finger down the slope of my cheek. Her voice is low and sweet. "Soon you'll crumple into yourself. The flesh will melt from your bones. You'll scream and cry until it's done. You have less than a handful of years."

I ignore the imagery. It is easiest to overlook the truth sometimes.

"Will you charge admission for that?" I say.

"No," she sighs, and tosses her spent cigarette over the edge. She looks small and incomplete without it. "I intend to make my customers forget these ugly things. No one will look at you and think about your expiration date. They will see youth stretching out like a canyon."

I can't help it. I look down. Most of the girls are sleeping through the day, but a few of them are up and about, bossing the children, tending the weedy gardens, flaunting themselves before the bodyguards for a bit of attention. Anything they can do to feel that they're alive. All of them hating me for being so high over their heads.

"You'll put on a good show for me, won't you?" Madame says. "There is only one rule. You and your boy must behave as if you are alone. My customers will not want to be seen. They are not behind the walls but are the walls themselves."

The idea of performing for "the walls" gives me no comfort. But I only need to play along until I find an escape, and there are worse things than being trapped in a makeshift birdcage with Gabriel, pretending we're alone. Right? My throat feels dry and swollen.

Madame reaches into the infinite bright scarves draped over her chest and pulls out a small silver compact. She opens it, revealing a single pink pill.

I eye it warily.

"It's to prevent pregnancy," she says. "There are lots of fake pills going around since the birth control ban, but I have a reliable seller. Manufactures them himself."

As though to mock us, a child screeches as one of the Reds drags her past the Ferris wheel by the hair.

"I can't waste them on all my girls, of course," Madame says. "Only the useful ones. I shudder to think what other horrors would fall from Lilac's womb if I let her reproduce again."

Lilac. Cynical and lovely and intelligent. She's a good mother, I think. As good as one can be in this place, and to a child like Maddie. But she hides this fact when the customers come in the evenings. She is one of the most sought after, and only offered to men who pay the highest price—first generations with the best-paying jobs, mostly. Madame told me this with pride. And yet, Lilac has not had a child since Maddie. I suppose the pink pill could be to thank for that.

Still, I don't want to take it. How can I trust anything in this place? Even the scents in the air can make me behave strangely.

Madame forces it into my mouth. "Swallow," she says, her sharp painted fingernail gagging the back of my throat. I struggle and jerk my head back, and the pill has been swallowed before I can register what's just happened. It hurts going down.

Madame cackles at my sour expression. "You'll thank me later," she says, and wraps her arm around my shoulder. "Look." Her murmur tickles my ear. "Look how the clouds have braided, like a little girl's hair."

The cold and the smoke and the pill have all caused tears to well in my eyes, and when I finally blink them away, the clouds have begun taking on a different shape entirely. But the wistfulness on Madame's face remains. *Braided, like a little girl's hair.* I think she misses her dead

daughter more than she cares to admit. I take bizarre comfort in this. The pain proves she is human after all.

The loose dirt is warm under my bare feet, humming with the life of Jared's machine. I'm loathe to admit that it feels inviting; my mind keeps going into a daydream about lying in it and falling asleep.

Gabriel and I are trying to force the spikes of our giant cage into the dirt. A few yards away Jared and a few of the bodyguards are setting spikes into the ground, preparing to raise a tent around it for tonight's show.

It's the first chance Gabriel and I have had to be alone all day, and even still, the guards are close enough to overhear our words at any given time. But I catch his glances at me, his chapped lips pushed together like there's something he wants to say.

"Here," I say, pressing myself against his back and reaching around him, helping him force a bar into the ground. "What is it?" I whisper.

"We're really going through with it, then?" he whispers back. "This show?"

I move on to the next bar, forcing it down. "I don't see how we have a choice."

"I thought we might try to run for it," he says. "But there's a fence."

"There's something off about it," I say. "Haven't you noticed the noise it makes? Like it's buzzing?"

"I thought that noise was coming from the incinerator,"

he says. "It couldn't hurt to check it out."

I shake my head. "If anyone saw us, we'd be trapped."

"Then, we'll have to be sure nobody is watching."

"Someone is always watching."

I steal a glance at Jared, who has been watching me but now looks away.

"I think we can stop now," I say, dusting the shimmering gold residue from my palms. "This cage is as rooted as it's going to get."

LES TOURTEREAUX. The sign, elegant in its crudeness, has been posted outside of the new peach-colored tent.

We're standing beside our cage while reluctant girls light incense and lanterns around us, making our shadows dance. Madame wanted a yellow tent originally, but decided the peach tarp would be most flattering on our skin. She says I'm as pale as death. Gabriel has just whispered something, but through all this smoke and my heart pounding in my ears, I didn't catch it. He's wearing the ruffled shirt Lilac spent the afternoon sewing. I am positively covered in feathers; they're in my hair, and arranged like giant angel wings at my back. The dye hasn't quite set, and watery streaks of color stain my arms.

He takes my face in his hands. "We still could run," he whispers.

I find that my arms are trembling. I shake my head. At this moment I'd like nothing more than to run, but

we'd only be brought back. Madame, in her fairyland of opiates, would accuse Gabriel of being a spy and have him killed. And who knows what she'd do to me. It's to my advantage that I look like her dead daughter. It makes her like me in a way that's unfair to the other girls. I can feel a tentative trust growing between us. If I can build on that trust, maybe it will grant me more freedom. It worked with Linden, but I'm not quite as hopeful here. Lilac is Madame's most trusted girl. She's trusted with the money, with the training, with the oversight of dresses and performances. But I've never seen Lilac any closer to freedom than the rest of them.

Still, it can't work against me to be on Madame's good side.

"Just kiss me," I say, raising the latch of our cage and backing in.

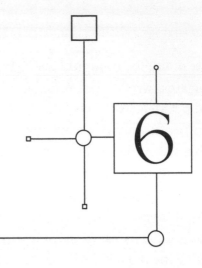

EXHAUSTED, I slide under the blankets in our green tent. The air is not so smoky here, though I've grown used to the constant haze of Madame's opiates and all the perfumes worn by the girls.

Gabriel sits beside me, freeing the dyed feathers clipped around my hair like a crown. He stacks them neatly in the dirt and stares at them.

"What's wrong?" I ask. It's late. When we left our cage, I saw the periwinkle sky giving way to dawn.

"Those men were staring at you," he says.

I push the thought away. I didn't let myself look outside of my cage. Rather than the rustles and the murmurs, I focused on the brass music playing in the distance. After a while it all blurred together. There were scarves hanging on the bars, brushing our skin. Gabriel kissed me, and I parted my lips, closed my eyes. It felt like one short, murky dream. Several times he whispered

for me to wake up, and I opened my eyes to see the dark concern in his. I remember saying, *It's okay.*

The words come out of me now. "It's okay." A mantra.

"Rhine," he whispers, "I don't like anything about this."

"Shh," I say. My eyelids are too heavy. "Just lie down beside me for a while."

He doesn't. I feel a light pressure on my back, and I realize he's unpinning the feathers from my dress, one by one.

Days flutter by, in purples and greens and crumbling golds, spilling from the gilded bars like empires collapsing. And all around me is blackness. I am in a kind of tunnel, sleepwalking through the time between sleep and performances.

Somewhere far away Gabriel's worried voice is saying that it is time to go, that this must end. But in the next moment he's kissing me, and his hands are under my arms, and I'm falling into him.

Ferris wheels spin, leaving streaks of light in the sky. Girls cackle and vomit. Children skitter like roaches. The guards keep their guns in sight like a warning.

Cold water hits me in the face, white and loud. I splutter.

"Are you listening?" Gabriel whispers harshly.

I cough, swipe my wrist across my eyes. "What?" I say.

We're in our green tent. There are feathers all around us.

"We have to leave. It has to be now," he says. I try to focus on his face. "You're becoming one of them."

I blink several times, trying to wake up. Our blankets are drenched. "One of who?"

"One of those awful girls," he says. "Don't you see? Come on."

He's pulling me to my feet, but I resist. "We can't," I say. "She'll catch us. She'll kill you."

"She's right, you know," Lilac says. She's standing in the entranceway, arms folded. The early morning light shines behind her, making her an elegant black ribbon of a girl. "Best not to do anything stupid. She's got eyes everywhere."

Gabriel looks at her and says nothing. When she leaves, he hands me a rag to dry off my face.

"It has to be soon," he insists.

"Okay," I tell him. "Soon."

I force myself to stay awake despite the heavy pull that's weighing me down. Gabriel and I whisper about our options, which are dishearteningly bleak. All of our ideas lead back to the fence. Ways to climb it. Ways to dig under it. He tells me that he and some of the bodyguards are going to be repainting the merry-go-round, and he will try to get a better look around then.

We sleep, eventually, when the sun is high and being in our tent is like being in the heart of an emerald. Just before I drift off, I feel his kiss on my lips. It's certain, sincere, and I return it in kind. Something stirs in my

chest, and I want more, but I force those feelings away. I cannot rid myself of the sense that we're being watched.

In my dream I follow the pink pill that Madame forced down my throat. I slide down the tongue that stretches into a dark cavern. I land with a loud splash, liquefied and startled.

Lilac tugs my hair, startling me awake with the pain. "Napping on the job?" she says. I open my eyes. All I can smell, once again, is the charred air and Madame's many perfumes. Lilac had been curling my hair. I must have drifted off.

Now she is grabbing my wrists and yanking me to my feet, fluffing my curls. "Madame wants to see you," she says.

"Now?"

"No, tomorrow, when she's hungover and all the cus tomers have gone. Put this on." She hands me a wad of sunny yellow fabric that I guess is supposed to be a dress, and doesn't bother turning the other way while I change into it.

The dress is so long that it drags across the ground, and Lilac has to help me figure out how to wrap it over my shoulder. "It's called a sari," Lilac says. "They feel a little weird at first, but trust me, Madame only lets a girl wear one when she wants to show her off."

"Show me off to who, exactly?"

Lilac just smiles, straightens the fabric hanging over

my shoulder, and takes my hand to lead me out.

She drags me out into the night, and the air is so cold, it's like a slap. Snow is whirling around in wisps that never accumulate on the ground. It's fitting that snow doesn't settle—nothing else does either. The girls are forever in motion, everything like cogs in a machine, gears in a giant wristwatch.

Madame runs toward me, arms out, her scarves and billowy sleeves trailing in oranges and purples and silky greens. "Now you look like a real lady," she says.

Jared stands behind her, arms folded, an orange cord draped over his neck, and a lantern in his fist. His sleeves are torn off, and his arms are muscular and smeared with grease. Earlier I saw him lying under a giant machine that looked like a heap of vibrating car parts strung with lights. Despite the cold, there are beads of sweat glistening on his face. He stares at me with dark deadpan eyes.

Madame pinches my cheeks, twists them between her knuckles. I cringe but don't withdraw. "You needed more color," she says, and cackles. "Come, come." She leads me by the wrist, and Jared follows at a distance. I can feel his stare boring into the back of my head.

Pebbles cut at my feet as I step on them. That's another strange thing about this place—nobody ever wears shoes.

We pass the Ferris wheel that's spinning, with no one to ride it. We pass tents that rustle and giggle and glow with flickering lights. The cold wind mutters words I

can't understand. The embers of Madame's cigarette fly at my eyes. Something is moving in the field of dead sunflowers, following us. At first I think it's some kind of animal, but then I see the white flutter of Maddie's dress. Strange child. Even Lilac says so. Says she's mad and brilliant and wonderful. Says she was meant for a better world.

We walk all the way to the chain-link fence, through which Gabriel and I were once dragged against our wills. From the corner of my eye I see Maddie parting the weeds with her hands. In the darkness her eyes are like sparks. She drags her index finger through the air in the shape of letters, but I can't quite make out what they spell.

Jared opens the fence, and he watches me the whole time, like he's taunting me. Like he's saying, *Go ahead and try it.*

But, just like the first time Linden took me outside of the mansion for that expo, I don't run. Something in me argues against it. Maddie writes furiously in the shadows.

I can hear the tide turning out in that darkness, can smell the ocean. My stomach lurches with longing and dread. I can hear something else out there. Something approaching us.

"You're going to meet someone special," Madame says, her breath hot in my ear. Her smoke coils around my throat like a hissing serpent.

I think I've stopped breathing, because the color emerging from the darkness, in the shape of a man much bigger than me, is all gray.

Nobody is sure exactly why the Gatherers chose the color gray for their jackets and vans. Sometimes the vans are poorly repainted, the windows globbed over with dribbling gray, the tires splashed with it. The jackets are not all uniform—I know that much. They are also hand-dyed, all different cuts and styles. The Gatherers are their own underground group, and while some say they work for the government, one thing that's certain is that they travel in packs; they find one another, form a shelter somewhere, and wait for opportunities. Maybe they split the money they make off us, and use it to fuel their vans, load their guns, indulge themselves in liquor and whatever else they want.

I think this man's smell hits me before the color of his coat. Like mold and liquor and sweat. It must be laborious for them, stealing so many girls. Must make them perspire. Especially those of us who fight, scratch, make them bleed any way we can.

His smile emerges next, his teeth rotten like the broken smiles of Madame's girls.

I take a half step back out of instinct, but Madame wraps her arm around mine, and her nails and cheap jewels are clawing into my skin until I'm sure I must be bleeding from it.

The man cups my face in his hand, and Madame ges-

tures to Jared, who holds the lantern up over my head. And I realize what's happening. This man, this Gatherer, is looking at my eyes, the way my brother and I would look through apples in the marketplace for the best pick. Something flashes in his eyes like delight. I struggle, though the realization of what's happening still hasn't quite reached me. Not until Madame names her price.

And finally, finally, I understand the word Maddie was writing for me.

Run.

Her hands are still moving, screaming.

Runrunrunrunrun.

The Gatherer is arguing, saying he can get girls much cheaper on the street. He looks so angry that he could spit. And Madame is laughing, smoke bursting out of her mouth, saying, "Not like this one, you won't."

Run.

I can't! Gabriel is still a prisoner here. Madame will kill him; I'm sure of it. Kill him when she realizes she can't turn him into one of her bodyguards. He doesn't have it in him to hold a girl against her will—to carry a gun, much less shoot one.

And even if I were to run, how far could I get? Jared is standing right beside me, shining the lantern on me, ready to grab me at a moment's notice. My breath hitches. My mind is in a fury.

Runrunrun.

Run where? Run how?

The Gatherer is indignant, but he isn't leaving. Madame knows that, one way or another, she will sell me. She's smug about it. And I should have seen it coming, really. What use does she have for yet another girl? All the girls in this place are wilted, dried out, used up. There's a whole tent just for the ones that are in all stages of the virus, and she offers them to her customers at a discount. The men leave them, wiping the blood of the dying girls' kisses from their stubbly mouths. Everything has a price. How long has it been since she had a healthy girl, whole and fully conscious, with clean teeth and all?

She told me I reminded her of her daughter.

The daughter she loved too much. The daughter whose death left a permanent scar on her soul. She will never, never love again.

I should not have loved my daughter as I did. Not in this world in which nothing lives for long.

The Gatherer offers a lower price.

You children are flies.

Madame doubles hers.

You are roses.

"Robbery," he spits out.

You multiply and die.

Madame triples it. "This one is a goldenrod," she cries, like that should mean anything to him. "She is a gem. She will make you a fortune in return."

"Eyes are eyes," the Gatherer says. "There's other girls with eyes out there."

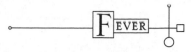

"Not. Like. These." Madame is red with fury. She wraps her arms around me like she's protecting me. "Her ring alone is worth what I'm asking! If you won't buy her, someone else will."

For one dangerous moment I allow myself a glimmer of hope. Hope that he will not buy me and Madame will send me back to a tent, and I can grab Gabriel and steal away.

But the Gatherer reaches for his hip, and in the next second I'm staring down the barrel of a handgun. And the lantern lights the rage in the Gatherer's eyes, more maddened even than Madame's, and he's shouting that he has changed his mind, he wants me for free, or he'll make sure no one else can buy me. And Jared has a gun too, pointed at the Gatherer, and the Gatherer points his gun at Jared.

I hear a wind in the tall grass like the whole world is gasping. But it's Maddie, launching out from the weeds. In a moment she's shrieking in that horrible way of hers, and then clinging like a leech to the man and biting into his leg. The Gatherer is clearly surprised by this. He tries to shake her off, but she has coiled herself around his leg and is biting and clawing and screaming.

The Gatherer is swearing and spitting, and I don't think he means to fire his gun—I see the surprise on his face when it goes off—but how can he concentrate with all this commotion? He gets Jared in the arm. There's a small explosion of blood.

Then another shot, this time from Jared's gun.

For the second time in my life, I watch as a Gatherer crumples and falls down dead in front of me. Maddie whimpers and coils herself around Jared's leg like a cat. He crouches down to console her, petting her hair with one hand and still aiming the gun at the Gatherer's corpse with the other.

"Bastard." Madame spits on the gray coat. The Gatherer's eyes are open and staring at her bare feet as she stamps out her cigarette. "One of the best customers. I give him all my best girls," Madame says. *One of ze best customers.* "This is the thanks I get?" She spits again.

Jared is whispering soft things to Maddie. Many of the women and bodyguards have a fondness for Maddie; they treat her as a sort of pet. But Jared is her favorite, and seeing a gun pointed at him clearly upset her.

"And you." Madame directs her anger to Jared. She paces toward him, dragging me tripping after her. "Look at the mess you've left me to clean up! How will I explain his death to his pack? He would not have shot her. It was a bluff."

Jared stands to full height, easily a whole head taller than me, and much taller than Madame, and still he looks small in the line of Madame's rage.

"I—" he begins, his fists clenching. Madame slaps him, first in the face but then again on the arm where he's bleeding and his skin has been ripped by the bullet.

"You've cost me too much business! You've cost me the sale of a lifetime!"

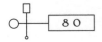

She's so furious that her accent is gone. She starts raving about there being spies, that she'll never be able to do business with the Gatherers again if they find out about this. She hits him again and again, the way I think Vaughn must have hit Gabriel the day he let me out of my room, which left him bruised and limping. But Jared is much bigger than Gabriel, and much stronger. He could rip Madame in two, but he doesn't. He doesn't because she is his only home, his only shelter. He's her technological genius, her favorite, and Madame is so broken from losing her child that even for him she hates where she should love. Hates brutally.

Jared takes it, doesn't cower, doesn't flinch. It's Maddie who is fuming. When she can take it no longer, she screams and throws herself at Madame with such a force that they both hit the ground. Fake rubies and emeralds scatter around them.

And then Madame is ripping Maddie away from her, standing over her, kicking her. And the girls have gathered around us and are all laughing or screaming—it's impossible to know which—and Lilac is running toward us, her skirt billowing out around her in slow motion, and Jared is grabbing Madame's arms, trying to pull her back. He's strong, but Madame is a woman possessed. He's yelling, "You're going to kill her." And she's yelling back, "I know."

Maddie folds in on herself, hugging her knees to her chest, her face hidden by her tangled dark hair. If she's

making any more noise, it's drowned out by all the girls, and by Madame's cursing and hissing.

Jared pulls Madame back by the arms, her feet still kicking at the air. Lilac and I kneel by Maddie, who I think for a second is dead, she's so still.

"Get her out of here," Jared is yelling over Madame's screaming. "Go! I'll hold her as long as I can."

Lilac, trembling with fear or rage, scoops her daughter's tiny body easily. I grab the lantern from where Jared left it on the ground, and I follow her, running to keep up. But as I turn in the direction of the green tent, Lilac says, "Not there. Madame will find her there."

She leads us, running, past the incinerator, which hums so loudly, it shakes my bones. Madame is so proud of that grotesque thing; it's welded together by street signs and bits of metal that advertise prices for popcorn and something called cotton candy. It makes popping sounds as though something is alive in there, hurling itself against the metal walls.

Makes ze messes easier to clean, Madame said. She was petting my hair, and her teeth were unnaturally white as she smiled. *Nothing but dust.*

What was going through that madwoman's head when she said those words? Was she thinking that she'd like to throw Maddie inside that machine's gaping mouth, listen as the child's screams became nothing but the mechanical popping and humming?

Her venom might even be worse than Vaughn's. My

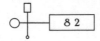

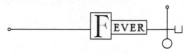

father-in-law was cold-blooded. He murdered my sister wife. But his approach was sinister and scheming, an approaching fin in murky water that you wouldn't see coming until the water had turned red around you. I never saw a fire in his eyes like there was in Madame's as she pummeled and kicked that little girl. She was enjoying herself. She wanted Maddie dead.

I'm short of breath, tripping over the ridiculously long sari, but I don't want to stop moving. I'm afraid that Maddie is dead and that once we stop moving we'll realize she's not breathing; she's so small, her limbs like dark limp weeds hanging over Lilac's arms.

We're past Madame's gardens now. The grass is waist-high and unruly. Lilac stops and sinks to her knees. "Bring the light over," she tells me, gasping for breath. I kneel too and hold the lantern over us.

Maddie's chest rises and falls. And now that I'm close enough, I can hear her little whimpers and moans.

"Shh," Lilac coos, and lays her daughter in the grass. "It's okay, baby. It's all right." Lilac unbuttons the front of Maddie's threadbare dress, and I wonder how it is that nobody in this place ever wears coats. I suppose the smoke and Jared's machine have something to do with it, because now that we're far from Madame's smoke and the lights of the broken carnival, I'm realizing how cold I am.

Lilac runs her fingers over her daughter's ribs and arms, cringing when she causes a cry of pain. She is mumbling angry profane things about Madame, and I see tears brimming in her dark eyes.

Maddie looks at me, irises the color of moonlight on snow. Almost not enough blue in them to make them stand out from the whites. I want to look away—Maddie's stares always unnerve me—but I can't. It's true that malformed children frighten me; I always stayed away from them in the lab where my parents worked. There's something far-away about their faces, as though they live in a world the rest of us can't see. There's even a popular theory that they can see ghosts.

Right now, though, Maddie's eyes are right here. She sees me, and I see her. I see that she's in pain, that she's frightened. "We aren't very different," I whisper. "Are we?"

Maddie closes her eyes in a long blink, and then looks back to her mother. Lilac gingerly buttons her daughter's dress back up. "I could kill that woman," she says.

"Has she done this before?" I ask.

"Not like this," Lilac says. "Never like this."

"It's cold," I say. "Let me go back and get blankets, at least."

Lilac shakes her head. "Jared will be here," she says.

It turns out that she's right. Within minutes we see the shadowy figure lumbering toward us through the weeds. There's gauze wrapped clumsily around his upper arm. He has brought blankets and gauze and liquid-filled bottles that look like props out of Vaughn's basement. "I

grabbed what I could in a hurry," he tells Lilac. "How is she? Is anything broken?"

The two of them talk in low voices, Maddie between them all lit up in the lantern light. She's propped herself up on one trembling elbow, and Jared is prying apart her eyelids, checking her pupils.

I stay out of the light, watching, worrying about Gabriel, whom I've left alone in that distant sphere of smoke and bright lights and music. I have to get to him. I have to get us both out of here, now that I can see how dangerous Madame is.

Before I realize I've moved, I'm up and walking.

Jared says, "Where are you going?"

Lilac says, "Come back here. Are you out of your mind?"

But their voices are too small and far away to stop me. I hoped before, stupidly, that playing by Madame's rules would give me an opportunity to escape. Just as I played by Vaughn's rules when I was trying to escape my marriage to Linden. But I could never have predicted the evil that chars those two souls. The bodies Vaughn collects. The maniacal delight in Madame's eyes as she closed in on Maddie for the deathblow.

I see it now.

There are no rules. It's survival of the fittest.

I break into a run, and I hear someone crashing after me through the weeds.

"Stop." The whisper is hot and angry. "Stop.

"Stop!"

An arm latches around my waist, lifting me off the ground.

"I can't leave him there," I cry. "You don't understand!"

I struggle to get out of Jared's grip. His arm is thick and as heavy as iron. I raise my elbow and manage to jab him—hard—in the gunshot wound. He drops me, cursing, and I hit the ground running. But he grabs the scarf of my sari in his fist and reels me in, and I can't break free.

"Just listen," he growls. "You want to help that boy? If Madame catches you right now, you won't be of any use to him. You'll never get away."

I yank the fabric from his hands and bristle, indignant, but I know he's right.

"Did you know?" I say. "Did you know that she was planning to sell me?"

"I don't pay attention to how she does business. But I do know this: If she sees you, she will not let you get away again. There's something about you that she thinks will make her a lot of money."

"I don't care what she thinks. I have to get him out of there," I say. "Let her try and stop me."

There's so much anger in me that I can feel it buzzing through my blood. I know I'm not being rational. I know that my rage won't transform me into something stronger and greater than what I am. I know that I am in over my head, that I've taken Gabriel down with me. But all I can do at this point is try.

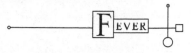

Somewhere behind me Lilac is calling out to Jared, saying that something is wrong, that Maddie's coughing blood. She's in a panic, telling him to come and help her, to quit worrying about me. And she's right. He knows it.

"Don't be stupid," he tells me. But the only stupid thing would be to stand around not trying to fix anything.

Jared goes his way, and I go mine.

Gabriel is half-awake in the green tent, his eyes wild and blue. When he sees me, he struggles to regain awareness. "They injected me with something," he says, slurring the words. "'Time to die,' they said. The horses all began to blur."

Madame must have been planning this. Incapacitate Gabriel so that he would have no way of saving me. Sell me off to the highest bidder.

I'm kneeling in the entrance. The wind is howling behind me, as though Madame herself has conjured it. I am certain she is running toward us, and then it will all be over. I don't know how, but it will be over.

"We have to go," I say, reaching for him.

He struggles to his feet and says, "Hurry up. We have no time."

The wind is screaming.

No. It's not the wind.

The girls. Madame's girls are screaming.

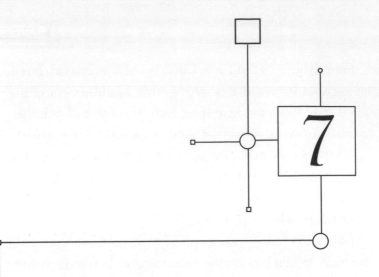

7

I HEARD SOMEONE running toward me. This much I remember. I turned and saw Madame, white hair all undone and wild around her. In the light of all the lanterns, bits of it were blond. She had her arm raised. *A knife*, I thought. She was going to pierce my heart. It was going to be the end.

But the thing glinting in her hand was too small for that. Slim and silver. I couldn't quite place it until she jabbed it into my shoulder.

A syringe. The word appeared in front of my eyes, before the darkness swept over it like waves.

Now there is something coming back to me. A pulse. The sound of breathing. Muttering.

Something brushes against my hand, and bit by bit I can feel my body materializing. But I can't quite open my eyes. Not yet. "It's done," a voice says. A voice that's dark and baritone. Jared. "She's dead."

Are they talking about me? Maybe I am dead. Maybe that syringe was full of poison, and now my spirit is trapped in my own corpse somehow. Will I feel myself burning in the incinerator?

"Let me see the body," Madame says. "Maybe the dress can be spared."

"I put her—it—in the incinerator, Madame. It was upsetting Lilac."

"Bah!" Madame says. "It is her own fault." *Her own vault.* "Should have let me drown that useless girl when she was born."

No, they aren't talking about me. I can still feel my heart beating, and it sinks when I realize what has happened. Madame and Jared are talking about Maddie. Maddie is dead. Incinerated.

How quickly the topic changes, though. Madame is more interested in Jared's gunshot wound, fussing that it may become infected and she cannot afford the medication.

"Where is that stupid girl?" Madame says. "She is good with treating wounds."

"Give her time to grieve," Jared says.

"Nonsense . . ."

Their voices fade. I feel myself slipping away.

When I wake up again, I can curl my fingers into a fist. In the dream I was holding something important, but now I can't remember what it was. I am only aware of the emptiness I feel gripping nothing.

I'm able to open my eyes, and everything is yellow. Buttercups, I think. They sprouted up in my mother's garden one year, an unexpected surprise. She'd been experimenting with seeds and compost. "Look," she told me, crouching down. I was so small back then—small enough that I could pretend to be lost in that garden, which didn't seem as big after my mother died. The sunlight burned my exposed shoulders. I dug my fingers into the cold earth, probing for worms. I liked dangling them, liked the way they retracted and expanded their beige-pink bodies between my fingers.

"Buttercups," my mother said. Buttery, rubbery little flowers were coming up in the dirt.

My brother was sword-fighting with a stick nearby, parrying and stabbing at the air. "They're just weeds," he said.

I hear the wind. The yellow undulates over and around me, and I realize with despair that I'm in one of Madame's tents.

I don't quite have the strength to raise my head; the edges of my vision are smeared, but I am aware of someone breathing beside me. A hand brushing against mine. A voice whispering my name. It sounds exhausted and terrified.

Gabriel. I try to answer him, but my lips won't move.

"Shut your eyes," he whispers. "Someone's coming."

I do, but I can still see all that yellow in my eyelids. Someone opens the tent, letting in a burst of cold air, but

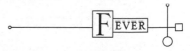

my body doesn't shiver. I can feel the cold in a detached sort of way.

"She can't keep them like this." Lilac's voice. "Look at them. They'll die."

"She wants to be rid of the boy by tonight." Jared's voice is even more menacing and dark now that he's talking softly. "She has another buyer coming to look at the girl."

I try to concentrate on what's being said. I know it's important. But my brain won't cooperate. I'm phasing in and out of darkness.

Somehow I will my fingers to move, and they brush against Gabriel's. He's more in control of his body than I am mine. He grabs my hand and holds on tight.

Something awful is going to happen to both of us. And how can I stop it? I can't even hold on to his hand.

This time when I wake, it's violent. My wrists are yanked upward, my eyes fly open, and my head jolts back so hard that I think my neck will snap. "Up, up, up!" the voice is saying. I stagger. I'm on my feet, but I can't hold the position. I fall forward, and someone pulls me back up.

"What?" I try to say, but I don't think anything intelligible has come out of my mouth.

I'm being pushed outside. Everything is dark. No carnival lights. No Ferris wheel. No music, either.

Hands are pushing me, and someone is saying, "Go!"

But I can't. My legs are rubbery and numb. My stomach is churning, and sure enough, I vomit before I've even finished my next breath.

Curses, muttering. I'm still coughing when someone throws me onto their shoulder and breaks into a run. I know it isn't Gabriel; he would never be so violent with me.

All around me I hear frantic whispers, bare feet pounding against the dirt as people run in all directions. I shut my eyes tight and try to keep my stomach quiet. It's all I can do. The carnival has ended. Madame's languid girls are running scared. Maddie is dead, her little body burned to ash. The world has gone completely crazy.

Then, suddenly, the person carrying me stops running. Sets me down. Holds me under my arms so I don't collapse.

I can't see much of anything in this darkness, but I recognize the outline of those wide shoulders. I can see the gauze tied around his arm. Jared.

"What have you done?" His voice is low, thunderous. "What have you brought to this place?"

"I don't—" I press the heel of my hand to my forehead, trying to get my bearings. "I don't know what you're talking about."

"There are people looking for you," he says. "Madame has ordered a blackout. She thinks spies are trying to break in and kill us all to find you."

"Madame is a lunatic," I say. I blink several times, try-

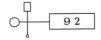

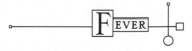

ing to regain my senses. The stars overhead all throb with unreal brightness, and then subside. The earth tips under me.

"Not this time," Jared says. His fingers are boring into my skin as he holds me up. "There's a man at the gate looking for you."

Wake up! I tell myself. Whatever was injected into my veins that made me sleep is holding my mind hostage.

"Who?" I say. There's a horrible, coppery taste in my mouth.

"A Housemaster," Jared says. "He claims you're his property."

I repeat the words several times in my head before they hold any meaning. And then my blood goes cold. It's impossible. How could Housemaster Vaughn have followed me here? My father-in-law played the role of a mad scientist, it's true, but his domain ended at the mansion gates.

I regain enough cognition to break away from Jared's grip on me. My stomach and head are swimming. There are insects buzzing and chirping around me. Dry grass is brushing against my bare legs. "Where is he?" I say.

I don't know where we are, but I can hear the incinerator, which means we must be far from the Ferris wheel and the tents. I hear whispers and rustles all around me. Either I'm hallucinating or everyone is hiding.

Jared looks at me, and I can only see the whites of his eyes.

Without lights and from a distance, the carnival in the moonlight looks like one of Linden's unfinished drawings. All lines and beams and angles. I feel as though I have tripped and fallen into the unreal world of his sketchbook.

"Madame told me to hide you until he offers a suitable reward."

She may be a lunatic, but she is all about business first.

The whispers around me are getting louder. The grass is growing high up over my head, bending over me, coiling around my arms and legs and throat. I blink, and it all stops.

"He's lying," I say. "Whatever he told you, he's lying. I don't know any Housemasters, and I'm not anyone's property."

"Really?" Jared says. He folds his arms, and his shadow doubles in size, then deflates back to normal. "He seemed to know an awful lot about you. Rhine."

My name. He knows my name. And all the whispering voices around me are repeating it now in a hushed chorus.

And then my name is being screamed from across the abandoned carnival. Madame. I whip in the direction of the voice, but Jared has no reaction to it. I hear footsteps coming at me, but no figures emerge from the darkness.

You're hallucinating, I tell myself. It's whatever was injected into my veins. It's the smoke that the cold air still carries.

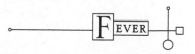

Jared holds up a giant net in which to trap me. But once he wraps it over my shoulders, I realize it's his coat.

A softer voice says, "Is that your real name? 'Rhine'?" Lilac is rising to a stand in the tall grass. Has she been hiding in this whispering field the whole time?

I don't answer.

Lilac grabs my hand. Her fingers are gentle, small, and cold. She runs her thumb over my wedding band and says, "Was marriage really so bad? Worse than this place?"

It's a good question, and my mind is so bleary right now that I can only answer honestly. "No," I say. "Not worse than this."

I had a comfortable bed. A husband who adored me. Sister wives to quell the loneliness—or, on most days, to share it with me. Maybe I should give up. Walk through this dilapidated carnival one final time to give myself to Vaughn, and sober up on the long drive back home.

Home. The whispers in the grass echo the word. Home.

Home is not in that mansion. Beneath the comforts of the floor I inhabited with my sister wives, something much darker lurks. I think of Rose's lifeless hand falling out from beneath the sheet, Jenna dying in front of me, the story of Rose and Linden's dead child. All the agony and devastation could be blamed on just one man—the very man, in fact, who somehow followed me here.

"I can't go back there," I say. I can feel myself returning to my senses. "You don't know that man like I do. If he doesn't kill me, he'll do something much worse. He *has* done worse." My voice cracks. "Where is Gabriel? We have to go." I hadn't wanted to say his name aloud in the presence of others, but what does it matter now? Everything has gone mad.

Lilac and Jared look at each other hesitantly.

"Don't," Jared tells her, in a voice so soft it's almost not there.

"Who are you protecting?" I snap. "Madame? Why?" I'm looking at Lilac. "She's a monster. She killed your daughter!"

"Shh!" Lilac says, and grabs my arm.

She starts leading me away, but Jared calls out to her, "She's brought nothing but trouble. We should just give her up and be done with it."

"You know I can't," Lilac says. She tugs my arm. "Come on."

I'm not sure if it's Jared's voice or my brother's, whispering angrily after us:

Your problem is that you're too emotional.

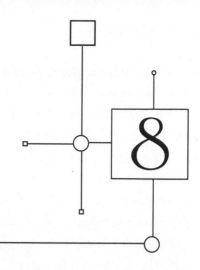

THE GRASSY FIELD goes on forever, it seems. It takes me a long time to realize that we aren't walking away from Madame's carnival so much as around it in a circle. Lilac leads, holding my wrist. The grass murmurs secrets in lost languages and grabs at my heels.

"What did she give me?" I say. I'm trying to be quiet, but my voice echoes and rattles the earth. Lilac doesn't seem to notice. "Why am I like this?" It feels as though the world is a giant bubble about to pop, spilling forth bees and words. I am walking lightly so as not to disturb it, all the while knowing something is very wrong with my perception.

Above us I can see clouds twisting and somersaulting in the dark sky, obscuring stars now. Thunder growls my name, a warning.

"It's angel's blood mixed with a depressant to keep

you asleep. You fought the hell out of her too. Damn near scratched her eye out."

"I did?" I don't remember any of it. But, then, I don't remember the nightmares Linden claims I had after the hurricane either. Memory loss may be the only wonderful part of this drug.

Lilac laughs, says, "Her Highness might've killed you right then if she didn't think you'd turn such a profit."

"She said I have her daughter's hair," I say. When I talk, the voices in the grass don't seem so loud; I'm beginning to feel more awake, if I can just keep talking, keep moving. I don't even care where we're going. "Did you know Madame's daughter?"

"Nope. Died before I got here," Lilac says. "Jared did, though. He grew up here."

"She says they were murdered."

"Her lover"—she says the word with disgust—"was some kind of respected doctor or something. He and their daughter were killed in some pro-naturalism protest. Jared says it really screwed her up."

I don't say that my parents were killed the same way. Pro-naturalists are against the pro-science research to cure the virus that afflicts each new child that's born.

"I can imagine what that must have been like," Lilac says, her voice grave.

She can imagine? She can do more than imagine. Maddie is dead now. Jared said so. Her body was burned.

That's how I know it's a hallucination when, once

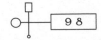

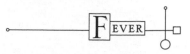

we've stopped walking, the grass parts and I see Maddie's surreal eyes peering up at me.

Lilac kneels beside her daughter, eases her to lie down, whispers nice things to her.

This isn't real. This is the angel's blood tricking me.

In the darkness I can just make out a body moving beside Maddie's. My mind, unreliable as it is right now, doesn't register who it could be until the body is up and standing in front of me.

I feel his fingers weaving between mine, squeezing tight. "Gabriel," I say. The word is as dire as my next breath. I say it again and again, until he pulls me to him and my knees buckle.

"I'm sorry." I can feel the heat of his skin as I whisper into his neck. "I'm so sorry."

"I should have been able to protect you," he says. His voice is hoarse, and it reminds me that while I've been in my hell, he's been in one of his own.

"No." I shake my head, grab his shirt in my fists. I don't recognize the threadbare shirt he's wearing. Maybe Lilac gave him whatever she could find as she hid him here, away from Madame.

God. I crush myself against him.

"I could hardly move," he says. "I could hear you crying out in your sleep. I could hear you fighting back against that woman. But I couldn't stop her."

"This is romantic and all," Lilac whispers sharply, "but get down or you'll get us all caught."

Maddie whimpers pitifully, and Lilac kisses her face and says, "I know, baby."

There's someone else kneeling in the grass too. I think it's the little blond girl who tended to Gabriel earlier. She is talking to Lilac, saying, "Her arm is definitely broken. I've done what I can to set it, but her fever isn't breaking. This air is only aggravating it." She's saying other words too, like "pneumonia" and "infection," and Lilac is keeping calm, just like I kept calm watching Jenna suffer and knowing I could do nothing about it.

"I thought Maddie was dead," I whisper so only Gabriel can hear me.

"They've been hiding her," Gabriel tells me. "Everyone is hiding. This woman—this Madame—has everyone scared for their lives."

"It's because of Vaughn," I say. "He's here looking for me."

I don't get to hear Gabriel's response to this, because all of a sudden the carnival lights up, and Jared is yelling for Lilac to come out, it's all right, Madame doesn't want to hurt her. She doesn't want to hurt anyone. Come out, girls, come on out.

Lilac flattens herself in the grass and gestures for us to do the same. The lights don't quite reach us, but I realize with despair that, despite what felt like miles of walking, we are still close to the carnival. There's a chain-link fence keeping us in.

Other girls reveal themselves, apprehensively.

"It was a false alarm!" Madame calls out. "There are no spies! Just a man looking to do business with me. But there will be no work until this is settled. Go on and make yourselves beautiful. *Vite, vite!*"

She claps. It turns into the next roll of thunder. *"Vite, vite!"*

Gabriel is half-covering me. I can hear his shivering breaths, can feel the rough stubble of his chin against my face. His arm tightens around me.

My hands are pinned under me, knotted into fists. I hold my breath. Vaughn is here. It's like I can feel him. Feel his footsteps coming for me, echoing as though in his basement hallways.

I can't let him get me. At least as Linden's bride I served a purpose. I kept my husband busy and alive and not lost in grief for his first wife, Rose. But if I go back there now, Linden will have turned his back on me for sure. Vaughn will be able to do whatever he pleases. Sedate me, kill me, cut me open, scrape the blue and brown from my eyes and study them under a microscope.

Without meaning to, I whimper.

We're far enough from the lights that we can hide in the shadow. But there's enough light for me to see Lilac staring at me. Jared is calling her name, and my fake name, Goldenrod, telling us to come out. She shakes her head.

Jared speaks again, in a lower voice that I have to strain to hear. I think he's talking to Madame. "—don't know where they could have gone. Not far. Everything's gated."

"—something of an escape artist—" Madame is saying, without an accent. Her real voice is craggy and dry. It sounds deliberately ugly. But I can't shake the thought that she was once pretty and maybe even kind.

Not that it matters, I tell myself.

The next voice is good-natured, with a hint of a laugh. "Darling? There's no reason to hide. Come on out."

Vaughn. It sets my mind in such a flurry that I miss the next few words he says, and pick up at, "—Linden is concerned about you. Cecily is sick with worry." I squeeze my eyes shut, wishing for the delirium I felt a few minutes ago, when words meant nothing on their way through my hearing. But Linden and Cecily won't go away. My melancholy husband; my withering younger sister wife, forever trying to shush the baby who is forever crying in her arms.

It's a trick. Even if I did make it back to the mansion, I wouldn't be reunited with them. Vaughn would see to it that nobody ever heard from me again.

I can't move. I don't think I'm breathing. I've never been this scared. Never. Not even in that van. Not even when I heard the gunshots.

Vaughn is saying, "Darling, come out," and, "Rhine, be realistic. You have nowhere else to go. We're your family."

Family. No. Unlike my sister wives, and unlike the

girls in this place and thousands like them on the streets, I know what a family is.

Jared says, "Is that them?"

Footsteps in the grass crashing toward me in a run. I wince, but Jared's dark, heavy form runs past me, leaps deftly over Maddie and Lilac in one bound, and goes on. But not before dropping something. I hear it hit the ground with a thud, and Lilac grabs it and stuffs it into her bag.

He's leading them away from us. I barely have time to process this before Lilac is crawling toward me and pushing Gabriel and me in another direction. I can just see her mouth forming the word "Go."

So we go, as quickly and quietly as we can, Gabriel and me tripping over each other as we move in a way that is both stooping and running. The wind is so violent that it disturbs the high grass as much as we do.

Lilac is following us, Maddie wrapped around her back.

Vaughn and Madame and Jared are calling for me, only me, my name everywhere like rain. Vaughn is trying other tactics too, telling me that Cecily's baby is sick, maybe even dying. And Linden hasn't come out of his room and he's wasting away.

"It's not true," I whisper as I run. "It's not true, it's not true."

Lilac says, "Shh."

The power goes out again, with a loud groan. Madame

starts cursing at Jared, who says, "The wind must have knocked out one of the generators."

There is no carnival music, no lights, no giggling girls, and without those things the nightmare of this place doubles and changes shape.

Then there's a crashing, swishing sound as my body hits something. I reach out to touch it, and my fingers move across the wire loops. A fence. Gabriel is feeling it too, maybe trying to determine if it can be climbed.

"It's electrified," Lilac whispers, gasping for her breath. "Normally you can hear it humming. But the power's out now."

"How long do we have?" Gabriel says.

"Not long," Lilac says. "Her Royal Stinking Highness will realize something's up if Jared doesn't fix it quickly."

I'm already climbing, looking back to see if Gabriel needs any help. But he's having no difficulty keeping up, and in fact he reaches the top of the fence before me.

Lilac is following, slowed down by the task of keeping Maddie secured to her back.

The fence isn't very high. Gabriel helps pull me to the other side. And then we both help Lilac, who is struggling because Maddie's broken arm is keeping her from holding on.

"Wait; it'll be faster this way," Gabriel says, and he grabs Maddie, who whimpers and cries out. Lilac tries to shush her, but the whimpers turn to sobs in a way that I just know is going to turn into a scream. I follow

Gabriel, jumping when I'm a few feet from the ground. Maddie is cradled in his arms, and I can smell the salt of her tears even if it's too dark to see them.

Lilac is just climbing over the fence when her daughter starts to scream.

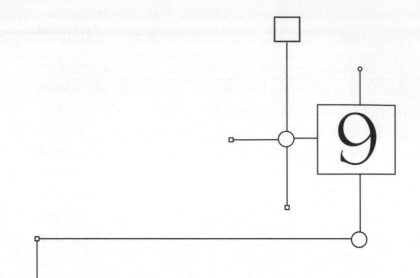

THE SCREAM is the siren that sets the carnival into a panic again. I hear shouts on the wind, saying, "That way!" and "There!"

I clamp my hand over Maddie's mouth. She's biting me, squealing against my skin, but I don't care. I'm so furious I don't even feel her teeth boring into my hand, and don't care how much I'm upsetting her.

I grab her from Gabriel, and I'm still muffling her screams as we run as far as we can before the lights come back on. The fence buzzes with electricity. We crouch in the tall grass, which is endless. Gloriously, wonderfully endless. I can see Lilac, a small outline in the distance, shuddering from the shock of the fence. And just when I think I am about to watch her die, she throws herself away from it, hitting the ground on our side with a thud I can hear over the wind. Even Maddie goes silent, watching.

Lilac moves, just barely, trying to pull herself up. Her last act of strength is to throw the bag that had been slung over her shoulder. It nips at Gabriel's ankle, and he grabs it without pause.

Lanterns are hurrying toward her like fireflies. Jared is shouting her name, but not with cruelty—with worry. She props herself up on one elbow and looks right at me. Right past the grass and across the distance, into my eyes.

Then she turns to Jared, who is standing on the other side of the fence, asking if she's broken anything.

"They got away," I hear her say.

Madame arrives at the fence, stopping just in front of its deadly humming, and cackles. "Stupid girl," she says.

Vaughn is there next, looking tall and calm, an aged version of his elegant son. But, unlike with Madame, I do not think Vaughn was ever kind.

For the moment they are all preoccupied with how to get Lilac back inside the fence. Lilac does not look back.

Maddie has gone silent, but I keep her mouth covered just in case she starts bawling again. Who could blame her if she did? My other hand goes to her forehead, and I try to smooth back her hair, to comfort her in some small way, but all I can register is how feverish she is, and how cold this January air is. She'll decline very quickly if we don't get her somewhere warm.

Gabriel seems to have the same idea, because he's moved closer, sandwiching Maddie, who is shivering, between his body and mine.

"Just hang on," I whisper.

It feels like everything is taking an eternity to unfold. Jared cutting off the power again and then scaling the fence to retrieve Lilac and return her to Madame, who is laughing like a croaking frog. They're all talking, not loud enough to be heard.

Eventually Lilac and Jared and Madame and Vaughn retreat into the carnival, and the lights and music return. From this far away it almost seems like an inviting place.

Gabriel says, "She's going to die—we all are—if we don't find someplace warm."

I can barely feel this cold. My mind is still not as sharp as I'd like it to be, this strange drug still coursing through my body. In a soft, chattering voice I tell Maddie that I am going to uncover her mouth and I need her to be brave and keep quiet. I promise her that she can scream all she wants later.

She understands. That, or she's too weak to protest. Either way she doesn't make a sound as I let go of her. Gabriel eases her into his arms, and we begin our escape through the tall grass, not knowing where it will end.

As we get away, I once again fight back the feeling that it came too easily.

The sign reads: YOUR FORTUNE FOR A DOLLAR OR TRADE.

Nearly every word is grossly misspelled.

The night ended gradually, with the sky becoming gray, then shifting with shades of brown and pink, the

stars rearranging themselves. My body moved, detached from my mind, as the world took shape in the daylight. I imagined the stars were the pearls and diamonds in Deirdre's sweater, desperate for the feel of its familiar knitted warmth against my skin. But I'll never get it back now; I'm stuck with this horrific yellow sari that trips me as I walk. Gabriel helped me tear off the sash so we could wrap it around Maddie as a makeshift blanket over her coat. It has helped somewhat.

There wasn't much in the bag Lilac threw to us before she was caught. There were boots and coats that Jared had dropped for us when diverting Madame. The coat is too big for Maddie, but I wrapped it around her like a blanket, and her teeth stopped chattering. There was also an old children's book. Soggy strawberries bleeding through a folded cloth. Stale bread. A rusty flask of water. A syringe and a glass vial of the ominous beige-clear liquid I know to be angel's blood. The water helped a little, but Gabriel and I were too sick to eat, and Maddie stubbornly refused food as well.

Now snow flits along the ground like enchanted dust. The field ended hours ago, turning into empty warehouses and skeletal buildings that had been picked of their insulation and contents. I said that there must be some civilization nearby, because it looked as though everything here had been stolen. Gabriel mumbled that they couldn't be *too* civilized. Maddie slept, her breath jagged.

But eventually I turned out to be right, because now

we're standing before a small building that has smoke billowing from its chimney. To call it a building is actually kind. It's barely taller than Gabriel, and made from pieces of scrap metal and boards. There's only one wall—the one with the chimney, which is a story higher than the roof—that is made of brick. The only remaining wall of a house. There are no windows, not even the outline of them.

Gabriel shifts Maddie to his other arm. All night he's carried her without a complaint, but he has to be tired. The morning light shows dark bags under his eyes, and his irises are not their usual bright blue. We had to stop several times because one or the other of us doubled over, sick from the angel's blood and fatigue. He looks like he's about to drop, and I doubt I look any better.

I'm the one to approach the door, which is a real door, with hinges that have somehow been welded to a piece of metal. I'm about to knock, when Gabriel whispers harshly, "Are you crazy? What if they want to murder us?"

"That would be unfortunate," I say, sounding more exasperated than I mean to.

He touches my arm like he means for me to step back, but I don't. I spin around to face him. "We have no other options. We're exhausted, and sick, and I don't see any luxury hotels around here. Do you?"

Maddie, her cheek against Gabriel's shoulder, opens her eyes. Her pupils are small, and her normally distant stare is eerie in an entirely new way. For the first time I

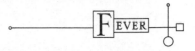

can see streaks on her face left by old tears. Was she crying all night in her sleep?

As scared as Gabriel and I are, it must be ten times worse for her.

"We don't have another option," I say. Gabriel opens his mouth to say something, but I turn away and knock before he gets a word out.

I've just realized what it is about Maddie that always leaves me feeling so unsettled. She reminds me too much of the children born in the lab. The small, malformed ones that clung to life for hours or days, or even weeks, but ultimately died. Her languid eyes just now confirmed it. I always ran past the rooms of those sad, hopeless lives, eyes averted, humming frantically in my head until the moment passed.

After I knock, the door rattles and then opens a few inches, with a horrible scraping sound. The metallic warmth of the building makes my nostrils flare. Gabriel has wrapped his arm around mine, and I can feel the rough burlap of his shirt.

The woman standing on the other side of the door is small and hunched. She's wearing glasses so grimy I can barely see her eyes through the lenses. Her mouth is open, her face nonchalant, as though the three of us are a delivery she was expecting and is now inspecting for damages. She looks me over—the torn fabric where my sash was, my muddy hemline, rumpled hair—and says, "You look like a broken empress."

"I've been called worse," I say.

She smiles, but it's a distracted smile. Now she's looking at Maddie, who is latched to Gabriel's hip like a baby koala.

"Your child?" the woman says. Then, "No, not yours."

It would not take a fortune-teller to arrive at this conclusion. Maddie has her mother's dark skin, though it is not *as* dark, and her smooth black hair.

"She has a broken arm," I say, as though that will explain her presence.

"Come in, come in," the woman says. But not before eyeing Madame's jewelry around my neck. As we follow her inside—me first, and Gabriel right behind me, still holding on—I cover my left fist with my right hand, hiding my wedding ring.

Inside, the small house is impossibly hot, the metal walls reflecting the light from the fire like we're in an oven. And there are things everywhere. Things that make no sense being near one another—a rusty lantern dripping strings of blue beads, a pink plastic Statue of Liberty, a jade dragon, a taxidermy deer head over the fireplace, a dresser that's plastered with stickers and missing its top drawer.

I am guessing that when she sells fortunes, the payment is more trade than dollars.

The dirt floor is covered by mismatched tiles—linoleum and stone and patches of carpet. There's a sleeping bag in the corner and a coffee table surrounded by couch cushions.

The warmth brings Maddie back to life. Her cheeks are flushed, her pupils expanded, her lower lip curled back in that brave defiance she showed Madame.

I look right at her, Maddie's unusual eyes against mine. I want to think our erratic features allow us some sort of telepathy. *Don't do anything crazy right now*, my gaze is saying. I don't know if she understands.

The woman, who introduces herself only as Annabelle and doesn't ask for our names, invites us to sit on the cushions. She offers us blankets, even though the fire is more than enough, and inspects the makeshift splint the blond girl at Madame's carnival made for Maddie's arm. It's just twigs and gauze, but it has held up pretty well, all things considered.

Maddie is so small that when she lies on the cushion, her feet hardly dangle over the edge of it. Her eyes are darting to all the things in the room, and the firelight lapping the walls and ceiling. I don't think she ever stops observing. Her mind is a bird that's trapped inside her skull, flapping and thrashing, never breaking free.

I take a strawberry from Lilac's bag and offer it to her. I have to dangle it over her face before she notices it, and then she raises her lip in a snarl, like it's toxic. "You need to eat something," I say. I feel absurd talking to her. She stares at me in a way that makes me remember the throbbing pain in my hand from where she bit me so hard that it's bruising. But she accepts the strawberry.

"Fruit, in this weather?" Annabelle says. She rubs some

grime from her glasses with both fists, revealing murky green eyes. She's a first generation, but her voice is light and young. Her house smells charred and sweet. It takes a second for me to recognize the smell. Incense, not overbearing like the kind at Madame's carnival, but sweet, similar to what burned in the hallways on the wives' floor.

For some indiscernible reason it's making me homesick.

Gabriel says, "They aren't very good."

"Actually, they're about rotten," I say. It doesn't stop Maddie from eating the next one I feed her.

Annabelle kneels beside Maddie's cushion, her frizzed white hair full of firelight. Maddie snarls at her, teeth stained pink with juice.

"I don't have anything for a broken arm," Annabelle says. "But I have something for fevers, if you wouldn't mind my taking those strawberries off your hands. You said yourself they were rotten."

"Take them," Gabriel says before I can interject. I shoot him an indignant look, but his eyes are on Maddie, whose cheeks are flushed.

I hand over the strawberries, careful to keep the stale bread hidden. Who knows when we'll be able to find food again.

We watch Annabelle eat every mushy strawberry, several at a time, then suck the juice from the cloth, and finally suck each of her fingertips. The entire process seems to go on for a very long time.

"Ah," she groans, sitting back on her heels. "That hit

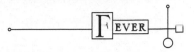

the spot. Hardly anything but dehydrated food in the winter." She doesn't ask where the strawberries came from, though, which I take as an act of consideration on her part.

She crawls to the dresser and rummages through one of its drawers, finally extracting a mason jar of white pills. Normally I would be wary of accepting pills from a total stranger, especially after Madame, but as she brings the jar closer, I recognize their oval shapes, the *A* stamped onto each individual pill. Aspirin. The same stuff my brother and I kept in the house. It's not hard to come by—if you can afford it.

Annabelle is so grateful for the semi-fresh fruit that, in addition to giving Maddie a dose of aspirin, she even offers us a spot on her floor to sleep. "Only until noon," she says. "That's when I start getting customers." She adds, "That sure is pretty, dear."

She's eyeing one of my necklaces, which bears yellow beads shaped like stars and moons. I pull it over my head and hand it to her without a word. And then I settle on the blanket, my back to Gabriel's chest. Maddie is already asleep on the cushion, which is why it's so easy for me to drape my arm over her. I'm a light sleeper. I'll know if she or Gabriel moves away from me.

Annabelle ignores us, humming as she pokes the fire and arranges the tarot cards on her coffee table. A few minutes later she leaves, I think to use the outhouse that stands a distance from her house.

"We shouldn't both sleep," Gabriel says the moment she's gone. "You go ahead. I'm wide awake anyway."

My cheek rests on his arm. In the abyss of my eyelids, I can see both of his arms wrapping around me, coiling and coiling, covering me head to toe. It's as creepy as it is comforting. I feel myself fading. How can he stay awake?

"Shifts," I agree. My voice sounds a million miles away. I'm not even sure if I'm speaking, or dreaming of speaking. "When you get too tired, move away from me and I'll wake up and take over."

He peels some hair from my face, and I can feel his eyes studying me. "Okay," he murmurs. It's not even a word. It's a white throb in my eyelids.

Living with my brother after our parents died, I trained my body to sleep deeply for an hour at a time, and to be alert for the hour after that so I could keep watch. But it's been so many months of crisp linens and down pillows, and the cadenced breathing of my sister wives across the hall, the *click-click-click* of my gold-rimmed bedside clock, the subtle shifts of the mattress when husband or sister wife crept in to sleep beside me. And though I try to maintain the urgency of this situation, sleep is pulling me back to that warm dark place.

"Good night," a voice says.

"Good night, Linden," I murmur as everything fades away.

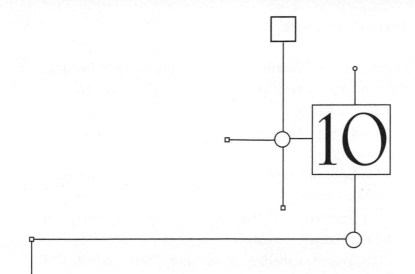

THERE ARE NO WINDOWS, and when

Gabriel wakes me, I have no way of knowing how long I
was out. "I just need a few minutes, okay?" he whispers.
"Wake me if you get tired."

But I'm feeling more rested than I have since I left the
mansion. My dreamless sleeps are always the deepest,
and the easiest to slip out of.

Maddie is awake, lying on her side so that she faces
me, her broken arm resting on her hip. The sheen of
sweat on her face tells me the fever is breaking. In the
firelight her too-light eyes are exhausted and serene.
She stares at me, and I stare back, both of us searching
out each other's faces as though there will be answers.

It occurs to me that I've just inherited this child,
that Lilac lost her daughter and her chance of freedom in one fell swoop, and gave both of those precious
things to two strangers. I don't know why. I can only

guess that if Maddie were discovered by Madame, she'd be murdered, and Lilac thought watching her daughter disappear was better than watching her die.

"I lost my mother too," I say. It's the only thing I can think to say.

Maddie blinks at me—slowly, wearily. Then she sighs, her chest puffing out like that of a tiny bird defending its territory before she deflates. She reaches with her good arm to stroke my necklaces.

"Where's Annabelle?" I ask her. "Still outside?" I don't really expect an answer, but Maddie's eyes dart to the door and then back to my necklace.

"She went outside?" I say.

I think she nods, but she might have been shaking the hair out of her eyes.

Annabelle returns a few minutes later with arms full of splintered boards that I guess she has foraged from nearby buildings. I didn't get a good look at the area, but I think most of it's abandoned.

"Your face is much nicer after you've had a little sleep," Annabelle says. She kneels by the fireplace and begins piling the boards into a triangle.

I sit up, necklaces swishing out of Maddie's uncurled fist. I can hear something ticking, and I have to scan the cluttered room twice before I finally spot the metal clock dangling from a nail on the wall. Ten o'clock.

"Thank you for letting us stay," I say. "We'll be out of here soon."

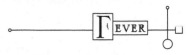

Annabelle, half-facing me as she works, smiles. "Off to your broken castle, Empress?"

"I thought empresses lived in palaces," I say.

She laughs, and the sound catches in the glass wind chimes outside her door.

"You were something great in a past life," she says. "A siren, maybe, or a mermaid."

I sit up fully, stretch my legs before me, and then cross them, lean back on my hands. I don't believe in past lives, or mythical creatures, but I indulge her anyway. At least it fills the silence. "I've always loved the water. In this life, anyway."

"There's a man who would drown for you, I bet," Annabelle says. Then, imitating my tone, she adds, "In this life, anyway." She smiles ruefully at Gabriel, and I can tell she isn't talking about him.

I don't respond. Part of being a good liar is never letting an apt guesser know when she's happened upon a truth. So I watch her hands moving, putting scrawnier boards into the fire. Her fingers are fascinating, freckled and shock white, covered in silver and brass and copper rings at every knuckle. The necklace I've given her blends perfectly with her mismatched motif. First generations are very sentimental about things, I've noticed. My parents were that way too. They had books and jewelry, and memories to breathe life into them.

A pang of jealousy flits through me. I'll never live long enough to feel that way about anything.

Annabelle stands, dusts off her hands, and moves to

sit on a cushion across the table from me.

"Tell me, Empress." She folds her hands, leans forward. "Is there anything you'd like to know?"

"About my past lives?" I say.

"That is my specialty," she says, and her hands break apart and flutter like a riot of birds. The shadows make them multiply. "But you, I suspect, have more pressing things in *this* life."

Maddie is sitting beside me now, coiling her finger around one of my necklaces. The plastic makes a dull grinding, like her thoughts turning. I hesitate; then I shrug the necklace over my head, and Maddie lets go.

I place it on the table as payment.

Annabelle makes a gesture for me to give her my hands. I do. Her thumbs prod my palms. Her rings are cold. She closes her eyes, settles more comfortably on the cushion.

I can see her eyeballs roving around behind her eyelids. Part of the show. My brother says fortune-telling is a form of psychology, and I know he's right. But a very small part of me—the part that is homesick, and tired, and afraid to die—wants to believe that I could have been an empress or a siren, that I was once destined for greatness. And that desire is why Annabelle has so many trinkets.

But she says nothing. She opens her eyes, narrowing them at me as though I've deliberately eluded her. "What is your sign?" she asks me.

"My sign?" I say.

"Sign, sign." Her fingers flutter as though the answer

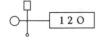

should be obvious. "Your astrological sign."

"How should I know?" I say.

"What is your birthday, child?" she says.

It hits me all at once.

Time stood still for me in the mansion. Looking back, those months now feel as small as minutes. But as I frittered away in Linden's dreamland, the world was going on nonetheless. Time was passing. My life span lessening. I've always known that, in some way-back part of my brain. As the Gatherers' doors slammed shut; as Linden pressed his face into my neck and breathed me in; as Cecily pounded out the notes on the piano; as Jenna let loose her final breath. And since my escape, as the date drew nearer and I remained no closer to my twin brother or my home, I have been dodging the reality of it. I spent an indeterminate period of time in a haze brought on by Madame's opiates, even opening myself up to terror and nightmares. Anything to escape the truth, which is that one side of the hourglass is much emptier than the other.

"January thirtieth," I say. "It's just passed." How long ago? Days? Certainly not more than a week. But I am sure we're into February now.

"Aquarius," Annabelle says, and smiles. "Ever the unpredictable one."

So I'm unpredictable. I decide to take it as a compliment. It's hard to capture the unpredictable, to keep it restrained.

"Ask me a question," she says.

Her voice is not theatrical. She has no crystal ball. (I've seen plenty of those with roadside clairvoyants.) Everything about the statement is ordinary.

I try to think of a way to ask my question without also giving away the answer. That's another bit of psychology right there.

"I'm trying to find someone," I say.

"That isn't a question."

"Where is the person I'm trying to find? then."

She smiles wryly at me, shuffles the deck of tarot cards. Maddie watches with interest, sitting up, the fingers on her good arm making swirls over her knee. Her hair is dank and wilted with sweat.

"Where is that person? Where is that person?" Annabelle murmurs as she spreads the cards facedown, sweeps them together, spreads them apart. When she has lumped the cards into three piles, she says, "Which pile?"

I randomly point to the one on my left. She pushes it toward me. "And another," she says.

I point to the one in the middle. She pushes it toward me. "Take the top cards from each pile," she says. I do. "Turn them over," she says. I do.

They land on the table before I've really looked at them. One, then the other.

There's a picture of a man on one card, a woman on the other. Both of them are dressed royally with red robes and crowns. I read their respective captions:

The Empress.

The Emperor.

Despite myself, I get goose bumps. Annabelle looks at me, eyebrow raised smugly. "Now I see why you've been eluding me," she says. "It's not just your unpredictable nature. You're missing your other half. Your Emperor."

I lean back on my hands, maintaining my neutral gaze. "I didn't know the cards were gender specific," I say. "What makes you sure I'm not the Emperor rather than the Empress?"

"Gender has nothing to do with it," Annabelle says, sliding the two cards toward me. "This is the card you chose first."

"Randomly," I interject, my voice cool to hide this new sense of intrigue.

"Would you like to know what the Empress is telling me?" Annabelle asks. She's grinning, showing a mouthful of yellowed teeth. Clearly she's enjoying her little accuracy.

I'm replaying the way she shuffled the cards, trying to remember if anything was strange about it, if she glanced at them, if she manipulated them so that they would read what she wanted them to read. But I can think of nothing, and even if this is all a scam, at least it's entertaining and all it cost was a necklace I didn't care about. I only say, "What?"

"The Empress is a good card. The Empress is nur-turing and loyal. Though"—she frowns at the Emperor card—"perhaps to a fault."

She nods to my hands, which are resting on the table, fin-gers interlaced. "I couldn't help noticing your ring," she says.

"If I have to give it to you to hear the rest of this, then forget it," I say.

"I was only going to remark on its patterns." She makes a gesture for my hand. I hesitate. "I won't ask you to remove it," she says.

I cautiously let her take my hand, and she traces her finger over the vines and flowers etched into my wedding band. "The Empress loves tending to living things, seeing them grow. But if a flower is overwatered, it wilts."

I think of my mother's lilies, how brilliant they were when she was alive, and how desperately I tried to revive them after she died, how important it was for me to keep that small piece of her going, and how I failed. "Perhaps," Annabelle says, "you love too fiercely."

Again I let nothing on my face reveal that she's stumbled upon a truth. That's how these things work. Fortune-tellers make guesses and then rely on the physical reaction.

"What about the Emperor?" I say, drawing back my hand and hiding it under the table.

"The Emperor is brave and in command," she says. "Because you drew this card next to your own, I believe it represents someone close to you. Someone as a part of your being as you yourself are."

Her eyes, on the other side of those filthy glasses, are knowing. "Is this person you're searching for your twin, perhaps?"

Easy guess. Empress, Emperor. A prickling sensation

crawls up the notches in my spine anyway. "Yes," I say. "My brother."

I don't even hear her immediate response because I am too busy figuring out how she's been able to predict me so well. My eyes go to all the things lining her walls, each one traded for a fortune she's told. She must have spun a thousand reasonable lies, all with her ability to read body language and faces. I thought I was a bit more clever than the rest, but she's cracked my code somehow too, and I am almost tempted to believe her. Bits of glass and plastic and metal wink at me in the firelight.

Annabelle snaps to get my attention. I look at her.

"I am having a hard time reading your twin," she says, exasperated, "*because* there is something about this person that you won't admit even to yourself."

"That's not true," I say. "I know everything about my brother. Except where he is now." Isn't that the point of this reading?

Annabelle eyes me skeptically. "The Emperor is a powerful card," she says. "It indicates a person who likes being in command."

That's Rowan, all right. After our parents died, he took charge of everything. He found work for both of us, made sure I got out of bed each morning rather than wallowing in my grief. He has always been the strong one, the logical one. In the months following my kidnapping by the Gatherers, I've been clinging to the hope that he has maintained that strength.

Even though I don't believe these cards hold any truth, I take comfort in the Emperor. It tells me that he's still fighting. He hasn't lost hope.

"Maybe the third card will tell us something," she says.

I draw the top card from the third pile and lay it faceup beside the Emperor.

The World.

"This card never comes up," Annabelle says. "Except, I remember, back when I was a girl doing readings in my hometown. Before we knew about the virus. It has not come up since then."

"What does it mean?" I ask.

"It's a good card," she says. "It means everything will fall into place. Your world will come together."

"That's a good thing, then, right?" I say.

She's frowning at the card. "When I draw three cards," she says, "it represents the three universal laws. Life, death, and rebirth. In fairy tales there are three wishes, three fairy godmothers. Every reading is different, but here the Empress symbolizes your life, and the World may symbolize your rebirth."

"And the Emperor represents death?" I say. That seems like an easy guess. We're all dying quickly enough.

"Not necessarily," Annabelle says. "Death doesn't have to be literal. It could mean change. A death of your former life, or your former relationships."

Like when the Gatherers shoved me into that van and

took me away from everything I'd ever known.

"Who's changed?" I say. "Me, or the Emperor?"

"Perhaps both," Annabelle says. "But what I can tell you is this: Things will get worse before they get better."

This is a saying that first generations seem to have. My mother used to say it, her voice cooing and soft as she stroked my forehead when I was sick. Things will get worse before they get better. A little more agony before the fever will break.

Of course they can say that. They live into old age. The rest of us don't have time to wait through the worse for the better.

"So you can't tell me where he is," I say. It's not a question.

"He is not as you remember him," Annabelle says. "That is all I can tell you."

"But he's alive?" I say.

"I don't see any indication that he isn't."

I hesitate, the next question staying on my tongue for a long time before I finally let it out. "Has he given up on me?"

Annabelle looks sympathetic. She gathers the cards back into one pile, tucks them safely away. "I am sorry," she says. "I don't know."

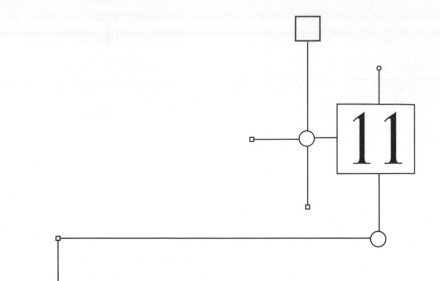

WHEN IT'S MY TURN to sleep again, I dream of fire. My parents' Manhattan house in flames. The open doorway reveals layers and layers of orange and yellow outside. The window is boarded up. I'm screaming for my brother. *Rowan!* The sound is raw in my throat.

I'm screaming for him inside my flames, crying out that I'm alive.

He doesn't hear me. The dream turns to blackness.

Maddie is hovering over me, shaking my necklaces so that they rattle aggressively. I open my eyes. My breaths are fluttery and shallow.

"You were having a bad dream," Gabriel says. He's kneeling beside me, offering up a stale piece of bread from Lilac's bag. "You should probably eat something before we get going anyway."

His eyes are tired, his skin stubbly and gray. I sit up,

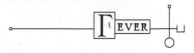

take a bite of the bread, and realize how hungry I am. I can't bear to think of the wonderful breakfast that would have been waiting for me at the mansion. "Did you eat anything?" I ask.

"A little, while you were asleep. Annabelle offered to boil some bathwater for us if I helped her carry it back from the stream. I was waiting for you to wake up first."

"I'll help," I say. But when I start to get up, he stops me with a hand on my shoulder.

"I can manage," he says. "You should rest. You look like you need it."

I could swear there's malice in the way he says it. I search his face. Faded bruises are still lurking beneath his skin. The distance in his eyes, I think, cannot be blamed only on the angel's blood still working its way out of his system.

He's upset with me. I can't blame him; I'm the one who talked him into leaving the mansion with me, and therefore I am the cause of every hardship that's happened since. The longer I stare at him, the more certain I become. My heart sinks.

"We've gotten off to a lousy start, Gabriel," I say. "I'm sorry. I promise it'll be worth it. Look, at least we're free—"

"Forget it," he interrupts, standing. "Just rest. I'll be back."

I hand the rest of the bread to Maddie, who gobbles it hungrily while I stand. "I'll go too," I insist.

Annabelle is inspecting one of her walls when we step outside. She's muttering about the wind always tearing the boards loose. She points us to the river and offers the stack of rusted, mismatched buckets she keeps for collecting and boiling bathwater.

Gabriel and I walk in a silence so tight, I can hardly stand it. Both of us are breathing too hard, from exhaustion and nausea and the trials of the past several days. And I feel guilt on top of all that too. Guilt for what I've put him through. And guilt for not being entirely honest when I convinced him to run away with me.

We sat on my bed and I told him stories about Manhattan, about freedom and fishing and tall buildings and my silly dreams of living a normal life. In my captivity the outside world became twice as bright in my memories, and wonderful, and so deliciously tempting that I wanted him to be a part of it. I wanted him to know what life was like beyond Vaughn's mansion. I was so swept up in these things that I forgot about how cruel the world can be. How chaotic and dangerous.

I open my mouth several times to say this to him, but eventually all that comes out is "How do you think Vaughn found me so quickly?"

"I don't know." Gabriel's voice is worried. "I've been thinking about it, and maybe we aren't very far from the mansion yet. He might still know people in these parts."

"It seems like a stretch," I say. "I thought we'd gone pretty far."

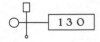

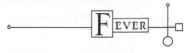

Gabriel shrugs. "We'll have to go farther." And then we go back to not speaking.

Hauling the water from the stream to Annabelle's house takes a toll on me. My arms are throbbing; my throat and skin are raw from the cold. My legs feel as though they're about to fall off. But at least I'm doing something useful.

Annabelle boils the water for us over the fireplace, one bucket at a time, and dumps it into a washbasin.

The warm water does wonders for me, even if I am sponge-bathing with a threadbare rag. It feels good to be rid of the layer of grime that accumulated on my skin.

I trade my yellow dress, torn sash and all, for a lumpy green sweater and jeans.

I think of the beautiful sweater Deirdre knit me; it's gone forever now, a part of Madame's demented circus.

Annabelle hugs me at the door when I leave, tells me to be careful. She says it in a hushed tone, like it's a big secret, the heaviness of the card reading in her eyes. I could swear she looks worried, even if she is rushing us out the door before her potential customers arrive. I see no promise of customers anywhere. We are standing in a ghost town, more dilapidated than Madame's carnival, every building plucked of vital pieces to be used in make-shift houses like Annabelle's.

Gabriel, still looking haggard, says, "Thank you for the accommodations," so formally, it's like we're still in the mansion. Then he takes Maddie's hand, and I

shoulder Lilac's bag, and we're off again.

Gabriel doesn't ask what our next stop will be. I think he's given up on structure. And I have no answers. I know we can't walk to Manhattan; I know we'll have to work something out before dark. Annabelle told us there would be a town a few miles up, if we stayed along the coastline. So we go, just close enough that we can smell the ocean, hear the waves rising and collapsing into themselves.

I think of what Vaughn said, about Linden wasting away and Cecily's baby dying. I hesitate, and then I say, "Do you think what he said was true? About Linden and Cecily and Bowen?"

"Doubt it," Gabriel says, not looking at me. I can feel his anger bristling under his skin, buzzing with an energy that's almost audible. The muscles in his face are tight, his lips chalky pale.

In the mansion he was always warm and alive. In the cold autumn air he'd bring me hot chocolate and hide for a while in the leaves, always red at the cheeks and hands. Vivaciousness under his suppressed smiles. Now he is not that boy at all. I can't recognize him.

"Let me see your eyes," I say.

"What?" he mumbles. He flinches but doesn't pull away when I touch his arm.

"Gabriel," I say softly. "Look at me."

Maddie stands beside us, watching, nibbling on the zipper of her coat.

He looks at me, his pupils lost, his blue eyes showing the empty sky behind me.

"You took more angel's blood." He looks away, to where the ocean is swishing out of sight, tossing mermaids and the corpses of empresses who jumped ship to drown if they could not have freedom. I wonder if we belong among them.

"I couldn't see straight," he says. "I was in so much pain."

"I was sick too," I say.

"Not like I was. I was having nightmares. You. Always you. Drowning. Burning alive. Screaming. Even when I was awake and you were sleeping next to me, it sounded like little earthquakes when you breathed—like the ground would split open and pull you in."

He looks back at me, and I don't see the drug or Gabriel in his eyes, but some sleepy in-between. Something I created. A boy I ruined.

I had a goldfish when I was little—a bloated orange thing my father gave me for my birthday. Days later I poured it into a drinking glass while I cleaned its tank and filled the tank with fresh water. Only, when I transferred it back into its tank, clean and crystal clear, the fish swam erratically for a while, tilted at an angle, and died.

It was too much too fast, my brother chided me. The transition from one body of water to the next needed to be gradual. I'd killed it with shock.

I wriggle my hands into Gabriel's sleeves, feel for his wrists and hold on tight. I can't be angry with him for this. I took him from the mansion, a virtual terrarium where Vaughn controlled everything but the weather, and I dumped him into a world of murderers and thieves and empty shells of people, with nothing for him but the promise of a freedom he didn't even want before he met me.

"Okay," I say gently. "How much is left?"

"Most of it."

"Let's try to ration it, to get you through until we find a place to rest. Then you have to fight it out of your system, okay?"

He nods, his head lolling back and forth. I wrap my arm around him and scoop up Maddie's hand, and we start walking again.

We pass through a town that at a glance looks abandoned, but I can hear footsteps running behind broken buildings, the sharp sigh of machines. I don't have to linger to know we aren't wanted here.

"Rhine?" Gabriel says after what feels like hours of silence. His voice is sleepy, slurred.

"Hm?"

"When are you going to acknowledge that we can't walk a straight line to Manhattan?"

Maddie breaks her hand away from mine and crouches in the dirt to inspect a cockroach that's skittering in circles. There are probably hundreds more of them; we're standing by a landfill, and the smell is making my eyes water.

"Okay," I say. "We can take a break and regroup. But not right here. Someplace with cleaner air."

"There *is* no place with cleaner air," Gabriel counters. "From the moment we left it's been one horrible thing after another." He looks right into my eyes, pausing purposefully between the words. "There is nothing better."

The earth rumbles with the weight of a garbage truck in the distance. The truck, shuttering and spitting fumes, hurls more trash into the landfill. It doesn't seem possible, but I swear the smell gets worse.

"It does get better," I insist. "Look. If there's trash, there's civilization. There's probably a city nearby."

Gabriel stares back at me, his eyes glassy, skin marbled and pale. And suddenly I miss him so much that it hurts. I miss his soft, unassuming warmth. His hands around my face when he brought me in for our first kiss. I know that I'm the one who took him from his element without preparing him first. He opens his mouth to speak, and I'm filled with hope that his words will be something familiar, something warm. But all he says is "Maddie!"

I turn to follow his line of vision. Maddie is running away from us, toward the small blue building that says WASTE MANAGEMENT in bold white letters.

"Wait!" I run after her, and surprisingly, Gabriel keeps up with me, Lilac's bag hitting his side like a broken wing. "Maddie! Stop. You don't know what's over there."

But she doesn't listen to me, and she's fast even with her slight limp. She darts to the back corner of the building, and then to my surprise she stops and waits for us. Gabriel and I finally catch up to her, gasping, and I am about to ask what the hell has gotten into her, when Gabriel catches my arm.

"Look," he says. Maddie brightens. There is a large delivery truck idling in a dirt clearing, its back door wide open.

"I think she found us a ride," Gabriel says.

I hesitate. My heart is hammering in my ears. From all the way over here, I can smell the metal air of the truck, remember the pulsing darkness of the Gatherers' van like a weight compressing my skull, the tendrils of madness that slither and coil around my arms and legs. "We—" My voice catches. "We don't know where it's going. It could take us in the opposite direction."

"Is there any way to know for sure?" Gabriel asks. The hope of this new possibility has brought a little color to his cheeks. I force down my fears. It would be selfish of me to deny him—to deny all of us—this golden opportunity.

"The lot code," I say. "My brother ran tons of deliveries, and when he was done, the trucks always went back to their lot. On the back there should be a lot ID number that begins with the state's abbreviation."

Gabriel has moved away from me. I watch him approach the truck as though he's moving in slow motion. "Is this it?"

"What does it start with?" I ask.

"PA . . . Pennsylvania? Is that far from New York?" he asks.

"It's right next to it," I say, trying to sound happier than I feel. I would rather walk than climb into the back of another dark vehicle. Maddie, of course, doesn't have any qualms about hoisting herself up into the abyss.

The side of the truck has a cartoon of a laughing baby chick, and the words CALLIE'S KETTLE SNACKS & SOFT DRINKS are formed around it in a circle.

Gabriel climbs in after Maddie and holds out his hand to help me up. He doesn't see the deep breath I draw to give me strength.

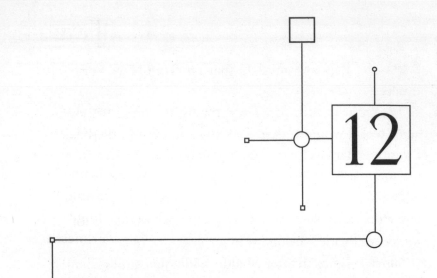

WE HIDE behind boxes of Kettle chips and pret-
zels. The driver slams the door closed, and then there is
the initial lurch and the truck starts moving.

There is no darkness like that of a confined space. It's
darker than the inside of eyelids, and darker than the
night. My eyes are open wide, trying to adjust, to make
out the outline of something, anything. But all I can see
are the huddled limbs of Gathered girls. I keep waiting
for the scream.

After a while Maddie falls asleep. I can hear her shallow little breaths magnified in these metallic walls.

Gabriel is silent, though I feel him beside me, his arm
pressed against mine, his head occasionally hitting the
wall behind us.

He just whispered something to me, but I didn't
catch it. Or maybe I imagined it. Maybe I'm dreaming. I'm suddenly finding it hard to know the difference

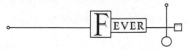

between nightmares and consciousness.

"Rhine?" he says.

"Yeah?" My voice sounds more tight than I mean it to.

"I asked how long you think it will take to get to Pennsylvania."

"What's the difference? It's not like we can tell time," I say. Then, worried that I might have snapped at him, I try to sound gentle when I ask, "How are you feeling?"

His body shifts against mine. I stare into the darkness of his direction. "You're shaking," he says.

"No, I'm okay."

"Yes," he says, "you are. I thought it was just the motion of the truck, but it's you."

I hug my knees to my chest and close my eyes, wishing for the beige redness of light against my eyelids. There is no reprieve from this blackness. It's a vise, squeezing at my brain.

Gabriel fumbles around until his hands have found my hair. He weaves his fingers through it, and I let my body lean against him. I can feel beads of sweat dripping from his face onto my skin, and I know it's because he's starting to go into withdrawal. He's in his hell, and I'm in mine.

"I should have known," he says. "It's because this reminds you of the Gatherer van, isn't it?"

I don't answer. His fingers make their way around the shape of my scalp, and brush down my forehead, to my chin, and back up again. When I was little, I used to wave a flashlight in the darkness to watch the hot streams of light it made, and that is what I imagine happening as Gabriel's fingers move against me. I imagine trails of light following his touch.

Then I surprise myself by saying, "I knew I wasn't going to die the day I was Gathered." I pause, looking for the right words. "I didn't know what was going to happen to me. I doubted it would be anything good. But still, I didn't feel like I was going to die."

"How did you know?" Gabriel says.

"I guess I didn't. Can you ever be certain?" I tilt my head, and I can feel his collarbone pressing against my cheek. I can smell Annabelle's strange little house in his clothes, and the heat of her fireplace. I can see her tarot cards arranged in neat piles before me. The Empress. The Emperor. The World.

"I have never thought I was going to die," I say. "My brother said that I just haven't accepted it."

"Your brother doesn't sound anything like you," Gabriel says.

"He's not, really," I say. "He's smarter than me. He can fix things, solve things."

"You can fix and solve things too," Gabriel says. "Don't talk yourself down. You're the smartest person I've ever met."

I laugh a little. "You haven't met very many people."

"Granted." I can feel his smirk. He tilts his head down, and his lips brush my forehead; they're chapped and warm, and all my nerves awaken. Gabriel is coming back to me.

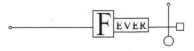

And just for a little while I feel like maybe Annabelle's fortune wasn't so crazy. I feel like everything will fall into place.

I awaken with the distinct feeling I've just been someplace safe. And someplace with light. But when I open my eyes, there's only the darkness of the truck, the rhythm of the road beneath us.

Something is shuddering next to me. It's Gabriel, I realize. I'm slumped against him, and when I fumble for his outline, my hands find his face, cold and perspiring.

"Are you awake?" he asks. His voice is creaky, almost inhuman.

"Yes," I say, straightening up, blindly pushing back his hair.

Somewhere else in the truck I hear the sound of bags crinkling, Kettle chips crunching. But Maddie's snacking on the truck's cargo is the least of my worries right now.

"You're in withdrawal," I say.

His rattling gasps are made all the more terrifying by the fact that I can't see him. "Gabriel?" The response is a pitiful groan. "Where does it hurt?"

It takes him a while to get up enough breath to say, "It's like someone wrapped twine around all of my organs, and pulled."

I touch his arm and am frightened by the tension of

his muscles. I swear I can feel his veins. "Keep talking to me," I say.

"I can't." He jerks away from me when I touch his hand, and I hear the thump of his clenched body hitting the floor.

"Gabriel?"

"You have to give me more angel's blood," he whimpers, actually whimpers, and it's so terrifying that I actually want to do what he's asking. "Just a little. Just for the rest of the way."

"I can't." I lie beside him and pretend that I can see him as I stare into the darkness. His cold breaths are brushing my face. They smell like blood and something sour. "I wouldn't be able to see what I'm doing with the needle. I could kill you."

"I don't care," he whispers.

I pretend I didn't hear that.

"It won't be much longer," I say gently. "Try to rest. I'll keep watch. It's what my brother and I used to do, to protect each other."

Gabriel makes a sound that could be a groan or a laugh. "Jenna was telling the truth," he says. "You think it's your job to take care of everyone."

"What are you talking about? When did she say that?"

"Before," Gabriel says. His voice is trailing off. I am sure he's delirious with pain and withdrawal.

"Before what?"

"Before she got sick."

I sit up, knocking over a box of snacks and creating so much noise that for a second I see white. "What did she say?" My voice is high, anxious. There's tightness in my chest.

He doesn't answer me, and I shake his shoulder. He grumbles protest, shifts away from me. "She said you were so busy trying to be brave that you just didn't realize. But Housemaster Vaughn did, and that put you in danger." His voice is fading as sleep begins pulling him down.

"Realize what?" I say. I'm getting desperate. I knew Jenna was keeping secrets from me, but they died with her, and I never thought I'd know any of them. But now, to hear her words from Gabriel's lips, it's almost, just a little, like having her back with me.

This was probably a conversation Jenna and Gabriel had in confidence, or else he would have told me about it when he was more lucid. But the withdrawal and the delirium have made him suddenly honest, and maybe I'm wrong for taking advantage of this, but I can't stop myself from asking the question again. "What didn't I realize?"

He answers me, just before I lose him to sleep. "How important you are."

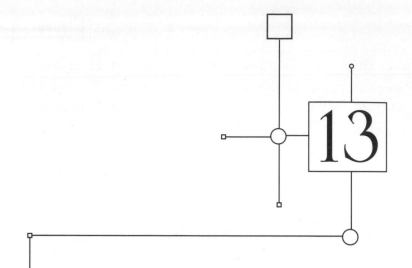

THE TRUCK STOPS. I don't know how long it has been. Hours. A day, maybe. I reach out into the darkness and find Maddie's small body and draw it to me. Thankfully she doesn't scream.

Gabriel's head is in my lap, and for the last several miles his measured breathing has told me he's been asleep, but now he jerks upright. "Shh," I tell him. "Stay low. We've stopped."

We huddle together behind piles of boxes. A bag crinkles in Maddie's hand; I close my fist over hers to silence it.

The sound of muffled voices makes my heart leap into my throat. Gabriel wraps his arm around my shoulders and stops breathing.

The door opens. I'm biting down on my lip, and there's a scream beating around the inside of my throat like a moth. I can hear the rustle of Gathered girls mov-

ing away from the sudden light, can hear their frightened murmurs.

The clang of hard shoes on metal, the truck shuddering with someone's weight.

"—could make it to West Virginia by morning to
drop off the rest if we drive straight through." A young
man's voice.

Boxes are being lifted, carried out.

Another voice says, "We could stop for the night."

"I can't afford it."

"One of us could sleep in the front, and the other
could sleep in the back."

A riot of laughter, fading as it gets farther away.

I crane my neck over the boxes and see the sharp yellow of the sun setting behind bare trees. The drivers
have disappeared into a building with a pink neon light
that reads FLAMINGO SIX in cursive letters. Below that a
handwritten sign reads OPEN.

"Come on," I whisper, shuffling Maddie ahead of me.
Gabriel is so out of it that he has to crawl after me on all
fours. I try to be careful about helping him out of the truck,
but I wind up pulling him a little harder than I mean to,
worried the drivers will be back before we're out of sight.

Maddie is holding her mother's bag, stuffed full now
with bags of Kettle snacks. I don't know why Madame
thought this child was stupid; so far she's been a step
ahead of me at every turn.

We wind up hiding behind a Dumpster while we

watch the truckers unload box after box of Callie's Kettle Snacks & Soft Drinks. It's a good thing we got out when we did, because the boxes that were hiding us are gone. One of the men slides the back of the truck shut, and the other gets behind the wheel.

Gabriel stares blankly at his lap, heavy-lidded, not minding the fly that's buzzing around his face. Maddie offers him a can of warm soda, and he brushes her off, muttering something I can't understand.

The graying light matches his skin, and dark bags are sagging under his eyes; his lips are chalky and pale; there's a ring of perspiration around his collar.

I don't want to allow myself to think about just how bad this situation is, but I have to face it. Though there's no snow on the ground here, it's cold. And nearly dark. We have no place to stay. I have a very sick person and a child to think about. Our only possible ride from one town to the next is about to leave. I squint and can see the hand gestures of one driver talking to the other.

"We're getting back into the truck," I say.

"You'll have nightmares," Gabriel says, so softly and with such a slur that I have to replay the words in my head before I understand them. "You . . . In your sleep you told me."

"I'll be fine. Come on."

Gabriel doesn't fight me when I pull him to his feet, but we don't move fast enough. The truck is gone before we even get close to it.

Maddie huffs indignantly, her hair fanning up around her forehead.

The door to the Flamingo Six opens, bursting with a laughing crowd of first generations who then scatter into cars. We must be near a wealthy area if people own cars, because only first generations can afford them. They seem to colonize in places, as though the rest of society is too difficult for them to face. There are those that boycott the birth of new children, pro-naturalists who intend to carry out the rest of their own lives without trying to bear or save us new generations, who are dying the day we are born.

Sometimes I envy them, to have lived seventy years already, to be so at peace with death.

I can hear distant city noise, and for the first time I look at what's around us. The Flamingo Six appears to be a type of restaurant, and we're standing in its parking lot. Farther off, down a little slope, there are buildings and streetlights and roads. "Look," I tell Gabriel. It is the first hopeful place we've encountered, and I want him to see that there is life worth living outside of the mansion.

But his eyes are unfocused, his hair jagged and a deeper brown with sweat. He leans against me, and I can actually smell the illness on him. I frown, murmur his name sympathetically; he closes his eyes.

"What are you kids doing, standing there?" a woman calls out to us from the open doorway. She is surrounded by warm light and the smell of sweet things. A man comes

up behind her, and Maddie darts behind me, clutching at my shirt hem.

The man, Greg, and his wife, Elsa, drew the conclusion that Gabriel is sick with the virus, and I didn't correct them. I suppose the symptoms could look the same, and they probably wouldn't have been so generous about feeding us if they'd known about the angel's blood working its way out of Gabriel's veins. Some first generations are opposed to our existence enough without thinking we're all addicts.

They take us through the kitchen, which is bursting with steam and wonderful aromas, and they let us sit at a small foldout table in the break room, and give us bowls of chicken noodle soup and grilled sandwiches. Gabriel doesn't eat. I can tell he's trying to stay alert, but his shoulders erupt with spontaneous convulsions and his eyelids are so heavy.

"We started this restaurant thirty years ago, if you can believe it," Elsa says, bringing us glasses of lemonade. Maddie gulps hers eagerly. "What a sweet thing," Elsa says. I suppose she wants an explanation, because Maddie clearly is not my or Gabriel's child.

"She's my niece," I say simply. Elsa doesn't ask for more than that. In fact, she seems more interested in Gabriel. "You should eat something, sweetheart," she tells him, sadness all at once filling up her dark eyes. "Tastes good. It'll give you strength."

"He just needs to rest. We're trying to get home to West Virginia," I say, thinking of what one of the truckers said. I'm assuming we rode as far as Virginia in the back of the delivery truck. "His family's up there. We thought it'd be best if—you know, if he's with them."

I immediately feel bad about my lie when Elsa's eyes fill up with tears and she excuses herself from the room.

"You're too good at lying," Gabriel murmurs, nuzzling his head against my shoulder. "You didn't even flinch."

"Shh," I tell him. "Try to eat something."

But a few seconds later he's snoring.

When Elsa checks in on us, she frowns at Gabriel's sleeping form. "Don't you have anyone you could stay with tonight?"

Maddie, mouth full of sandwich, looks at me inquisitively.

I weave a lie, and I'm so tired and my mind is so muddled that I'd be surprised if it makes any sense. Something about a bus breaking down, and there not being another ride out until morning, and no, we have no place to stay. But Elsa believes it, which is when I truly begin to suspect that something is a bit off about her.

And when she invites us to stay the night in the home she and her husband have above the restaurant, I'm sure of it.

As Gabriel rests against me, in some worrisome twilight that has him mumbling and twitching his leg (which only stops when I rest my hand on his thigh), Elsa pulls up a chair to talk to me. But while her words are for me, her eyes are on Gabriel. Thoughtful, even adoring. "Poor thing," she coos. "He hardly looks twenty-five."

This is because Gabriel is eighteen, but I don't say that. In fact, that might not even be true. I have known him for nearly a year, and perhaps he let his birthday slip quietly by, the way Jenna did. The way I did. One year closer. I tighten my grip on him, knotting the fabric of his pants in my fist.

I open my mouth to say that he's managing it, that he's holding on longer than I'd expected, but I stop myself. I no longer want to carry on this lie. There is so much death in the world, everywhere, every day, looming over this lovely new fake generation that Gabriel and I were born a part of, that I don't want to contribute.

In fact, out of nowhere, I feel like crying.

But I don't. I finish my soup and listen to Elsa talk about a boy named Charlie. "My Charlie." As in, "My wonderful, sweet, poor Charlie." I guess he's her son. Or was her son, because now Elsa is saying how much Gabriel looks like him, and how hard it was in his final weeks, and how she can hear his ghost in the halls. His words, she says, got trapped in the wallpaper, and they leap between the little blue flowers of it, echoing, playing with one another.

Maddie is transfixed by this woman's words, her head canted all the way up, watching Elsa's lips move. I wonder if Elsa and Maddie are on the same wavelength. If

Maddie could speak, would she tell of laughter in clouds, or ghosts in her hair?

Elsa assumes Gabriel is my husband when she sees my wedding ring, says her son never married. She says she'd love to find a girl for him, one day, who can reach him in death. And then she asks me if I know how to sing.

But she doesn't ask about my eyes, how I got them or if I'm malformed, which I appreciate. Maybe because in her world everything is out of sorts.

Greg, who heard Elsa speaking, comes and leads her away, saying, "Come on, dear. There are tables to bus." His presence breaks whatever magical spell Maddie was under, because she freezes when he approaches, and slinks under the table when he goes. She won't come out, no matter how many times I ask, so I give up. I make a game of tapping my foot against the floor in the rhythm of a song I remember from one of Linden's parties, and then, without warning, I'll tap Maddie's leg instead.

She likes this. I can hear the bubbling breaths that, I come to realize, are her way of giggling.

"Important," Gabriel murmurs into my neck, too far gone for me to reach him. I know it's going to be a difficult night.

"You'll have to excuse my wife," Greg says, returning and wiping his hands on a dishrag. "She has a hard time discerning people from stray kittens." I suppose this is supposed to be a joke, because he laughs. Maddie

is clinging to my leg under the table, and when Greg crouches down and waves at her, I can feel her nails digging through my pants like talons, and I'm sure she's drawing blood.

"We do have a spare room she likes to rent out," he says. "We'll expect payment, but that's something we can work out in the morning."

He has a kind face. Sad, dark eyes like his wife has. Laugh lines. Gray-brown hair and a close shave. But when he smiles at me, something about it makes me want to climb under the table myself. Not to hide with Maddie but to protect her.

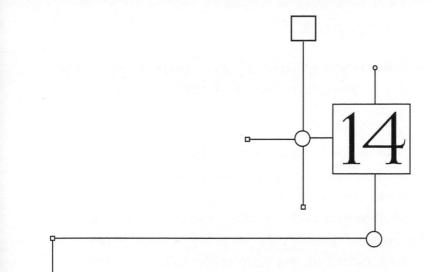

AFTER the restaurant has closed, sometime after ten p.m., I rouse Gabriel from where he's been slumped over the table for hours, spluttering in a lake of drool. I coax a little of someone's leftovers into him as we wash dishes. Maddie, standing on a lemon crate, dries them with surprising care. Something tells me that the sound of shattered glass would set her off and that she knows it.

Elsa skips her way up the steps to their upstairs apartment, which consists of two bedrooms, a kitchen, and a small bathroom on one long hallway that sections off into a tiny seating area with couches and a television.

The wallpaper in the hallway is patterned with tiny blue flowers, and Elsa taps them with affection as she shows us to our room. Gabriel raises his eyes to me, and I shake my head.

The bedroom has only one creaky twin bed, and I'm about to suggest we let Maddie have it, when she takes

her mother's bag, yanks a pillow from the pristinely made-up covers, and climbs under the bed. Used to the perpetual state of hiding that Madame forced on her, I guess.

I let Gabriel shower first, thinking the hot water might help him come out of his torpor a little. I leave the bedroom door open, listen to the odd splashes of the water falling off his body. Maddie scuttles around under the mattress, and then she pokes her head out at me.

"We need to get you cleaned up," I say.

Using the first aid kit from under the kitchen sink, Elsa re-dresses Maddie's broken arm. Maddie lets her, sitting on the edge of the pale blue counter that's a shade darker than her eyes. She holds her little arm up in offering, starry-eyed while Elsa hums and smiles at her and says she always wanted a granddaughter. She washes Maddie's smooth dark hair over the sink, and then she even takes a pair of scissors to it, fixing all the mismatched angles Lilac must have cut herself. She scrubs the layer of grime from Maddie's arms and face, humming, sometimes singing in a language I've never heard. Perhaps she made it up. Maddie moves her lips, and I almost think she's going to sing too, but of course she doesn't.

I stand in the doorway all the while, arms folded, knowing that as long as I'm in this place I won't allow myself to sleep. Not while Gabriel is too beat to keep watch.

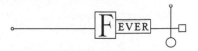

Back in the bedroom Elsa has laid out some clothes for us to sleep in, all the clothes of a young man—a baggy T-shirt that swallows Maddie whole, and a shirt for me that falls off my shoulder, and sweatpants that don't quite stay on my hips even with the drawstring pulled taut.

Gabriel is still showering, and when I sit on the bed to wait for him, Maddie climbs up beside me with the book from her mother's bag. It's a children's book, dog-eared, the brittle pages barely clinging to the spine. I check the copyright date and see it's almost as old as my parents. And in a child's unsteady handwriting, in blue crayon, is the name Grace Lottner. Maddie points to it, sweeps her fingers along the roller-coaster path of angles and edges. Then, her eyes watching me, she turns the page. The title page blooms with erratic flowers and scribbles and what I think is meant to be the drawing of a bird. But then, in all that chaos, there's something else. Something I am just barely able to read, it's so faded and messy.

Claire Lottner, followed by numbers and a street name, and *Residential District, Manhattan, NY*.

"Who is that?" I ask Maddie. "Do you know who lives there?"

She sighs the hair out of her face. Now that it's clean, it's like the fine fuzz of a dark baby chick.

She turns the page, points to the first word there, above an illustration of two children jumping through puddles, and waits for me to read.

When Gabriel returns from his shower, there is a folded pair of plaid pajama bottoms waiting for him. They fit perfectly, like he's stepping right into the ghost body of Elsa's son. There's also a T-shirt he's too flushed and achy to bother putting on.

After Maddie has gone to bed—or rather, under bed—he lies on the mattress facing the wall, I think in an attempt to conceal his agony. But I can hear his strained breaths, see his muscles jumping under his skin.

After I've finished washing up, I return to the bedroom and lie beside him, rubbing gentle circles on his back. His body is all locked up, like Cecily when we found her on the bedroom floor in the early stages of labor. She had been so stunned by the feel of it, so horrified, that when she'd finally opened her mouth, it was to scream.

But Gabriel makes no effort at sound; I know the wheezing and gasps are beyond his control.

"Am I hurting you?" I whisper. "Want me to stop?"

It takes him a while to get out the word "No."

My wet hair has dampened the pillow, but I'm too tired to do anything about it. Gabriel mumbles something about it smelling like apricots. "This?" I say, using a piece of my wet hair to paint a watery circle on his bare shoulder. He makes a small noise, like the trickle of water has brought him some relief, so I draw some more wet-hair swirls on his arm, over the hill of his shoulder, across his throat. From where I lie behind him, I can just see the smile swelling his cheek.

I inch closer, the coils creaking with the motion, so that my stomach is not quite touching his back, my forehead pressed against his skull. When I let out my next breath, his skin bristles with goose bumps. And I think: *This is his skin. This is the person I wanted to share my freedom with.* I should be happy that we have the freedom to be as close to each other as we'd like, to figure out our feelings for each other without worrying about noises in hallways, or my ominous father-in-law, or a basement of human remains, but it seems that a pall still hangs over us both even though we've escaped.

I know that I need to focus my attention on the present. I have been too selfish. While he was dealing with the shock of a world without holograms, and bearing the poison of that awful drug, I have been worrying over my sister wives and dreaming of down comforters, missing the taste of June Beans. And that is no good. I left those things behind. It's time to let them go, tuck them someplace safe in my memories and never speak of them again.

But before I do that, before I leave them behind, there is something I need to know. "Gabriel?"

"Mm?" He is weary, but fully conscious. I feel some hope that the angel's blood can soon release its hold on him for good.

"When we were in the truck, you said Jenna had talked to you before she got sick. She told you that I was so busy trying to be brave that I didn't realize I was in danger."

Gabriel raises his head a little, but doesn't turn to face me. "I said that?"

I feel disappointment rising up from my stomach. "Did it ever really happen, or was it the drug talking?"

"It happened," he says. "But I shouldn't have told you about it. I didn't know what I was doing."

This confirms my suspicion that this is none of my business, but I can't stop myself from saying, "Jenna was keeping secrets from me." And then I realize the reason I can't let this go is because I'm angry. "She was a sister to me. I confided in her. What could she tell you that she couldn't tell me?"

Gabriel takes a long, measured breath. His shoulder spasms; he grips his pant leg, and I manage to weave my fingers through his so that he's clinging to me instead. He makes a spluttering sound, and my heart wrenches for him. I am about to say I'm sorry for bringing this up, that he should rest, when he says, "She knew that Housemaster— that Vaughn was going to kill her."

Vaughn. The cause for all the suffering my sister wives and I endured. Of course I knew that he had somehow brought a premature end to Jenna's life, but hearing it out loud, getting actual confirmation, hurts in an entirely new and brutal way. I barely get out the word "How?"

Gabriel says, "She snuck into the basement just to find me." That was the afternoon she disappeared, and later, when we talked in the library, she would say only

that she had been to the basement, would answer none of my questions, and yelled at me for trying to prod her.

"What—" My voice catches. "What did she say?"

"She knew that we were planning to escape, and she was worried. She said that you were always trying so hard to take care of everyone, to be in control, that you didn't pay any attention when you were in danger. And that place was full of dangers. She asked me to take care of you even when you didn't let on that you needed it. The rest of it, she asked me never to tell you. But—and this is the truth—I would if I thought it would help you. But for your own sake, Rhine, let it go."

Let it go. Let Jenna's secrets die with her.

I say nothing more, but I reach behind me and turn out the lamp. Maddie rustles under us in the darkness, perhaps dreaming her strange, wordless dreams.

Just when I think Gabriel has drifted off to sleep, he says, "I don't trust these people." I don't either. Elsa is lost in the wistful wasteland of her own mind, and Greg seems to terrify Maddie. I've tried to reason this out by considering that Maddie, after spending her young life watching the customers come and go through Madame's carnival, has come to fear men. But no, that doesn't make sense. She showed affection to Jared, and Gabriel has never managed to upset her.

"I'll keep watch," I say. "I'll wake you if I get tired."

His shoulders shake with a soft laugh. "Liar," he says. But there's no malice to it. The next second, he's gone.

Gabriel's sleep is a fitful one. Through the night I grip his clenched fists to stop the thrashing, sop up the perspiration with my sleeve, bear it when he snarls hateful things in his semiconsciousness that make me wince. I know the words aren't for me. What frightens me is that I don't know who or what he is speaking to. Something is visiting him, and maybe it really is the ghost of Elsa's son pulsing in the walls, because at one point he opens his eyes and looks right past me, as though there is someone standing over the bed.

I turn on the light, both to show him there's no one there and to prove it to myself. But instead I notice the wild things his blue eyes have become, the pallid skin, the white lips that make him look dead. "Rhine?" he says, as though he's surprised I'm here. As though whatever trip his mind has taken him on has made me invisible all night while I've tried to console him.

"Hi," I say, and push the sweaty hair from his face. "Do you need anything?"

My voice seems to relax him a little. I'm sitting over him, and when I put my hands over his, his fingers unclench. He watches me a long while, bewildered and weary, and then he says, "Were we just talking about flying back to the mansion in a helicopter?"

I can't stop myself from laughing. I shake my head. "No."

"Oh," he says. "I could have sworn. And then your hair turned into bees."

I dangle a piece of my hair over his face, the multi-hued blond waves bouncing like tangled, coiled wires. "No bees," I say. "Are you thirsty?"

"A little," he says, and his eyes roll back as they close. He will be okay, I tell myself. This will pass.

This will pass.

This will pass.

"Be right back," I whisper.

I make my way down the hallway, which is pink from all the rosy night-lights Elsa has plugged into its sockets. Perhaps she thinks it will keep her son's ghost at bay, or guide him.

The kitchen is dark, though, aside from the moonlight and the glow of the fridge when I open the door and find a plastic bottle of water. Plastic, my brother says, is the most brilliant chemical invention because it never deteriorates; once it has served its purpose, it can be melted down and made into anything else, or left to rot forever in a landfill.

Scientists could make bottles, he says, but not humans.

"Your husband's not long for this world, is he?" Greg says.

I start, and the refrigerator door slips out of my hand and closes. In the darkness I can just make out Greg's form hunched over the kitchen table. "Didn't mean to scare you," he says.

"It's okay," I say, my voice not quite as steady as I'd like. "I was just getting some water."

"For your husband?" Greg asks. His tone is deadpan, almost dazed.

"Yes," I say.

"It's nice that you take care of him," Greg says, and his head turns toward me, though I can't make out his face. "But don't forget to take care of yourself, too. When they're dying like that—it just sucks the energy right out of your soul. It makes you feel like you're the one dying."

My next breath catches in my throat. Gabriel is not dying; his body will recover from the aftereffects of the angel's blood, and he'll be all right. But Jenna *was* dying. And, kneeling beside her in her sickbed, cradling her head, sweeping the blood from her mouth only to have it return, I did feel like I was dying along with her. I promised myself to let my sister wives go, but that is a pain that will never leave me. It's trapped at the back of my mind, always, and now, to hear Greg describe it, I feel sick with it.

"I know," I say.

"Our boy died over thirty years ago," Greg says. Then he repeats the words, slower and with more punch. "Thirty years. Elsa's still not quite right about it."

He takes a sip from his drink, and I hear the ice clinking against the glass. At once I can smell the alcohol, and realize that he's been slurring his words. "We failed you kids," he says, and the chair tips and then crashes to the ground as he stands. He is unfazed. He comes toward

me, and I press my back against the freezer to be out of his way as he opens the refrigerator door. The blue glow shows me the sadness in his dark eyes, the messy hair, the misery just radiating like an awful song. He turns to me and says, "What does it feel like to know exactly when you'll die?"

I am inching away from him, blood cold, my palm sweating around the bottle of water I came in here for. I don't think Greg even expects an answer. He's smiling at me, a distant, sleepy, awful smile. Maddie's letters flash into my mind: *Run.*

I take a step, and he grabs my arm. "Wait," he says. "Just—wait. You have so much life in you still. You're the warmest thing I've seen in years."

I jerk my arm, but his grip tightens. His eyes darken. "Let go," I say.

"In a couple of years you will be nothing but ash," he says.

He kisses me. It's a hard, forceful kiss, his tongue prying my mouth open, attacking me with salt and cheap liquor and hot, coppery breaths. My struggle is immediate, my body moving on its own, pushing, kicking, resisting. None of it eases his grip. None of it takes his mouth from mine. I feel like his tongue is slithering down my throat, choking me. His other hand moves past the drawstring of my sweatpants. He has calloused papery fingers like Vaughn has in all of my nightmares, and they're traveling down, gripping the fleshiest part of my thigh.

I scream, but his mouth is suffocating me and the sound gets trapped in his throat. The room is eerily silent. My heart, pounding in my chest and head and all my fingertips, can't make a sound.

I don't even hear the water bottle hit the floor.

Then there's a cracking noise, bone against bone, and Greg has moved away from me. No, not moved. Fallen. He lands on his hands and knees, a stream of blood trailing after him. Is it possible that I did this to him? I stare at my hands, unbelieving. No, I'm sure I was pushing him, but I hadn't been able to hit him that hard.

Then I see the other form moving in the doorway, panting with rage, his foot poised over Greg's crumpled form as though to kick him if he tries to fight back.

"Gabriel?" I gasp.

"Are you okay?" he asks me, not looking away from Greg.

"I—yes," I say, blinking, pushing down a sick wave in my stomach. Suddenly the room is full of sound again. Life, which had inexplicably paused, has resumed. And that awful moment feels so much smaller now that it's behind me. I wipe my mouth and tongue on my sleeve as Gabriel takes my hand and pulls me from the room.

"I could kill him," he's muttering as he pulls me down the hallway and into the bedroom. "I could *kill* him."

"It's the withdrawal talking," I say. "This isn't you. You aren't like this."

"Oh, it's me," he says. "Maddie, get up. We're leaving."

He's reaching under the bed and tugging the poor girl to her feet before she can even register awareness. I grab Lilac's bag from where Maddie dropped it on the floor, and I'm surprised to find that my hands are shaking. The room tilts. I have to close my eyes for a second to get my bearings.

We can hear Greg in the kitchen, and before I can stop it, Gabriel runs toward him. "Don't!" I whisper. "You're going to wake Elsa! Let's just go."

"I'll meet you," he says. "Take Maddie and get outside."

The only way out is through the restaurant, though. I run down the steps, clinging to Maddie's hand to help her along. But she's faster than me; she's used to running for safety, but has she ever truly been safe?

Have I?

She bolts away from me when we make it to the bottom of the stairs. I'm just forming the word "wait" when she tugs open the door, triggering the security alarm, which blasts through the ceiling. It's like the sound of the tin cans all crashing together in the trap my brother and I set, magnified by a hundred, a thousand. It's so loud that I'm seeing red. And there is no catching Maddie after that. I see her for an instant in the door frame, bounding into the darkness and disappearing, a bird in flight.

There's no point in being quiet anymore. I shout her name, and in all the chaos I think I hear someone answering me. Maddie, or a ghost. Hands are pushing me forward, and I'm running for the door, and still running when my feet hit the gravel. Someone, or something, is guiding me behind the Dumpster, our original hiding place.

It's quieter there, and I realize Gabriel was the one spurring me into action. He's wearing the shirt that Elsa had laid out for him, and somehow I am holding the bundle of clothes we got from Annabelle. But none of this throws me off as much as the fact that, crouched in the shadows, I am still shaking.

Maddie has been waiting for us here, smart girl that she is. She's hugging her mother's bag. Over the noise Gabriel is asking me what authorities the alarm will summon. He is still expecting some rule maker, some god, some Vaughn to come and punish the offenders.

"None," I say. "No one is coming. The alarm is meant to wake them up if anyone breaks in." Wispy, frail Elsa, and dark, staggering Greg, who is in his own way just as gone as his wife. They are the keepers of their own little restaurant. The only ones who can protect it. Just as Rowan and I were the only ones who could protect our home with the cans and string we placed in our kitchen.

Everyone wants to defend what belongs to them. I must have said that last part out loud, because Gabriel answers with "Not well enough" and opens his fist to show me a wad of crisp green bills.

Gabriel. I didn't think he had it in him. And I might have been unhappier about the fact that he stole from the

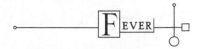

people who took us in if I couldn't still feel Greg's hand on my thigh. If my bottom lip weren't quivering.

"It should be enough for bus fare," Gabriel says, after the restaurant is behind us. "So you won't have to hide in the back of another truck."

It would have been easier for him to work out his withdrawal simply lying in the back of a truck, in the cool darkness. But he did this for me, because he could feel how I was reacting to that dark place and knows I don't care to relive it. I feel a wave of something I can't explain, but it makes me happy and weak and nauseous at the same time.

The alarm cuts out in the distance. Greg knows that nobody has broken into his restaurant, of course, and he's in no condition to chase after us. If he even wants to.

We walk along a rocky paved road that takes us downhill and into a sleeping town lit only by dull streetlights. All of the houses seem to be in good shape, their yards not overrun with weeds or covered in dirt. This just reaffirms my belief that first generations make up the population. I use that to convince myself there will be no Gatherer vans. Still, though, I gasp when a car passes us, and Gabriel asks me what's wrong and why did I stop walking. I assure him I'm fine.

"I'm more worried about you," I say. "How are you feeling?"

"Tired. Not so bad." He stoops to pick up Maddie,

who is dragging her feet, but she resists, and he lets her carry on.

"Any more hallucinations?" I ask.

"I keep seeing snakes in the shadows."

Snakes. In the worst of my medicated delirium, Vaughn always became a snake. But I thought that had more to do with Vaughn than anything else. There was one time when Vaughn, Linden, my sister wives, and I were holed up in the basement during a hurricane. I'd started falling asleep, and as Vaughn spoke in the distance, he transformed into a giant insect. A cricket, I think. Not as damaging as a snake but still unsettling. And every time he spoke to me, I could feel cockroaches running down my neck. But that's no surprise. Vaughn has never seemed human to me.

As I'm thinking about this, we find the bus station. It's one of the few buildings still lit. I don't think about what could be in the shadows, and Gabriel says nothing of what he sees lurking in them. I admire him for that.

In the mansion he was meant to be subdued. And he followed the rules, ran mechanically on a schedule. But there was always something more under the surface, held in the bright wrappers of the June Beans he brought me. And his arms opening to catch me when I flew from the lighthouse in the hurricane. I always knew he was stronger than he had cause to be in that place.

And now that we are stepping into the bus station, the neon lights remind me how pale he is, show me the

bruises under his eyes. I figure it's the least I can do to read the glowing map on the wall and find the fastest route out of here. "You should sit down and try to eat something," I tell him. "There are still some Kettle thingies in Lilac's bag."

"Kettle thingies," Gabriel says wryly. "Yum."

But he doesn't go. Rather, he watches me as I trace my finger along a green line on the map, the same way I traced my finger along my blanket back at the mansion when I was telling him my delusion of grandeur—that there was still hope for the world.

"Why aren't you resting?" I say.

"Why aren't *you*?"

"What?" I say. "Me? I'm okay." I purse my lips, trying to focus on the city names but finding they all look the same. For some reason I'm not comprehending what I'm looking at.

Gabriel puts his hand on my shoulder. "Rhine," he says. "You're not okay. Just admit it."

"No." My teeth are chattering once I've said the word. I swallow hard, take a deep breath as he turns me to face him. "I'm all right. Really. I just need to think."

He pushes the hair from my face. "Just admit it." His voice is so gentle, and I feel so sad all of a sudden. I put my head on his shoulder, and he draws me in, and my knees give way, but it doesn't matter; he's holding me up.

"It's okay," he whispers. My lips brush against his neck, and I can feel the sweat, taste his fever, the sickness

seeping out of him. This is all wrong. I should be comforting him, not the other way around. But I'm the one
who's shaking. And those are my hot tears plopping onto
his collar.

He's rubbing my back, and as he whispers to me, his
lips are moving right against my ear so that the words
tickle and buzz. "It's okay. I won't let anyone touch you
like that ever again. I won't. Not ever again."

"Gabriel—" My voice is a whimper.

"I know." His voice is low, soothing for me, but it
serves as a warning for anything dangerous that might
try to slither up between the hold we have on each other.
Maybe he's still seeing snakes.

I sob. And when the tremor rattles from my body to
his, there is true pain in his voice. "I know, Rhine, I know."

I can't get the feeling of that man's hand off my skin.
Over and over again I feel his fingertips boring into my
thigh. But it isn't just that. It's his words, imbedded so
deeply into my brain that I'll never be rid of them: *You
will be nothing but ash.*

How could Jenna have known me so well, even in
death? How could she have known, when she asked
Gabriel to take care of me so very long ago, that at this
moment it would be the only thing I wanted?

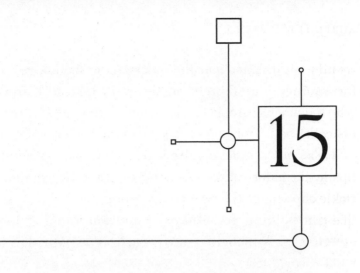

SOMETIME AFTER DAWN we board a bus that will take us to Pennsylvania. After that we'll have enough money to take another bus to New Jersey, and from there, Manhattan. Gabriel told me all of this before the bus even came, but still the name of my home is echoing through my head. Like a gift. Like an unattainable thing. I can't believe we're so close.

I take the seat by the window, and Gabriel takes the aisle, with Maddie wedged between us. My mouth has gone dry. I try to contain my smile, and can feel it inside of me anyway, tightening the muscles of my face and neck, making me giddy. Manhattan. Home. The engine is thrumming under my legs.

When I crane my neck over Maddie and rest my head on Gabriel's shoulder, he says, "I'll take first watch."

"Okay," I say. But I doubt I'll be able to get any sleep, even when I feel my eyelids becoming heavy.

I do not dream about the mansion, or about Greg, or the haunted blue flowers on the wall. Instead I dream that the bus has stopped, that when I step outside, there is a wealth of people. Not first generations or new generations, but people: children, teenagers, young adults, adults, the elderly. Like a moving snapshot from a newspaper clipping of the twenty-first century.

I am holding something in my hand, and I look down at it. Annabelle's tarot card: The World. The whole world.

Something is not quite right about it, though. I can't find Rowan. I have a horrible thought that maybe nobody has told him that the world is saved, that I have the proof right here in my hand. *Too late*, a voice is telling me. *You got here too late.*

I recognize the voice just as the people recede into blackness, and I do not get the word out in time.

"Mom?"

My eyelids are rising on their own, and the daylight is unwelcome and harsh. I shield my eyes with my forearm. "Where are we?" I mumble.

Gabriel doesn't answer right away. He leans forward just enough to look at me, where my head rests lazily on his chest, and he peels some hair from my eyes. I repeat the question.

"Just making sure you're really awake," he says. "You were talking in your sleep."

"I was?"

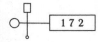

"You've been doing it a lot lately," he says, and for some reason he looks unhappy before he tilts his head back so I can't see his face. He works his fingers through my hair. I close my eyes, lulled back toward sleep by his touch and the whirr of the engine. And I've forgotten my question by the time he answers it. "You could sleep a little more if you want."

"I'll take next watch," I mumble. "Thank you."

His fingertips tap the rhythm of the engine. They're warm and alive with his pulse, his energy. And I drift into a half sleep, listening to the voices on the bus, sometimes dreaming of faces, street signs passing by too fast for me to make out the words printed on them.

I dream of where I am, and what lies before me. I do not dream of where I've been or what I've left behind. I tell myself that this is what I've wanted from the moment I was captured, and that I should be happy.

Despite the nagging feeling of emptiness, I should be happy.

At the bus station in Pennsylvania, Maddie and I leave Gabriel only long enough to use the women's bathroom and to wash up. Gabriel is waiting for us outside the door, looking tired but not as beat-up. We wait on the plastic chairs, eating Callie's Kettle Snacks and warm, flat soda.

"How are you feeling?" I ask.

"Okay, I think," Gabriel says. "My head hurts a little bit, and my back."

"It's because you were so clenched up," I say. "Your muscles are stiff."

"I know," he says. But there's something he's not telling me. Hallucinations, horrors that he endured while I was sleeping peacefully on his chest. Or more secrets he shared with my sister wives. More things I'm not meant to know.

While he's chewing on a Kettle chip, I search his eyes. I see a bright and youthful blue, the boy who brought me June Beans in the early hours of morning. I see none of the darkness of the angel's blood holding him hostage, but when I glance, subtly, in Lilac's bag, I see that the vial of liquid is still there.

On the bus Gabriel is asleep even before we've started moving. He's directly beside me, head on my shoulder. His lips move against my neck and form words that have no sound. "Dream of good things," I whisper, and hope my voice will reach him. I imagine it as a mist entering his nightmares, coiling around the monsters and then tightening, causing them to burst into oblivion.

"Rhine," he whispers. "Look out."

The seat in front of us is empty, so Maddie makes a game of hooking her knees over the back of it and hanging like a bat. It seems to entertain her, at least, even if she is annoying some of the first generations that are eyeing her. I can feel the stigma they've placed on Maddie. And on me, and on Gabriel. For our youth. For our looming deaths. As though it's our fault we were born into this world.

Still, I don't want us to draw attention to ourselves, especially after Vaughn was able to find me at Madame's carnival.

"Maddie," I say. "Come and read with me."

We read from her worn children's book, and after that we read the pamphlet in the pocket of the seat before us. We read about how many miles it is from a top-rated hotel to the water, and where to get the best seafood. But eventually that gets old too, and we're back to the book. Only this time Maddie opens it to the page with the crayon scribbles. She traces each letter with purpose. *G-R-A-C-E L-O-T-T-N-E-R*. Then she turns the page, and she follows the blue scribbles for a while, and traces the other words too. *C-L-A-I-R-E L-O-T-T-N-E-R*. I stare at the address, which would only be a few miles from my district of Manhattan. I think it once used to be called Queens. But it could be a coincidence. This book is probably secondhand, something given to Lilac by one of Madame's customers who couldn't pay in cash. A small trade for a piece of her flesh.

Still, I ask, "Maddie, who is that?"

Of course she doesn't answer.

The bus has only just stopped, and its brakes are still squealing when I shake Gabriel awake. "We're here." I'm pressing, as though if we don't run from this bus to the next, we'll never leave this spot. The next bus will take us straight through to Manhattan. Manhattan. The word sends chills and prickles through every nerve in my body, making me shudder with it. I can feel the hairs on the back of my neck bristling. I cannot remember the last time I was so excited.

I ignore the other thing too, intermingled with all this exhilaration. Some dark worry that has been within me this past year, threatening to turn my giddiness to anxiety, my hopefulness to fear. "Gabriel!"

He swats me away at first, muttering, "I hear you, okay?"

"Sorry," I say. "I'm sorry. But we have to get off now. The next bus leaves in ten minutes and this is the only pit stop."

"What's a pit stop?" he asks. We're shuffling down the aisle now, him yawning as I resist the urge to push him along.

"I don't know, something my parents used to say. Rest stop. Bathroom break. Food break."

Gabriel is hardly interested in food, though. While we're standing outside waiting for the next bus to arrive, I manage to coax some warm soda into him. His trembling hand is rattling the can, and I put my hand over his to steady it.

This is the last of it, I think. These small tremors are the drug leaving his blood. I'm about to suggest we throw away the bottle still in Lilac's bag, when the bus appears. It stops with a squeaky, whinnying sigh, and the doors open for us. I'm ahead of everyone, already sitting, my fists squished between my jumping knees, by the time Gabriel drops beside me.

It is late in the day. The interior of the bus is full of

searing yellow light, like we're inside a halogen lamp. Gabriel squints. He is bronzed, the fine hairs on his arm glowing with white as he traces his finger along the curve of the seat before him. His lower lip is held between his teeth, and pink with color again. Fine brown hairs along his face have frizzed like tiny baby versions of my own curls.

I watch his finger move, first along the edge of the seat but then away from it, making shapes, charting paths.

"Where are you?" I ask softly.

"Sailing," he answers. "Right here are the waters of Europe." I lean close to him, my chin on his shoulder, and I watch. "This is the North Sea, and then here is Germany." He trails his finger down, down. "And the Swiss Alps."

He is remembering Linden's atlas. I can see it in his faraway expression, not lost to drugs but to something captivating. Lost like me when I am dreaming of what the world once was, what it should be.

"I'm following the Rhine River," he says.

"Am I there with you?" I ask.

The concentration leaves his face. He looks at me, and I raise my head from his shoulder. "You're everywhere," he says.

"Because there is no more Germany," I say. "No more Swiss Alps." Just bits of river broken off into the choppy sea; like Gabriel said, everywhere.

Neither of us gets any sleep. Maddie, who is not used to being made to sit still, begins crawling under the

seats, much like the way she crawled from tent to tent at Madame's carnival, stealing berries from the garden and biting the ankles of customers.

Gabriel and I do nothing to stop her. She has lost her mother, and she has quietly put up with being dragged around, ripped from sleep, and huddling in dark places for hours at a time. I have a feeling that if we took this one harmless liberty from her, she'd throw a fit, and I can't say I'd blame her. So the annoyance of the other passengers is meaningless to me. Some of them don't seem to mind her; they say "Hello, little one" and "What an unusual ribbon," meaning the length of toilet paper she took from the bathroom and fashioned into a sorry-looking flower for her hair.

It's all I can do to sit still. I try not to think of Manhattan, because that will make the ride there feel even longer. Instead I start thinking of the page Gabriel opened to in Linden's atlas. France, Luxembourg, Belgium, and the Netherlands climbing one another like a ladder alongside the English Channel and the North Sea. Those flat illustrations could never do justice to what once stood in that part of the earth, what is now just waves.

Somehow this leads to thoughts of my mother, part poet, part dreamer, but all scientist. She wore a small wooden globe the size of a grape on a silver chain. My father had carved it for her. When she'd lean forward to kiss me good night, it would swing down and hit my chin.

I think of the way her brows knitted, magnified and

stretched out when she held a beaker to her face. She worked so hard, and was so passionate, that at times her eyes turned a different shade of blue. I remember worrying for her, that she might be too eager and too sad sometimes. That the globe around her neck really did bear the weight of the world she wanted to save. I remember a time when I found my mother sitting on the bottom step, just staring into her open hands like they'd failed her.

Maddie emerges from under our seat, killing my daydream. She climbs over me, kneeing my thigh, elbowing my stomach as she wedges herself between the window and me. If I didn't know better, I'd think she was excited too.

It's going to take a lot of convincing for my brother to accept Maddie. He'll want to stick her into an orphanage, which is a death sentence, since she's malformed. He'll say she's not our problem. Then again, maybe he'll be so happy to see me that he'll let it slide.

Or he'll be infuriated by my absence. We've never been apart for this long, and I don't know how he'll react. I don't know how this past year has changed him. It startles me even to think how this past year has changed me.

"We'll figure out a plan for you," I tell Maddie. She looks at me, no expression, her finger tapping her lips. Then she turns away, presses her hands to the glass, and watches as our bus ascends over the ocean on a bridge. Manhattan is in the distance, all gray, like a thought starting to emerge.

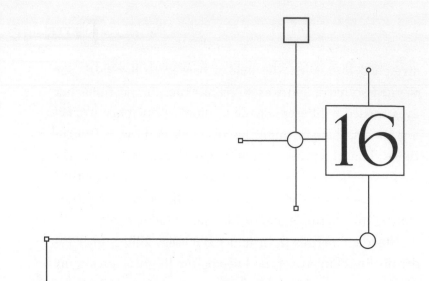

IT'S DARK when our bus stops at the station, which is grimier than the ones before it. The neon lights are struggling, full of moth wings. There is the dull, persistent smell of ocean, and of exhaust, and there's the roar of delivery trucks lumbering through the night. My brother used to drive among them in the daytime. Does he still?

There are other vehicles too, of course. But I prefer not to think about those.

A quick look at the map on the wall confirms that I am not very far from home. Home. The word fills me with so much hope that I can't bring myself to say it aloud. "We can make it there tonight" is all I say.

But Gabriel is against it. We have enough money for a night in the motel that faces the bus station, its neon *M* flickering, its *L* out entirely. It's not ideal, he says, but it's safer than taking our chances at night. He doesn't

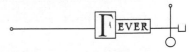

need to say anything more than that. I know exactly how dangerous the venture would be.

I don't sleep. Maddie burrows herself under the double bed and uses the emergency flashlight to read her book.

I sit on the window ledge, watching the lighthouse gleam moving across the water. I can tell by Gabriel's breathing that he isn't asleep, but he says nothing, lying in the darkness. I know he's exhausted, that he's being strong to help me hold it together.

"You should come to bed," he whispers after what feels like an hour has passed. The mattress creaks as he sits up. "Or is something on your mind?"

Lots of things are on my mind. My brother. The state he'll be in. This sick feeling of dread that won't go away. The world hanging around my mother's neck, and the feeling that, somehow, her death passed that world on to me.

I don't know how to explain these things in a way that makes sense. Maybe that's because they don't. So, without saying anything, I get into the bed beside Gabriel. We don't get under the blanket, because the sheets are questionable, and we use our extra clothes as blankets.

He drifts off, and his breathing is more even. I listen to him for a while, worrying when a breath catches or a limb thrashes, but his dreams don't seem to escalate into nightmares. I lie on my side and stroke his forearm for a while, noting that his muscles are no longer clenched.

Eventually I settle down and close my eyes, and when I open them, suddenly it's morning. Gabriel lets me take a shower first, and when I turn the knob, the pipes shudder and the water comes out yellow. After nearly a year as Linden Ashby's bride, the reality beyond the holograms and bright gardens is bleary. Only my wedding ring seems to shine.

This is home, though, and as I struggle to wash my hair under the thin trickle of water, I'm smiling.

We're close enough to my neighborhood that we can walk. It's windy and cold, but not freezing, at least. Gabriel asks why the snow is so gray. "It's not snow," I tell him. "It's ash from the factories and the crematorium."

Maybe I shouldn't have been so honest about that last part, because he winces, and I catch him rolling up his collar as though he could use it as a mask. "Is it safe to be breathing it in?" he asks.

"You get used to it," I promise him.

"People breathing in ashes?" he says. "Now I've seen everything."

"No, you haven't," I say. "Not even close. Come on; I know exactly where we are now." I hook my elbow around his and pull him toward the concrete platform that overlooks the water. Maddie presses her stomach against the railing, her arms outstretched, the fingers on her good hand wriggling over the water.

"I'd come here with my father all the time," I say. "And

this is where my brother tried to teach me how to fish. Right here."

The water is gray and unceremonious, and probably nothing like the picture I painted that afternoon when I lay in bed telling Gabriel about it. I can see in his eyes that he's not very enchanted.

"This used to be the East River, more than a hundred years ago," I tell him. "Before so much of the land around it eroded."

"Now it's just the Atlantic?" he says.

"Right," I say. Gabriel, a lover of boats and the idea of sailing, only had the outdated maps and atlases in the mansion to teach him. A hundred years ago there was nearly twice as much land to our country. Some of it was ruined by warfare, but most of the land loss was natural, the land deteriorating slowly and sinking into the ocean. But rather than relay this dreary history lesson, I show him the figure standing out in the middle of the water. A woman all in pale green, with a spiked crown on her head and a torch in her hand.

"There's the Statue of Liberty," I say. "You could get a better look if you wanted to put five dollars into one of these telescopes."

Something changes in Gabriel's eyes as he stares out at the Statue of Liberty. "I've seen this before," he says.

"In books?" I ask.

He stares a moment longer, and then he shakes his head, clearing the dazed look from his eyes. "Must be.

In my orphanage, I guess. I don't remember much about my time there. I was still young when I went to auction."

He was nine years old when his orphanage decided to auction him off for profit to the highest bidder so that he could live the rest of his lifetime in servitude. Young, but more than a third of the way through his life.

Maybe Maddie is picking up on my approaching somberness, or maybe she's completely oblivious to it when she grabs my hand and pulls me away from the water. As we press on, I tell her about the billowing black clouds that erupt from funnel-shaped factories, how they are producing everything from plastics to smelted iron to food. The trees are small and bare, confined to cedar patches in the sidewalks. They aren't the brilliant orange blossoms of the mansion, nor are they the blood-red petals of the rose garden, but still I've missed them. I've missed the coppery smell of this air. I've missed this horizon of buildings. Always buildings. Some towering factories, some apartments, and others crumbling brick houses that all complement one another. A sepia photograph of a city.

Among my father's books there were antique postcards of the Manhattan cityscape in the twentieth century, taken from the Hudson River. They were all taken at dusk, with the buildings' corners glinting as though on fire, windows lit up like a circuit board, everything close together. It was a city that didn't sleep, my father said. But, bit by bit, it crumbled. A later postcard shows

the same cityscape in an afternoon fog, looking less com-
plete. And while it's still the busiest, most crowded city
I can imagine, it's merely a ghost of those old pictures.

We take a turn down a decline, at a brick crater that
was a church when my parents were children, and I can
feel the anxiety knotting in my chest. My street is just as
I left it. There is still that robin's-egg blue colonial with
the collapsing porch, and the high oak tree where the
man in the smallest house ties his barking collie, thinking that tiny creature will keep him safe from thieves.
And there is the three-level brick house where my little
neighbor girl used to live, her window so close to mine
that we could reach out our arms and touch.

Next to her house, of course, is mine.

I see my house, and my breathing stops. First in triumph, then realization. Because this isn't my house, not
really. It's a skeleton, charred black. The windows are
broken through, or else murky with some type of brown
grime.

I can do nothing but stare at it. At these bones that
used to house my family. The front door is missing, and
the steps—I used to count them every morning and
every evening, one, two, three—are littered with glass
and bits of blackness.

This can't be right. There should be color here. And
then I'm sure I have it wrong, because the charred blackness becomes bright white, and then, for just a moment, I
can see the color of the bricks, and the burlap curtains in

the windows, and the house shudders as it draws a breath.

I feel my knees buckle, a hand gripping my arm so I don't collide with the pavement that's rushing up to meet me.

Something cool and rubbery brushes my face. I blink, and Maddie is sliding a wet leaf along my jaw. She plucked it from one of my mother's evergreen shrubs that have all managed to stay alive beneath the kitchen window. They don't die as easily as flowers; you can grow them nearly anywhere. My brother says they're like weeds that way. But after our parents' death, even he didn't have the heart to uproot them.

I'm sitting on the top step—number one in the morning, number three in the evening—staring at Maddie's unreal blue eyes. Blackbirds take flight and rush across the skies in them. The world is slowly coming back into focus. The familiar street where I grew up. The overcast sky. Lifeless branches shaking at a gust of cold February wind.

I moan, stretch my legs in front of me, and raise my palm to my throbbing forehead.

"Careful," Gabriel says. "There's glass."

"I blacked out," I say. I meant for it to be a question, but my voice can't summon the wherewithal required for inflection.

"For a few minutes." Gabriel is rubbing my shoulder, as though trying to coax my blood back into circulation. His eyes are dark with worry.

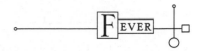

"This is wrong," I say.

"Here, drink some of this."

"I—"

"The sugar will help." He's holding a can of soda in front of me, but I only stare at it.

"I don't understand. How . . ." I don't finish the thought. The word flutters around me and echoes into the atmosphere. *How, how, how . . .*

Gabriel tilts the can to my lips, and I choke for a second and then force myself to drink.

I let the sugar and the calories spread through me. I let strength and thought back in. It takes a while, but I convince myself to turn around and look at my house. It's so ruined that even the century-old ivy imprints are gone.

"Oh, Rowan," I whisper. "What did you do?"

I tread carefully, upsetting the cockroaches that spread out and rustle in the shadows. There is nothing left of the soft orange wallpaper in the kitchen. The linoleum tiles—the ones still here, anyway—are scorched. The tip of my shoe knocks against an empty can, causing it to roll into a pile of ash.

No, not ash. Paper.

I crouch at the hill of crumpled pages by the door frame. They reek of gasoline, and the black oval on the wall beside them tells me the fire must have started here. I tear through the pages, searching for one that isn't destroyed, that doesn't crumble to dust in my hands, and finally I have one. I uncrumple it and read the words that are scrawled outside of the lines:

crossbred flowers
cilium
eggshells and chloroform
my sister's ideas
greenhouse gases
my mother's hands
one hundred days
but still no sign

The fragments are delivered one atop the other, like a chaotic madman's poem. The rest has been crossed out by a frustrated hand; the pen nearly dug through the paper.

"My brother wrote this," I say.

Gabriel crouches behind me and reads. The words make no sense to either of us, but they can't hurt him like they hurt me. Because this page is one of dozens. And maybe all of the pages together would bring this story into focus. But I will never know if that's true.

My brother set fire to his words. There's no message here for me because he didn't think I would come back to read it.

I feel dizzy. Numbly I allow Gabriel to take my arm and guide me to my feet. There's no place to sit down,

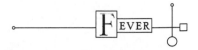

so I lean against him and look around the room. There is nothing for me here. Over the threshold I can see the living room in the same state.

"Maybe it was arson," Gabriel says. "And your brother was forced to evacuate."

I know he's trying to make me feel better, but I am too drained right now to allow false hope. "No, I'm sure he did this," I say. My brother can be ruthless about defending what's his; one winter he let a dead orphan lie on our porch for days as a warning to trespassers. He would not have been driven out of this house against his will. "He wasn't planning on coming back, and he didn't think I would either."

"But why burn it down?" Gabriel asks.

I have no answer.

There's a memory of my mother, shrouded in light. Light and blue. She was hanging blue glass doves over the kitchen window with kite string. A sort of wind chime. Her voice was so melodic, humming the words to me while I sat on the counter making soap bubbles through my fingers. "Always look after your brother. He isn't strong like you are."

I remember giggling at the absurdity. Rowan was stronger than me. Of course he was. He was always taller, and he could bend tree branches down so I could pluck their best autumn leaves. He could hold a fishing rod against the resistance of a struggling catch without letting go and losing it to the ocean. I relayed this, and my mother told me, "A different kind of strength, love. You have a different kind of strength."

A loud creak jars me from my thinking. I recognize it as the last floorboard before the basement door.

"Maddie, wait!" I cry. "It's dangerous!" But she has already pulled open the door and is descending into the darkness. Gabriel and I follow her. She still has the flashlight from the hotel, and now she's waving it around as she goes. I'm surprised the steps are able to hold our weight, but the basement looks as though it has been spared.

One step, two, three, four. With each one I wrestle with hope. That when I get to the bottom, something will be waiting for me. Or that my brother is still here. But ultimately I'm wondering why my mother said those words to me. I must have been very small, because my bare feet were in the kitchen sink as the tap water ran between my toes. I remember that. And the smell of something baking. And how pretty the walls looked in that slant of daylight.

Rowan's note crinkles in my palm, and I fold it and tuck it into my pocket.

Gabriel holds my arm, probably thinking I'll black out again and fall. Maddie waves the flashlight around when she reaches the bottom of the steps. Instinctually I reach for the pull cord that will turn on the hanging light, but of course there's no power.

I take the flashlight and point it, first into the cor-

ner of the room where the cot still stands. My brother and I slept here in hourly shifts, keeping each other safe through the night. Then I find the courage to move the light to the tiny refrigerator, which is empty, door open, without electricity. As I am sweeping the light to yet another corner, I find something more troubling than the emptiness I expected.

Rats. Dozens of rats, lying everywhere. On their backs, on their sides. Some in lakes of blood and others decomposed to near nothingness. All of them dead. And scattered among them are rotted stems and wilted flower petals. I'm so horrified that I don't even hear Gabriel's reaction.

My brother had concocted his own poison to take care of our rat problem, but I had only ever seen it kill one or two at a time. And then there are the flowers. Lilies, shriveled like earthworms. The ones from my mother's garden. Every spring I would try again with seeds I bought at various markets in Manhattan, and even from flower shops out of state if my brother's deliveries took him away.

The only seeds I didn't dare to try were the ones that my mother had kept in a pouch in her dresser drawer. They belonged to her, and I felt I had no right planting them. I remember that I pressed them between the pages of one of her notebooks and buried it in the backyard with all the other things my brother and I didn't want to have stolen.

The backyard. I move the flashlight until I find the shovel that's resting under the staircase, and I hurry upstairs. I run through the living room, trying not to see the mess that's become of my father's desk and wicker chair, or the couch that still, just barely, bears brightness from its daisy print.

By the time Gabriel has reached me in the backyard, I'm jamming my weight onto the shovel to break the earth. He helps me, even though he's not sure what we're looking for, and I can tell, by the way the dirt has been disrupted, that it's already gone.

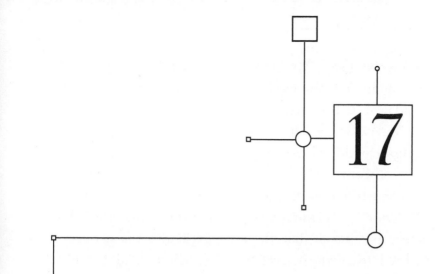

MY BROTHER left some things in the trunks we'd buried. Probably because they were too much to carry wherever he was going. Or because he didn't think they'd be useful. Clothes; my parents' lab coats; my father's glasses; a flightless paper kite I made when I was young; yellowed books about war or romance; my father's twenty-first-century atlas.

I flip through all the pieces of my childhood, and the books my parents read to escape work for a while, and I ignore the memories and the pain that fly up with the dust, because there is something more pressing that I want.

"What are you looking for?" Gabriel says. He helps me, carefully unfolding and refolding the clothes, checking the jewelry box and finding it empty. Even the globe necklace is absent. I hope my brother didn't sell my mother's necklaces and rings for money, though hope seems stupid at this point.

"Seeds," I say. "My mother's lily seeds."

Maddie is a few yards away, studying an abandoned wasp nest on the ground.

"Maybe we dropped them while we were moving things around," Gabriel says.

"No," I say. "They aren't here. And neither are any of my parents' notebooks, which is where I left the seeds."

I search everything a second and third time, though, before putting all but the atlas back into the ground. Gabriel takes the shovel from my hands, and I don't object when he reburies my parents' things so I won't have to. I just stand there, useless, my fingers worrying over the edges of the atlas, fighting back the emotions that come at me like bullets. Better to feel nothing. Better not to think.

And that's when the memory comes back.

She was baking a cake for Rowan's and my birthday. Our ninth birthday. And the other side of the sink was full of dishes that I was helping to wash. Dinner had just ended, and with his mouth full of food, my brother turned to me and said, "Next year you'll be middle-aged. But I won't be." At first I thought he was trying to compete with me, but then he averted his eyes, and I knew he was hurt.

Once he had gone upstairs to take his bath, after my mother had hung the blue birds, she said to me, "You have to look out for each other."

Look out for each other. That was our theme. I could

almost believe my parents had had twins on purpose, rather than by chance, just so we could each fulfill that promise.

But I didn't follow through on that, did I? I left him here alone. I don't know where he has gone, just like he doesn't know what happened to me. The only thing we seem to know is that the other is not coming back.

There is something about this person that you won't admit even to yourself. That's what Annabelle said when she laid the tarot cards before me. Something about my own brother that I wouldn't admit.

I stare at the hole I made in the earth, which was already pliable from my brother's efforts.

"He thinks I'm dead," I whisper.

Gabriel says something, but his voice comes to me as though underwater, and I don't make out the words. My pulse is throbbing in my ears. My blood is waves of hot and cold.

When our parents died, my brother became all about survival. He took care not to let me sink too deep into that endless cavern of despair. He worked us both into a routine of doing and surviving. And all that time, while he was keeping me afloat, it never occurred to me that I was doing the same for him. That he needed me every bit as much as I needed him.

That, without me, the routine would fall apart.

I held fast to the hope that he'd go on here without me, waking himself in the morning, having tea, working through the afternoon, setting the traps and sleeping on our cot. But I've been gone too long, and there are new ashes billowing up from the incinerators every day.

He has given up on me. What is holding him together? The answer is the same as what he's left behind. Nothing.

Mind racing ahead of me, I run into the house. *Search every corner,* something is telling me. This can't be everything. This can't be all. The stairs shudder and creak under my weight. A separate fire had been lit upstairs; it ate all the doors, charred the walls. And though these rooms have been empty since my parents' death, they seem emptier still. Black like craters. Nothing. More nothing.

I don't know how long I stand there, panting. I wait for tears, but they don't come.

"Rhine?" Gabriel is starting to climb up after me.

"Don't," I say, descending the stairs. "There's nothing to see up there."

He tries to put his arm around me, but I walk ahead of him, through the scorched doorway and into the ruined yard.

Some distant part of me is trembling. I can feel it. I don't think my legs will hold much longer, and so I sink into the high grass. I feel orphaned all over again.

Gabriel is kind enough to not say anything when he sits next to me. He offers me soda, doesn't press me when I refuse, and lets the time go to slow motion as we watch Maddie entertain herself in the high, dead grass.

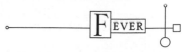

In fact, it's not until rain clouds threaten the sky that he asks, "What now?"

I lean my head on his shoulder. "You must think I'm so stupid," I say. "To leave the mansion behind for this."

He swallows, and I'm so close to his throat that I hear it. "I didn't understand it at first," he admits.

I close my eyes. I don't have to remind myself not to daydream about the mansion, because right now I see nothing.

"And then Jenna came to the basement to talk to me," Gabriel says. "She told me that, after everything that had happened—the hurricane, the expo—you still wanted out, and that I shouldn't let you go alone."

"But you still tried to convince me to stay after that," I remind him.

"I didn't want you to be hurt. Or killed," he says. I feel his weight shift. "But maybe you felt like it was better to die trying than to stay trapped, and who was I to argue?"

"I didn't think I would die trying," I say.

"Because you don't think about death."

"Right."

A new thought has occurred to me, though. Why did Gabriel come with me? Because I'd convinced him, or because he felt he had to protect me at Jenna's insisting? In either instance it doesn't sound as though he wanted to.

"And you don't care for plans, either," Gabriel adds.

When the next breeze washes over me, it brings

something like guilt with it. But I do have a plan. Even if it is a long shot.

I open my eyes, sit up, brush the dirt from my knees.

"Maddie," I say. From where she's crouched in the grass, she raises her head to me. "Let's show Gabriel your storybook."

Claire Lottner's address is in the residential district of Manhattan. "Right now we're in factories and shipping. It's just across a bridge. We could be there before evening."

"Who is she?" Gabriel asks.

"I have no idea. Maybe she's not even there."

But it's the best idea either of us has. And it's better than sitting here breathing in the burned smell of what was once my home, so we start moving.

My neighborhood no longer looks the same to me. I keep my eyes on the street, recognizing the more substantial cracks, trying not to think about anything. It never works, though. The thing about hope is that it doesn't go away even when it serves no purpose.

There's no need to look at the pamphlet map Gabriel picked up at the bus station; I know where we are. I recognize every crumbling building, every withering excuse for a park, every turn of the ocean. I even know its fish, the rainbow scales, the deadpan eyes, the toxicity that makes sport fishermen throw them back. I lead, and the others follow me through streets that will take us to the

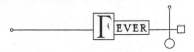

bridge that leads to the residential district.

We become aware of a crowd that has gathered about a half mile from the bridge. There are balloons every-where—white and royal blue, the trademark colors of President Guiltree's family. The distant thundering sound becomes drums and music as we press on. Maddie claps her hands over her ears, and her whimper of distress is drowned out by all of the commotion.

"What's going on?" Gabriel shouts over the noise. He picks up Maddie, who is rigid in his arms, her eyes round with alarm. She shakes her head frantically, covering her face with her hair.

"Maybe the president is giving a speech," I say. Manhattan is so technologically advanced that most of the president's news broadcasts are filmed here. It's not unusual for select roads to close to accommodate them. Not that his speeches are worthy of closing a road, my brother would say.

There's a trumpet blast that sets off the percussion of parade music, and through the crowd I can make out the drummers deftly spinning sticks between their fingers as they march. And then there's the president on a high platform that's decorated in gigantic fake flowers, in honor of spring. I remember one winter his bulletproof dome was aflutter with artificial snow. He never ventures anywhere unless he's encased in that dome.

Today he's dressed in a bright leafy green suit, his white hair crowned with laurel.

His platform stops. He holds up his arms. Cameras loom over the crowd on vertical lifts.

"How will we hear what he's saying in that thing?" Gabriel asks me.

I don't have to answer him, because immediately President Guiltree's voice comes booming and echoing through speakers that have been fastened to the surrounding trees. "What a large turnout!" he says. There's the squeal of interference in one of the speakers. Maddie is a furious shade of red, her hands pressed against her ears. I try to comfort her by stroking her hair, but she jerks back and hides her face in Gabriel's neck.

Gabriel loops his arm through mine, drawing me close. Between the orphanage and his time at the mansion, I doubt he's ever seen a crowd like this—stretching along every pathway like the legs of a giant spider. And I doubt he's ever heard the president speak. He isn't missing much. President Guiltree is more of a figurehead than anything else. A symbol of a pointless tradition that's been carried on for centuries. America is a country. A country must have a leader, even if its people are scrambling around like ants without their queen, going through the motions but to no end.

Behind the president, in his dome, are all nine of his wives, each wearing a different shade of pastel dress and a crown of laurel. Three of them are first generation; four of the younger brides appear to be in various stages of pregnancy. They were chosen from a long

list of applicants, bright-eyed and willing. I often wonder if they regret their decision. The luxurious life of a
wealthy man's bride has its appeal. I know that. But it
even took its toll on Cecily, who'd spent her childhood
dreaming of it. There was a desperate undercurrent to
our marriage—a feeling of being in a dream from which
I couldn't seem to awaken. A nagging sense that my life,
laid out so neatly like the clothes Deirdre left on my
divan, was no longer my own.

The president is saying something about the
approach of spring and newness, but it's hard to pick
out his words when they keep echoing. The drummers
have all stopped to listen. A hush falls over the crowd
in time with a gust of sea air, and the president's voice
becomes a mumble and then nothing at all as the speakers are readjusted.

"Technical difficulties, folks," he says, laughing good-
naturedly. Someone behind me growls.

I'm just opening my mouth to tell Gabriel we should
leave, when the president starts up again.

"As everyone is aware," he says, "spring will soon be
upon us." And then he dips into a speech about how spring
brings newness and life, and with the birth of the dog-
wood blossoms that surround his home, and the anticipated arrival of his new sons, he would like to restore
some hope to us as well. "That is why," he says, smiling
so brightly I can see his teeth all the way from my place
in the crowd, "I am announcing the rebuilding—no, the

re*birth*—of the laboratories that stood in Manhattan's shipping district."

He wants to rebuild the laboratories in which my parents worked—the ones that were bombed in protest of further research for the antidote. My brother and I heard the blast as we were walking home from school. The ground rattled under our feet, and we held hands as we ran toward the billowing smoke in the distance.

There were hundreds of buildings there. It could have been any of them. Still, we knew. Some survivors were crawling from the rubble when we arrived. I had to wrap my arms around Rowan like a vise, pleading for him not to join the civilians who rushed in to help. In the end he stayed with me on the sidelines, and we watched until the last rescue effort had evacuated. And later that evening, what was left of the structure collapsed entirely.

Not only did that explosion take my parents, it took the city's pro-science ideals, left us all thinking we had no choice but to accept our meager life spans, that nothing could be done.

A new lab. It is the first thing the president has ever said that has made me feel hope. But that hope only lasts for an instant, because as the president is starting up his next sentence, the angry cries from the crowd drown him out.

Gabriel tightens his arm around mine. In the distance someone hurls a rock that hits the president's dome. No, they don't want more research. They don't want chil-

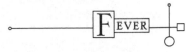

dren to be tampered with more than they already have been. Isn't it bad enough, they ask, that we've already been given death sentences?

The first generations are the angriest, but, then, they make up the majority of the pro-naturalist mentality. They've already watched their children wither away; they've seen the consequences of science, and will have no more of it. "Use that space to build a hospital!" someone yells. Hospitals are a luxury only the wealthy can manage. However, there are some who have studied medicine and offer makeshift health care out of their homes. If they're able to find a usable abandoned building, they might set up a broader practice. I've never heard of the president shelling out a dime to help fund these ventures. Why would he? What would be the point in saving a life that will end in a few years anyway?

"We should go," I tell Gabriel. I'm not sure if he can hear me over the commotion—the drums have started up in an attempt to drown it out—but he is pulling me away anyway. The crowd is everywhere, tightening on us, and I'm craning my neck to see over the heads and find the proper route.

Then the explosion happens.

I freeze. Gabriel tugs me, but then stops when he realizes I won't move. Can't move. I'm transfixed by the tiny gray cloud that has formed in the distance. And then another blast. And another. Someone is bombing the trees. One goes off behind me, knocking over a camera lift.

The screams in the crowd are not only terror. They are outrage. The president's dome is framed by hands pressed and pounding against it in anger. His wives, in their row behind him, are steely and brave, their chests pushed forward, their chins high, their hands roped together. The president tries to speak, over the blasts and the drums and the microphone interference, but eventually he gives up. His platform starts moving slowly forward through the crowd, and people scramble out of the way and then follow it. Follow it all the way to the pier, where it connects with a ferry that will take him out to sea before his helicopter comes to retrieve him.

The blasts are small. Nobody appears to be injured. But as the thin smoke spreads through the crowd, all I can think is that these explosions are only a taste of what's to come.

When we finally break free of the commotion, I quickly steer us in the direction of the residential district. Most of the crowd has headed to the pier, leaving only a dwindling number of people for us to push through. More than half of the crowd, though, was opposed to the new lab. More than half of my home city believes we are a lost cause. Believes I am a lost cause.

My hands are shaking, and Gabriel clenches his fingers around mine. Now that the noise is in the distance, and not so immediate, Maddie has lowered her hands from her ears and is blinking owlish eyes at me as though for an explanation.

"I don't think anyone was hurt," I say, swallowing the catch in my voice. "It was just a . . . demonstration."

Gabriel is working through his shock, I can tell. His sharp breaths are accented by clouds, small versions of the smoke plumes. "What," he says, "were they trying to demonstrate?"

"More than four years ago protestors bombed the research labs in the name of pro-naturalism," I say. "They didn't want any further experiments to be done on children to find an antidote, because they don't think there *is* an antidote. They think we should just accept what has happened."

I start walking, unsure what else to do, and Gabriel follows alongside me, Maddie latched to his chest. It takes a lot to rattle her, but I'm guessing even the freak show at Madame's hadn't prepared her for something like this.

"So they blow up trees?" Gabriel says.

"To demonstrate," I repeat, slowly, deliberately. "They are saying they will do the same if the lab is rebuilt. I don't know how they were so prepared. Maybe someone knew what the president's plans were in advance."

"Or they hate him enough to blow up trees no matter what he said," Gabriel offers.

"That's possible too," I say. "I've seen that happen."

He shakes his head, mumbling something I don't catch. High above us, we hear the chopping of helicopter blades, and Maddie tilts her head to watch as the

president and his nine wives fly into the blue, far away to someplace that's safe.

The houses in the residential district attempt to be more colorful than the ones in shipping. Bubble gum pinks, sage greens, an ashy gray that was probably once cerulean. We get lost a few times, because here the streets are not numbered the way they are in the shipping district; they have names. Jennifer. Eileen. Sarah Court. A century ago several of the crumbling factories in this area were demolished to make way for new houses, to encourage families to grow. I wonder if these streets were all named for someone's daughters.

Normally this amount of walking wouldn't bother me, but my head won't stop swimming, and several times I have to blink away the bright spots that crowd my vision. I open a bag of Kettle chips, hoping the empty carbohydrates will aid my brain as it works through the shock of this afternoon. First, the lost brother. Then the hope of a new lab, which was immediately destroyed. But the chips don't help, not really, and Gabriel keeps asking me if we should take a rest.

Eventually we find Dawn Avenue, and we begin working our way down the house numbers. Maddie is watching the numbers descend, all of them big and gold on the doors. She's paying better attention than I am, because I bump into her where she's stopped before the number 56. Claire Lottner in blue crayon in a faded children's book.

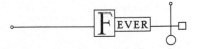

The building is bright green, three stories high with white and pink polka-dot curtains. The lawn is scraggly but decorated with colorful gnomes and wooden statues of cartoon animals arranged as though they're playing a game of catch. A red wagon is capsized on the pathway that leads to the front door.

It's the sign that really gets my attention, though. It's hand-painted in deliberate cursive, a couple of feet in from the sidewalk: GRACE'S ORPHANAGE.

Gabriel is the one who walks ahead of us and knocks on the white painted door. Inside I can hear piano keys. But not a skillful melody like Cecily used to play; this is more like a cat walking across all the low notes. The playing stops, and a child shrieks with laughter, and a muffled voice is approaching us as the door opens.

Maddie latches herself to my leg. I can't tell if it's in affection or fear.

There's a young man standing on the threshold, shirt-less, a pair of sweatpants hanging from his hip bones. His light curls are frizzy and disheveled, but somehow they complement his angular face. His eyes go immediately to Maddie, who has tightened her fist around my pocket, causing Rowan's note to crinkle.

There is something in the young man's expression that darkens. Something like suspicion, then pain. But when he opens his mouth, all he calls back into the noisy room is "Claire! We've got another one!"

Claire is a first generation, tall and heavyset, with dark skin and a deep, mellow voice that spills out like molasses. There is a cloud of children at her feet wherever she walks, her feet artfully dodging wet paint projects left to dry on the floor, roller skates, teddy bears, xylophones.

She calls everyone "baby," and she smells like fresh laundry. Her paisley peach dress has long sleeves that funnel out like bells.

She does not ask us about Maddie right away, or how we came to acquire her. Instead she offers us green tea in chipped, mismatched mugs.

The children at her feet multiply and dwindle, scatter and assemble. One of them pulls out a chair for her, and she sits across from us at the folding table in her kitchen. She offers us sugar for our tea, but we both refuse, used to the blandness for our own separate reasons. Gabriel was never allowed the luxury of sugar when he worked in the mansion, and I never cared for it. In fact, the only sugary things I liked were the desserts at Linden's parties, and the June Beans.

"Did you hear about us from one of our signs?" she asks.

"Signs?" Gabriel asks.

"We don't have anything so high-tech as a printer," Claire says. "So we handwrite them and tape them to streetlamps."

I don't remember any signs, but then again, I had my head down so much that I don't remember a lot about the trek other than the street names.

"It was in a book," I say, my voice surprising me with its frailty. It's the voice of a spirit that has been crushed, a girl one tenth her normal size. I look into my tea.

"A book?" Claire says. "That can't be it. We've never advertised in the phone book." She looks at the young man who opened the door for us. He's leaning against the refrigerator now, arms crossed. "Silas, baby? Did we?"

Even without raising my eyes, I can feel him staring at me with his sleepy, distant gaze. I feel judged for some reason, and hunch my shoulders to my ears. "No," Silas says.

"It wasn't a phone book," I say. I reach into Lilac's bag, extract the book, and slide it across the table for her. "In here."

The book is called *Pram's Ponies*, and it's about a little girl who can speak to foals, and a little boy who doesn't believe her. In the end the boy drowns and the girl grows a pair of wings. Morbid, but Maddie never seems to tire of it.

Claire does not take the book at first. She presses her fingertips to it, withdraws them, presses them to her chest.

Maddie, who has been crawling under the table, now forces her way into my lap. Silas's eyes bore into me. My vision flutters with strange metallic bits of light. My chair rattles with a laboratory explosion that nobody else can feel.

Apparently I missed the part where Claire asked how

we got this book, because next thing I know, Gabriel is answering. "It belonged to her mother." He indicates Maddie.

Maddie is wriggling against me, burying her little fists in my armpits, the bones in her face pressing on my neck. I don't understand why. We have never shown each other much affection. But it helps me back to reality.

Claire leaves her seat and kneels beside me. In a soft voice she's asking Maddie to look at her. And at first the response is a head shake that grates on my collarbone, but eventually she looks.

Claire extends one finger and doesn't quite touch Maddie's forehead, but manages to brush away a wisp of that smooth dark hair. "What's your name, little one?" she asks.

"Maddie," I say, surprised by the protective tone in my voice. "Her name is Maddie. She doesn't speak."

"And where do you come from?" Claire is still directing her questions to Maddie, but her eyes dart to me for a second.

"A scarlet district in South Carolina," I answer. Or was it Georgia? Even though it was only a few days ago, my memory of it is muddled and oddly lacking in color. Even Madame's scarves and jewels are registering as gray and chalky when I think back on them.

I know that this is grief, creeping up on me. I am grieving my brother. The notion astounds me.

"Her mother's name is Lilac," Gabriel says.

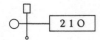

"No," I say. "All the girls were renamed for colors." I can see where this is leading now. Maddie clinging to me. The anxiety on Claire's face. Claire's resemblance to Lilac. Claire's resemblance to Maddie.

G-R-A-C-E L-O-T-T-N-E-R in blue crayon. Claire's daughter. Lilac's real name.

Lilac's book has found its way home without her.

"How is this possible?" Claire whispers. It's a question I'm getting used to myself.

It takes Maddie more than half an hour to release her grip on me, and it's only because Claire has set a dish of oatmeal cookies on the table.

There's an empty can in the corner of the room, collecting drips from a blackened patch in the ceiling. One drop, then another, pieces of thoughts that never pool into anything substantial.

I know Gabriel is feeling better, because he grabs a cookie immediately. But I am feeling nauseous as Maddie twists herself around in my lap and reaches for the plate. Claire's eyes are red and weepy, and so the orphans look weepy too. They tug on her dress like they're trying to climb her.

While the cookies were baking and cooling, Claire began the story:

Once upon a time there was a girl named Grace Lottner who wanted to be a teacher. She helped care for the orphans that lived with her and her mother. Read to them, cooked for them, tucked them into bed. By age twelve her pretty eyes and easy smile, coupled with her long limbs and coffee-dark skin, had made her a thing of beauty.

She left for school early one morning and never came home.

The rest Claire cannot bring herself to say. But that's all right. I can figure it out myself. Lilac—Grace Lottner—was Gathered and sold into prostitution. She wound up pregnant, and maybe she tried to escape, but she only made it as far as Madame's.

I watch the water plinking into the can. Claire sits across from me and watches me until I raise my eyes to her. Then she says, "You all right, baby? You look flushed."

For some reason I'm unable to respond. I don't think I have the strength to so much as open my mouth, and suddenly all I want to do is cry.

Gabriel comes to my rescue and says that I am probably just exhausted. Then he gets into something about how far we've walked, about Lilac—no, not Lilac—Grace having tried to escape with us but not making it over the fence.

Grace. At first I cannot see Lilac as a Grace. Rubbing glittery lotion on her arms and long, long legs, sweeping up her hair, smiling a bright red lipstick smile. But then I think of how cooing she was with Maddie, and how gentle she was when arranging my hair, and I start to just ache for her. How alive she was compared to Madame's

rainbow of other girls. How intelligent, lovely. And how destroyed.

Silas, who never approaches us, is now standing else-where in the room, watching me. "Why didn't you go back for her?" he says.

I can feel Gabriel bristling at the accusatory tone, but the question was for me, and he lets me answer it.

"She covered for us," I say. "We were hidden, and she told them we'd gotten away. She knew we had Maddie and that it was better for us to take her than to risk her being caught."

Silas makes a sound that is between a laugh and a sob. When I look at him, his pale face is red, his light eyes are shiny with tears that don't come. "Noble," he snorts.

"Madame was going to kill her!" I snap. I'm not sure where this anger comes from. It's like sitting back and listening to some other girl who sounds like me. "You didn't see that place—I did! We did the best that we could; if you want to go after her, you're more than wel-come to try."

The room throbs, twice as bright, and I force myself to calm down before I black out again, or cry. Silas turns away, muttering about weakness and Grace only having less than a year to live.

Claire sits back, one hand resting on the other. She does not let her emotions get the better of her. She does not force Maddie to acknowledge her as her grand-mother, nor does she make a fuss about Maddie's broken

arm. She does not tell Silas to stop muttering, nor me to stop breathing so angrily.

Instead she takes a long moment, then says, "I would love for Maddie to stay with me. Is that why you brought her here?"

And there lies the heart of my anger, and this persistent heartsick feeling like a lead weight on my chest. "We brought her here," I say, very carefully, working through my disbelief, "because we have no place else to go."

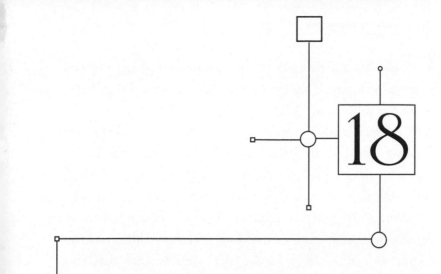

CLAIRE'S HOUSE reminds me of my own.

It's one story higher, but the structure is about the same. Crumbling. Vaguely colonial. The floors and door hinges creak with the presence of past lives. My parents grew up at a time when houses like these were robust, the wallpaper not peeling. How were they to know what would happen to their children? And to the world as a result?

Maddie clung to the table when Claire offered to lead us on a tour of the house. Maddie was absolutely unwilling to budge, when a moment before that she wouldn't let go of me. I will never understand that girl. I left her sitting there, gnawing pensively on cookies.

Claire leads Gabriel and me up the steps, past toys and art projects and a piano with sticky keys, on the first floor. The second floor is mostly bedrooms, but the main area holds a chalkboard on its wall and more than a dozen chairs arranged into a classroom setting. Papers everywhere. More tin cans and glass jars catching drips from the pipes that leak through the ceiling.

The attic makes up the third floor. The ceilings are slanted into the upside-down V shape of the roof, and there's a double bed, a dresser, and a bathroom. This is where Claire sleeps, and it is the only room not entirely overrun with children's things. There is also a mattress on the floor, made up with sheets and a threadbare comforter. It's under a stained-glass window that fills the whole room with warm pink and yellow light. "When one of the little ones is very sick, I let them sleep up here with me so I can care for them," she says.

Up here the cacophony of piano keys and child shrieks and leaky pipes is far away and subdued. I would love nothing more than to collapse into Claire's double bed and sleep. Or turn my thoughts off for a while.

But Gabriel and I will be sleeping on the second floor, on a thick down comforter that doubles for a mattress. We're welcome to stay here as long as we help out. She assumes we're married, glancing at my wedding band, and that we'll want to be kept together, though she strongly implies that any marital activities would be a bad idea, as there's no such thing as privacy with so many kids running around. Plus, we'll be in Silas's bedroom. Maddie is welcome to share a bed with anyone she likes; there are more children than beds, and they're used to squishing together. But I have a feeling that if Maddie

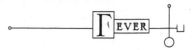

doesn't find a corner all her own, she'll end up sleeping with us.

Silas's bedroom is really more of a closet that was just big enough to hold a bed. When we spread the comforter out, it covers every bit of the floor. Silas seems less than enthused when he crosses the threshold and sees that Gabriel and I have taken over his space, but all he says is "Dinner is in a few minutes. After that, feel free to wash up." He wrinkles his nose, like we're the most offensive creatures on the planet. "Then it's lights-out."

I'm not hungry for dinner, but I feel a little better after I've taken a quick shower. I'm wearing pajamas that are threadbare, but well-fitting and comfortable. I'm trying not to think of the white sweater Deirdre made for me on Madame's hunched, wrinkled body.

Gabriel climbs onto the blanket beside me, his hair still damp, and for a while we lie in the darkness, staring up, saying nothing. The house is full of noise as Silas—who is the oldest orphan here, at roughly my age—and Claire get the orphans into bed. This apparently involves a group song at the piano. When I last saw Maddie, she'd made friends with another malformed girl with clear green eyes and no left hand, and she didn't try to follow me to bed, so I left her to whatever game they were playing, which involved crawling under the couch.

"I'm sorry," I say. My voice is tight. My eyes are sore with the threat of tears.

Gabriel rustles beside me. "Sorry for what?"

For what? I don't know, exactly. I can't say that I'm sorry for bringing him out of the mansion with me, because the thought of being alone right now is crushing. And I'd only be worrying for his safety, all alone in Vaughn's basement of horrors, among the corpses of my dead sister wives.

"It wasn't supposed to be like this," I say.

Gabriel is quiet for a while, and then he says, sounding surprised, "Did you have a plan for how it would be?"

"No," I admit. "I thought we'd make it home, and my brother would be waiting for me. I thought, maybe—I don't know. I thought we'd be happy. Now I realize how stupid I must have sounded, after every possible thing has gone wrong."

"Wanting to be happy is not stupid," Gabriel says.

It's quiet for so long that I think he must have fallen asleep. But then he asks, "So what now?"

"I find my brother," I say. "I'll start looking near home." The word hurts in a way I never imagined it would. "Check the factories first, see what kind of jobs he might have had while I was gone, and if he let anyone know he was leaving." It doesn't sound like something my brother would do. Outside of me, there was no one he trusted with the details of his life. But it's all I've got to go on.

"Okay," Gabriel says. "I'll go with you. But for now try to get some sleep, okay? You're starting to worry me."

And because he does me the courtesy of playing along,

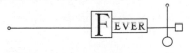

letting me hope for something that is clearly futile, I pretend to sleep.

After the rest of the house has gone silent, I hear the floorboards creaking as Claire moves about upstairs. Silas stumbles into his bedroom, and in the darkness he manages to step around the bodies of the strangers who have taken over his floor. Water from his freshly showered hair drips onto my face as he passes.

Gabriel has moved onto his side, facing away from me, his breaths even and clear now that the drug has left his system.

The coils of Silas's mattress creak, go silent awhile, creak again. I hear his blankets rustling. And clearly my fake sleeping isn't fooling him, because eventually he whispers to me, "Is Grace really alive, or were you saying that for Claire's sake?"

"It was true," I whisper back. "We were climbing down the other side of the fence, and she fell behind. But she was friends with one of the guards there, and I don't think he'd let anything happen to her."

Silas is quiet, taking this all in. Then, "How was she?"

"Brave," I say. "Smart." I decide not to mention the angel's blood.

He hesitates. "Did she mention me?"

"She didn't mention anyone. I didn't even know her name was Grace."

I know I should be kinder, but it's the truth. Lilac—or, Grace—is not the twelve-year-old girl that was Gathered away seven years ago. Time may have let her retain some of her old traits, and her pretty face, but it has changed her. If only one year away was able to turn my life upside down, seven could obliterate a girl entirely.

I inch toward Gabriel, close enough to smell the still-damp hair that is almost, just a little, like the ocean. I tell myself that if I ever get to sleep tonight, I'll dream of the North Atlantic. I'll dream of catching rainbow trout while coasting on a ferry that takes me toward Liberty Island at high noon, my skin warm with the sun.

But instead my dreams are of nothing but blackness, and the smell of burned wallpaper.

I wake earlier than the rest of the house, and I reach over my pillow and into Lilac's bag. My hand fumbles around until it finds the page with my brother's notes. By the green glow of Silas's bedside clock, I hold the page over my face and try to read it. I can't make the words out too well, but it doesn't matter. They still wouldn't make sense.

"Have you been up all night?" Gabriel murmurs. I look over and realize his eyes are trained on me in the darkness.

"No," I say. "Go back to sleep."

But he doesn't close his eyes until I've returned the note and settled down again.

I listen as Claire's footsteps ease down the creaking staircase, and then I hear her moving about in the kitchen. I wonder if she's slept at all either. What must

be going through her mind, to know the fate of her missing daughter? Seven years is a long time. Long enough
to presume a person dead. Long enough for the shock
and the hurt to scab over. I still miss my parents, every
day, but I've stopped seeing their faces in crowds. I've
stopped expecting them to come back to me somehow.
How must it feel to discover a loved one presumed dead
has been alive the whole time?

Probably the way my brother will feel when he sees
me again. If he ever does.

I close my eyes, try for sleep. I know I'll need the rest
if I'm going to spend the day searching Manhattan for
traces of my brother. To deal with the shock of how the
tables have turned.

But sleep doesn't come. I lie there for what feels like
hours, until the light makes the insides of my eyelids
bright beige and a toddler starts wailing in his crib, setting off a chorus.

Breakfast smells delicious, but the food is like paste
in my mouth. Those bright spots of light are swimming
in my vision again. But I know that Gabriel is watching
me, and so I smear extra jam on my toast and force it all
down.

Maddie and her new friend, Nina, have become
inseparable. I last saw them spinning circles around the
piano as though they could hear a song the rest of us
couldn't.

The news is on the small TV that Claire keeps on the

kitchen counter. More about the outrage at the president's idea to rebuild the labs. There are some supporters, of course, but the news favors the angry opposition. For instance, the first generation woman who has buried all six of her children, having conceived them with the hope that there would be a cure in time.

Silas mutters about the stupidity of trying, and I glare across the table at him. "Have something to say, princess?" he coos.

I gather the plates from the table, taking his just as he was reaching for the last bit of waffle drowning in syrup, and bring them to the sink.

The news story changes to a segment about President Guiltree's lineage, how more than a century ago, citizens could vote for their president. It worked for a while, so the story goes, until opposing sides began battling among each other. Now the presidency is inherited. The shortened life spans of the new generations threaten this tradition, but Guiltree seems to think he can solve this by having as many children as possible. The fact that all of his children are sons is also suspect. Many have speculated that he is running his own private genetic lab to manipulate the gender of his children. Some speculate that he already has the cure, though I don't see why he'd keep that a secret.

There's a crash in the living room, followed by the hiccup and wail of a child, and Claire dashes to the rescue.

Once she's gone, Silas says, "They should leave well enough alone," to no one in particular.

I spin around to face him. "You call a death sentence 'well enough'? There's nothing wrong with pursuing a cure."

Silas snorts, turning up his nose at me as he crosses to the fridge, takes out a carton of milk, and drinks straight from it. "Rebuilding that lab will create jobs, and that's all the good it'll do. After that it'll do nothing but give people hope."

"Hope is a bad thing?" I say.

"When it's false hope."

Gabriel starts to say something, but I cut him off. "Who's to say? There are talented scientists, talented doctors, and maybe hope isn't such a bad thing. Maybe it's what keeps us together."

There's rage stirring in me like paint spilled into water, making everything red. But just a few weeks ago, I was lying beside Cecily on Jenna's trampoline, telling her there was no cure and to get that through her head. I wish I could undo that; I'd been so stricken by grief that for a while I'd forgotten myself. It goes against everything my parents fought for. Everything they died for.

Silas laughs without any humor. His eyes are languid like the eyes of Madame's girls. There's a sort of dead passion in him. A spark that, had he more years to live, would be a wildfire. And I can see that he's given up. "You're so naïve, princess," he says.

I have been called so many things this past year. Sweetheart, Goldenrod, Empress, Princess. I used to have only one name; it used to mean something.

"I know more than you think," I say.

He comes close, his nose inches above mine, and I can hear his lips parting when he says, "Then, you know that you are going to die." His eyes are searching my face, challenging me. I can't argue, and he knows it.

All that comes out is a small "Maybe."

"Maybe nothing," he says. "That lab explosion was a blessing in disguise. It made us all face facts. Live for today, while you can."

That's enough for Gabriel, who grabs my arm and moves me away. I'm shaking all over, and there's something angry that won't make it to my lips; all that comes out is a frustrated grunt that seems to shake the walls as I stomp from the room and up the stairs. Maddie and Nina move to approach me, but quickly think better of it and go back to their game of trying to weave through the banister.

There's nowhere to go but Silas's room. Gabriel trails after me and closes the door. He reaches for me, but I'm pacing, moving my mouth and trying to get the words out. I can barely see straight. Finally I blurt out, "Smug."

I ball my hands into fists. "He has no right—who does he think he is?"

"He shouldn't have called you naïve," Gabriel offers, trying to help.

"It isn't that," I say. "I mean, yes, that's part of it, but—he said the explosion was a good thing." I stop pacing and chew on my knuckle, feel the bone between my teeth. "My parents were killed in that explosion, Gabriel. They were killed because they believed they'd find a cure. And they were doing such good things in the meantime! They were caring for newborns, and taking in pregnant girls who had nowhere to go, and—" My voice cracks. Through tears I glare out the window, where Silas is going into the shed. He breathes into his red hands for warmth, fidgets with the lock, and disappears inside.

From up here he seems so small. He's a petal of ash tumbling toward the sky, all that's left of the flames.

Strange how easily things disappear.

Once upon a time there were two parents, two children, and a brick house with lilies in the yard. The parents died, the lilies wilted. One child disappeared. Then the other.

"It's okay," Gabriel says. His hand hovers near my arm, but I think he's afraid to touch me.

"My parents would have done more good things," I say. "Great things."

"I know," Gabriel says.

"They didn't want this for Rowan and me. My brother—he's smart. They were teaching him to become a scientist, but after they died, he gave up. He gave up because we had to take care of each other."

I stare at my reflection in the glass, and I can see two versions of myself: the twin sister, and the bride.

"It was supposed to be better than this," I whisper.

When Gabriel and I announce our plans to head into the shipping district, Claire doesn't question it. Silas mumbles something into his tea about how he'll never see us again. He thinks we're abandoning Maddie. But Maddie either knows this isn't true or doesn't care, because she can't be interrupted from her game when I pass her on my way out.

The walk feels twice as arduous as it did yesterday. My legs are stiff and heavy, and I keep my head down to avoid the blinding sun. Gabriel doesn't press me for conversation. Sometimes he'll reach over and rub circles on my back. I think he expects me to cry or something, but I am beyond crying. Beyond feeling anything. Beyond thinking of anything but the most immediate of actions: Cross the bridge. Start with the factories closest to my home and then work my way along the shoreline. Do not pay attention to the water—it is full of memories and sunken continents, and many places in which a person's mind can drown.

In every office of every building, I deliver the same quick speech. I'm looking for my brother. His name is Rowan Ellery. About this much taller than me. Blond hair. One blue eye, one brown eye. You'd remember him if you saw him, probably.

But no one does. Over and over it's the same thing.

Until we reach a food processing plant, and a first generation man with freckled skin, a hairnet, and a stained shirt with the word "supervisor" on the chest knows who I'm talking about. He goes on an angry tirade about how Rowan—he's made up a less-than-charming nickname for him—worked for him right up until he stole one of the delivery trucks with a rather expensive supply of canned soups inside it. This man is so angry, his words so heated, that he ignores my next question each of the several times I ask it. Finally Gabriel takes over for me, places a hand on the man's shoulder. Manages to calm him down with his placid, easy expression, his blue eyes making contact but holding no aggression. "How long ago?"

The man blinks. "Months," he says. "I knew something was off about that kid. Always muttering to himself, disappearing for an hour once. But he got deliveries done quick enough, so I kept him around."

I try to reconcile my brother with the person this man is describing. Rowan always had a quick temper, and if he was particularly upset, he would mutter under his breath the things he wished he could have said to fix the problem. Mostly unkind things, but lucid at least. He would only stop when I put my hand on his arm, talked softly to him. After the Gatherer broke into our home, my brother was furious for days. Pacing. Worrying. And just when I thought he was calming down, he shattered a window with his fist. But I never considered how deep his anger could go, or if his tirades could stop making sense if he went about it long enough.

Just as he had always been there to protect me, like that night the Gatherer held a knife to my throat, I had always been there to calm him back down. I was the only one who could do it.

A lead anchor of guilt sinks in my stomach. He's out there somewhere because I couldn't reassure him. I couldn't bring him back from the darkness beyond the edges of his own mind.

My voice sounds a thousand miles away when I ask, "What did the truck look like?"

The man is all too happy to show us his delivery trucks, and to end the tour of the parking lot with "If you ever see that kid again, tell him he'd be an idiot to show his face around here."

If. If I ever see him again.

On the walk back to Claire's, I'm the one who's muttering angrily. About Gatherers. About months and trucks and nonsensical notes left in a burned-down house. And about time—always time—because that's what it all comes down to, isn't it? Time frittered away at the mansion. Time waiting for a twin who isn't coming home. Time until I die.

I must look as disgruntled as I feel, because when I return, Silas holds back whatever smart comment he was going to make. For a moment our eyes meet, and he gives me a look that isn't disgust, or pity, but rather of solidarity.

I think he knows my search was a fruitless one. I think he understands how that feels.

I would love nothing more than to go upstairs and bury myself in the nest of blankets and fall into a deep, dreamless sleep. This is what I did when my parents died. But there is some small, logical part of me that keeps going, like a lone gear in a broken watch. I move into the kitchen. I help Claire with the dishes. I boil water for the spaghetti. I wipe sauce dribbling from toddlers' chins. I dust a menagerie of trinkets on mantels and shelves. I shrug Gabriel off when he asks, over and over, if I'm okay.

And over the next several days, I fall into a routine. I begin sleeping normally. The food is still tasteless and it sticks going down, but I eat it. More than once, going into the shed for canned food or the tool kit to fix a leaky faucet, I find Silas pressed against the wall and tangled in the arms of a new girl. "Come to join us?" he teased the first time, and the girl hit his chest. But after that we learned to ignore each other.

Gabriel is popular among the youngest children because he knows how to play a few songs on the piano. I never knew this about him, and when my chores aren't very taxing, I sit on the bench and watch his fingers move over the keys. He shows me how I can enhance the song by simply pressing the same key over and over. *Ping, ping, ping.* I focus on just that one note as the rest of the melody washes through the room.

It does not leave me, even after my index finger has

left the key. *Ping, ping, ping* as I gather dirty laundry and haul it to the washing machine. *Ping, ping, ping* as I am climbing the stairs and trying to be quiet, because it's dark now and the children are all still with sleep. I can hear the mishmash cacophony of their breathing, and the water hissing through the pipes as Gabriel showers.

Ping, ping, ping—the notes catch with my next breath, and before I know what's happening, I've lost my footing and I'm tumbling forward.

I never hit the next step, though, because Silas has grabbed my arm. I can see his pale skin reflected back in the moonlight. Does he ever wear a shirt? His face is in shadow, but his eyes are light enough that I can see them watching me. They roll to every angle of my face as though deciding something.

"Thanks for catching me," I mumble.

I remove my arm from his grip, and he lets go, but for some reason I am rooted to this spot.

"You got dizzy, didn't you?" he whispers. "It's been happening every day."

"I'm all right," I whisper back

"You're not all right," he says.

I say nothing, stepping around him to go to the bedroom. How can I explain to him that what he perceives as dizziness is, in fact, a creeping form of madness? Like how the tendrils of ivy probed their way up the exterior of my brick house (the one that is now uninhabitable), I am being overtaken.

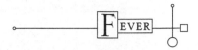

How can I explain that the reason I fell was because of the aftershock of a laboratory explosion that killed my parents years ago?

In the morning, while I'm making the beds in one of the children's rooms, I reach out to close the window. I can see Silas staggering behind the shed several feet below, a girl in his arms. The wind picks up her long dark hair and drops it as though in frustration. I see his lazy smile as her arms coil up around his neck. Her sweater sleeves are striped like the Christmas candy in old storybooks.

For just a second, as I'm stretching up to lower the window's frame, he raises his eyes to me. He taps his nose, then tumbles around the corner of the shed, the girl laughing all the while, and disappears from sight.

Confused, I touch the skin under my nose, trying to find meaning in the gesture. When I move my hand away, it's smeared with blood.

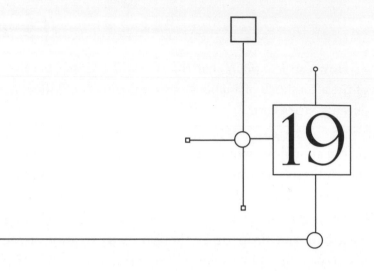

BY MID-FEBRUARY the air starts feeling warmer. The fine layer of frost melts, giving the grass a freshly watered look, and softening the earth. I sit on the curb in front of the orphanage, watching the layer of early fog that swirls above the concrete. I try not to think of the orange blossoms. They would be sleeping in the trees now, waiting to be born.

This time last year I lived in the shipping district of Manhattan. I was barely sixteen. I did not know that I was just days from being Gathered.

I rest my hand on my raised knee and look at my wedding ring. I follow the vines and petals that don't begin or end.

There are so many thoughts in my head. Ones I should avoid. Ones I should gravitate toward. All of them fluttering like orange blossom petals in this morning fog. I can no longer discern which thoughts are useful and which

are dangerous; all I know is that I'm sick of being stagnant. So, not knowing what else to do, I start walking.

Even a few yards down the street, I can hear the children and clattering dishes inside the orphanage. I turn off Dawn Avenue, though, and they vanish. There is nothing but the distant whoosh of city traffic, the far-away tide. A gust of wind picks up, and I hug my chest.

I'm wearing a brown-and-pink-striped sweater that itches everywhere. It was not made especially for me. It is not inlaid with pearls and diamonds.

I'm so busy trying not to think that I don't hear him calling for me—not until the sound of my name echoes against the empty street with his footsteps. "Rhine! Wait up."

I stop walking, don't turn around, and wait for him to catch up.

"Oh, good," I say, once Silas is beside me. "You're wearing a shirt."

He huffs indignantly and shakes the curls from his eyes. They're blond almost to the point of being completely white. They take on the soft blue morning glow, and the frizz gives them a frothy ocean look.

This is what girls like about him, I guess. The too-cool-to-care thing. Normally this would be the time he'd disappear from the house to be with one of them. In the toolshed or elsewhere in this neighborhood, letting their hands swing between them as they walk away. But that's his business, and I don't care. I'm only happy he's considerate enough to keep his escapades out of Claire's home, especially since we share a bedroom.

"Thinking of running away from our fine establishment?" he asks as we start walking again.

"No. Just going for a walk," I say.

I try to stay out of Silas's hair. If he goes to bed before I do, I busy myself with chores until I'm sure he's asleep. And if I go to bed first, I pretend to be asleep as he tiptoes over my body. I have also done my best to give him no indication of the bright bits of light that swim around before me at the worst moments, when hope feels impossible. Right now, for instance.

Gabriel has been concerned about me too, but I don't need to avoid him, because he isn't intrusive. He asks, I change the topic, and that's the end of it.

If Silas questions my state again, I am fully prepared to run away from him. I am scouting potential alleys as we go.

It's not until he speaks again that I realize there is another reason I've been avoiding him. It's so I won't have to try to answer his question—the one that's been hiding in his sleepy, disinterested-looking eyes from day one. "Gabriel's not really your husband, is he?"

The least exhausting thing would be honesty. And I have so little energy to spare these days. "No," I say. "But you knew that."

"Mm," he says.

"How?" I ask. "You always look at us like you know, but how?"

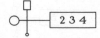

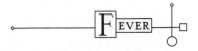

"It isn't a lack of affection; you obviously care about each other, or whatever," Silas says. "If I say this, you're going to think I'm crazy."

"No," I say. "Trust me, I won't."

"How do I explain it?" he says. "It's like there's an invisible cord on that wedding band, and it doesn't lead to him. It's like you're tethered."

Tethered. That's a good way to put it. Thoughts of my husband and sister wives, and even my deranged father-in-law, seem to never truly leave me.

"I ran away," I say. "I was Gathered, and I escaped, and I came home, and my family was gone."

I don't realize how badly I've needed to say those words until they've left my mouth. They hang in the air. And all I want now is to be away from them. To leave the truth behind. Because if I can't do anything about it, I certainly don't want to face it.

I turn off the main road and start walking downhill, careful not to slip on the grass that's slick with dew. In a brighter city, with cleaner air, this would be a place flowers might bloom. Instead there's nothing at the bottom other than a trickle of a river and some bony tangled shrubs. I thought about that when I came here the other day. I needed to get away from the chaos of the orphans for a while, and this little area seemed safe to me, shrouded in sun, bearing the damp, earthy smell of spring.

Today there is a different smell. I don't recognize it,

not right away, until Silas is gripping my arm and telling me not to look.

But it's too late. I've already seen the dead girl lying faceup in the shallow water, her eyes full of clouds.

There are so many bright pieces of light that it hurts my eyes. I just stand there, mouth shut, staring through them. I do not see this girl's features, the color of her hair. A bizarre thing happens. I see her bones instead. I see right through her skin, to the blood and tissue that's blackened and still. I see the torn muscle that used to be her heart. That's where the Gatherer's bullet hit.

Silas talks to me as though through glass. He pushes me, tries to make me move. I can't feel my body, though, and I'm like his marionette, arms and legs moving limply as he forces me uphill. Then he sits next to me on the sidewalk curb, watches as I brace my hands on either side of me.

Gradually the blood starts flowing again. The bits of light dwindle and disappear.

"That could have been me," I whisper.

Silas is watching me.

"There were three of us," I add. "Three who got chosen. They shot the rest. Threw them somewhere. Left them to rot in a ditch until someone came to cremate them."

The words sound so awful when said out loud. I should probably be crying, or even hysterical. But I can't seem to feel anything. I shake my head violently at nothing in particular.

Silas says, "You have to be careful of ditches. You never know what you'll find."

"Maybe it should have been me," I say.

"Why?" he asks.

"Because I never wanted to be married," I tell him. "One of my sister wives did. The other—she could at least acknowledge that it was better than death, and she accepted it. But I . . . threw it back. I could have been murdered right there in the lineup, but for some ridiculous reason I was chosen, and I threw it back. I almost got killed, once, trying to get away."

"Guess you didn't let that stop you," Silas says. "I mean, because you're sitting here now."

I shake my head. "I didn't."

I look over my shoulder, down the ditch, but at this angle I can't see what's coasting on the shallow water. Silas places a finger tenuously under my chin, waits a moment, and then turns my head toward him. "Maybe that girl chose death over imprisonment," he says. "Maybe she looked right down the barrel of the gun and said 'Screw you.'"

"Doubtful," I say.

"Stop it. So you ran away. You don't deserve to die for that."

I smooth my jeans against my thighs, watch leaves scuttle against the pavement. I think of Linden's hot, sobbing breaths against my skin. Rose, languid and elegant on her deathbed, ascending gracefully to her end. The blood on the sheets when Cecily was in labor. My heart pounding, sometimes in terror, sometimes in exhilaration. Sharks in the pool. Road maps in my husband's paper houses. Kisses that tasted like June Beans and autumn winds and stale laboratory air. Permanent. Inescapable.

The girl lying in the ditch will not have memories like these. Her skin will dissolve down to bone, her skull emerging with its grin of teeth. Her hair will fall away. Her ribs and hips and elbows will stay together for as long as they can, but ultimately she'll be nothing but pieces, in a heap of other pieces, on their way to becoming ash.

"I'm sorry," I whisper, but she can't hear me.

"Come on," Silas says, getting up, pulling me along by the wrists. "Let's go do something fun."

"Like what?" I say.

He throws an arm around my shoulders in an exaggerated gesture of camaraderie, but I think he's trying to keep me from falling over. And it's a good thing, because my head is starting to feel hazy.

"Like fix the broken toilet in the downstairs bathroom. Someone flushed some of the ABC blocks this morning."

I laugh, in spite of myself. "I'm supposed to be washing the sheets," I say.

"Lucky," he says.

We make our way back to the house, prattling about chores and the sticky messes the children leave on piano

keys and under tables. The dead girl follows me, a ghost hanging on my back, whispering in my ear, over and over, *It should have been you.*

Tonight I can't even force myself to eat. Just looking at this hot chicken soup makes bile churn in my stomach. The noodles, I think, are arms and legs and fingers, pieces that can never be made whole. I excuse myself early, promising Claire I'll help with the dishes once I've taken a quick shower.

She frowns, and the edges of her lips drip down her face like they're melting. I shudder and hurry up the stairs.

Sore. Every muscle of my body is sore, as though they're just now reacting to all those surges of angel's blood, and the running, and the sleeping on the hardwood floor with nothing but a comforter to soften it. I step under the stream of hot water, and it only intensifies this new wave of dizziness. The tiles jolt under my feet, so hard and in such rapid succession that I have to sit down.

As the water rushes over me, I think that maybe I was wrong about springtime coming so soon. Maybe I should have worn a coat over my sweater when I went outside, because this hot water is doing nothing to ease these chills that have found respite deep in my bones, this feeling that if I let go of the towel rack, I'll completely lose my grasp.

I'm in the bathroom for so long that Gabriel starts knocking on the door, calling my name. I guess he's been knocking for a while, because I open my eyes and find that I'm still sitting on the wet tile, but the water is cold, and he's saying, "If you don't answer me, I'm coming in there."

"No," I say. My voice rebounds off the tiles, amplifying the weak, wispy word. "I'm all right." I reach forward, twist the knob until the water stops with a whinnying jolt. "I'm just getting dried off."

I must look truly awful, because when I reenter the kitchen, Gabriel's arm around mine, the orphans scatter. Claire sets down her sponge, towels her hand, and presses the back of it to my forehead.

"You're burning up, baby," she says. "Don't worry about the dishes. Go to bed, and I'll bring you some aspirin."

Ascending the stairs is a chore, even with Gabriel's help. He sets me on the floor and leaves me so he can go find more blankets.

"I saw a dead girl today," I murmur when Gabriel comes back and starts arranging the quilts on the ground like a mattress.

He pauses only to frown at me, like I'm not making any sense.

"It's true," I say. "She was lying in a river in a ditch. She looked at me."

"Come here," Gabriel says. He's holding up a blanket

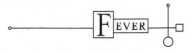

for me to climb beneath. I crawl into place, and he tucks me in.

He's running his fingers through my hair, and I lean my head against his thigh, sighing something about music as I start to drift off.

But I never feel as though I am truly asleep. The night is nothing but darkness, arms and legs and elbows emerging in the glow of Silas's clock. At one point I think they're waves rising up to drown me, and my scream sets off an echo of hiccups and baby cries. Someone turns on the light, and it stays on until morning.

In the early hours, the sky still a predawn blue, I awaken. My head is in Gabriel's lap, cushioned by a pillow, his fingers still in my hair, twitching sometimes with the memory of his gentle strokes. He's asleep, though, sitting up against the wall, mouth open, breaths rasped. I stare up at the curve of his chin, and I reach my hand out to touch it, but suddenly he's miles away. I try to call for him, but I have no voice.

I open my eyes again, and I must have been asleep, because now the sun is brighter and Silas is no longer in his bed.

"Hi," Gabriel whispers. His voice is a cool breeze through luxuriant trees. It's so sweet that I close my eyes, let it rush through me.

"Hi," I say. My voice is a broken violin string. "Still think I was lying about the dead girl? Ask Silas. It's true."

"I believe you," he says.

"Maybe it was too cold for me to go out." I press my temple against his knee. "I caught a chill."

"Being around so many kids can make you sick," Gabriel says. "Germs. Someone was always sick in the orphanage. I remember that."

I nod, and after a while I allow myself to be helped up. Claire brings me apple sauce and cranberry juice and aspirin. I force myself to down all of these things at her insistence, but a few minutes later, when it all comes back up, she gives me a look so worried that all the light drains from the room. I stare at her as the shadows engulf her dark face, leaving nothing but the whites of her eyes.

I'm aware of Maddie and Nina frequenting my doorway, holding hands, thinking themselves unseen while I'm in this hazy state. Nina whispers something, and they skitter away like cockroaches.

Gabriel only leaves me in the evening to help Claire with dinner, or maybe to shower—he told me, but I can't remember. When I finally awaken, I feel as though I'm baking in the blankets. I kick them away, sweat making my clothes stick to my back.

"I'm a mess," I say when Gabriel comes back. "I need a shower."

He helps me to my feet, and we start off down the hall, but Claire stops us. "You're too tired to be on your feet," she says.

Silas is just coming out of one of the rooms, biting into

a sugar cookie and watching me worriedly as he chews.

"I just need a shower," I say. "The water will clear my head."

Claire gives in, but on a compromise. I'm to use the bathroom in the attic because it has a tub and I should be sitting down. I even let her draw the water for me; she sprinkles it with eucalyptus oil. "I'll be just outside folding laundry if you need me," she says. Every few minutes she calls my name to make sure I haven't fallen asleep and drowned.

The tub is probably as old as the house, a white claw-foot that is poetically chipped and yellowed. My toes play with the chain of the drain plug.

The water feels so relaxing that I soak until it has gone cold. And then, teeth chattering, I towel myself off and slip into the pajamas Claire laid out for me.

When she offers to move the spare mattress into Silas's room so I can be more comfortable tonight, I try to refuse, but next thing I know, Silas is hauling the thing down the stairs.

I follow him, taking slow, careful steps, my wet hair dripping alongside my footsteps.

"Silas?"

The mattress hits each step with a thud, a small explosion, jarring my vision. I cling to the railing.

"What?"

Because he has already asked me a question that was difficult to answer, about my wedding ring and Gabriel, I decide to ask him something that has been weighing on me since the day I arrived.

"You blame yourself for what happened to Grace, don't you?"

Thud, thud—the mattress drags down the steps. "Yes," he says. He sits at the bottom step, the mattress splayed on the floor at his feet, and I sit beside him. "I tried to blame you, for not bringing her back with you. But it's my fault she was taken in the first place."

He pauses, granting me the opportunity to tell him he's wrong, but I say nothing, and he goes on. "We were fighting. We fought all the time. But that morning was different. Ominous. I still remember how blue the sky was. Is that strange? We were walking to school, and I looked up into all that sky and I felt like something had changed."

"I don't think that sounds strange," I tell him.

"She tripped on a tree root that had grown over the sidewalk. She dropped her books, and she was swearing as she picked them up. I laughed at her. She shoved me. The truth of it is, I wanted to kiss her, but I knew she wouldn't let me. So I said something stupid instead, but I don't even remember what it was. She ran ahead of me. 'You're an idiot, Silas!' she said. That was it. She turned a corner, and I never saw her again."

"She might have let you kiss her," I offer.

Silas laughs. "That's your response?"

I take a moment to think about it. "Yes."

"Kiss or no kiss," Silas goes on, "I never even saw the van. I never heard a scream."

"You were only a kid yourself," I say. "Believe me, you wouldn't have been able to overpower the Gatherers even if you had."

"Maybe not," Silas says. "But I'll never know, will I? And that's what stings."

"Do you love her?" I ask.

"I don't know who she is now," he says. "Or what she's gone through, or what she must have been thinking all these years. She had a daughter." He drops forward on his knees. "A daughter. Who doesn't even speak."

"Would you talk to her if she could?" I ask.

"No," he admits.

I put my hand on his shoulder, causing him to start. I don't know why; he should be used to girls pawing at him by now.

"Maybe you can get her back," I say.

"I've been thinking that," he says. "But she's nineteen now. And Claire—it would be too much for her to lose her only daughter twice. The second time so permanently. And she needs me here besides."

He shakes his head lightly, and his curls chime like bells in my mind.

"It's best to let her go," he says.

No, no, that's wrong. It's never right to give up on someone.

But then I think of my brother, so consumed with loss

that he set fire to our things and took off on a mission either to find me or to escape any memories of me.

And here I've been, staggering through the days like a zombie, wondering how I'll ever find him.

It would be easier to let go. For me. For Rowan. For Silas and Claire.

I don't know. I'm so confused, and the bells in my head are so loud that all I can manage to say is "Maybe you're right." Even though I know he's wrong. I get up, clinging to the railing, and nudge the mattress with my foot. "Would you mind setting this thing up? I'm really tired."

Silas drags the mattress into the bedroom for me, and I arrange the blankets and pillows for myself after he leaves to take care of some crisis involving maple syrup on the piano.

The mattress is not big enough to comfortably hold two people, but when Gabriel lies down on the floor, I ask him to get under the blankets with me. "I promise I won't throw up on you or anything," I say.

He fits himself behind me, and I close my eyes. He's trying to hold still, but the subtle shifting of his body indicates he isn't comfortable like this. I reposition myself, edging over to give him more room, though he never makes a word of complaint.

I say, "When I'm feeling better, maybe in a day or two, I'm going to start looking for my brother. I don't think I'm going to find him. There are a hundred trucks like the one he stole. But I'll hate myself if I don't try." Because

what Silas said is true: the not knowing is what stings. I can't live with that. It might be too late for Grace, but there is still time to find my brother. "You don't have to come with me. I'd understand. I've already dragged you all this way, and it's not fair to drag you any farther."

Gabriel is quiet for a while, considering. He tilts his head, and his face brushes the back of my neck, and something like exhilaration fills my exhausted body. "You didn't drag me out of the mansion," he says. "I wanted to go."

"Because Jenna asked you to protect me," I say.

"Is that what you think?" He leans over me so that I can see his face. My back is cold where his body was just pressed to it. "She asked me to, yes. But I had made up my mind before then."

"Why?" I ask.

"You fascinated me," he says, settling back down, gathering my body to his. "You had so much faith in the world, and I wanted to see it the way you did."

I laugh painfully. "Now that you've seen it, you must think I'm crazy."

He doesn't answer, but he tightens his arm around me, places a kiss on the back of my neck. It's not long before I fall asleep.

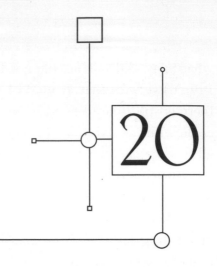

IN MY DELIRIUM one night I dream of our escape boat, feel it rocking me into a deeper sleep, to a place with long stretches of hot pavement. Frail lilies grow, weary and flushed, their soil heavy with the scent of blood. And everywhere are the girls, gaping, their black eyes full of clouds, the smiles of their slit throats crusted red. Their mouths don't move, but I understand what they want to say. *You could have been one of us. Don't forget.*

My twin has gone, but he was here. His presence lingers, sweaty and fragrant, filling over with dust. He has searched these girls for me, so hardened to the sorrow that he can feel nothing for them, cannot even see that they are girls; he only sees that they don't belong to him, are not his only sister. And he's on to darker roads, to scarlet district brothels and idling gray vans, covering the continent as quickly as he can, for the years are moving rapidly

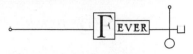

beneath his feet. And as he searches for me, I search for him, and I feel him only after he's gone and only when I'm dreaming. Does he feel me?

Sometimes I think we are about to touch.

My vision fails; I see colors in blurry, undulating spheres. My eyelashes are wet and heavy, and my eyelids can't lift them. "I'm here," I say, but my voice escapes me in foreign syllables, a drunken murmur. "I'm here. Turn and look." Or maybe I'm the one who's supposed to turn. But which way?

Another voice answers me, saying, "Can you hear me?" Then, more urgently, "Can you open your eyes?"

I try, and this time my eyelashes aren't so heavy. The colors wobble and then align, forming one solid image. A jam jar filling up with water that comes through a crack in the ceiling. Then Gabriel's eager eyes, his hand coming close and sweeping across my cheek. There are tears dampening my face.

"Hey," he whispers. "Welcome back."

More fitting words he couldn't have chosen. As I slept, I moved far, far from him. And once again I've returned empty-handed.

"Hey," I say. My voice is my own again. I clear my throat, prop myself up on my elbow, and ignore the bits of bright light that flutter into my vision.

Distantly I hear Claire making noise downstairs in the kitchen, all metal against metal, ceramic against ceramic. The orphans talk in hushed voices as they flit through the house, giggling. Someone's eyes watch me through the crack of the door opening, round and curious, then disappear. In another room some of the younger ones are learning their alphabet; if they can learn to read recipes, maybe they'll become cooks, and a wealthy housemaster will buy them. If the girls excel and also grow to be pretty, maybe they'll be brides or— dare they dream?—actresses like in the soap operas. These options excite them. Anything to avoid dying without purpose. They recite the letters in unison with verve. "*A, B, C, D . . .*"

I think of Cecily calling letters through my bedroom door, asking me how to pronounce things like "placenta" and "uterus."

"How long was I out?" I ask.

"You slept all morning," Gabriel says. "You were talking in your sleep."

"Was I?" I rub at the tears on my cheeks, but already they're drying away as the dream begins to escape me.

"It looked like you were having a nightmare." He runs a cold wet cloth across my forehead, and I can't help the groan of relief that escapes my mouth. Cold water trickles down my temples, winds paths along my scalp. Gabriel purses his lips in what I suppose is meant to be a smile, but he looks very worried, and I know my fever must be spiking again.

When I was a child, I caught pneumonia, and I still remember the gurgle of the humidifier mimicking my

rattled breaths, the phlegm grinding in my chest when I coughed. I remember feeling absolutely miserable, but in a way that was natural. A real, human ailment that had been around for centuries, and one that my parents knew how to treat.

This, though, is an entirely new sensation. One that does not feel natural, or treatable. One that makes my mind bend into bizarre nightmares, leaves me burning and parched while my arms and legs lose sensation. My body isn't craving hydration, or medicine, or even the warm puffs of air from devices meant to aid in breathing. I don't know what this is. I don't know what is happening.

Gabriel's touch is soft. I close my eyes, and his hands begin to murmur nonsensical lullabies to me. I nod as if I understand; I don't want them to think I'm not listening.

"Rhine. Stay with us, baby."

I open my eyes, and Claire is standing behind Gabriel. There is a little orphan on either side of her, one with a jam jar full of grass, another with a bowl of oatmeal on a tray. They seem excited to see me, but afraid to get much closer. Maybe they think I'm contagious.

"You need to eat now," Claire says. I'm not allowed to question this. It's her orphanage, and—She. Is. Queen. I've heard her bellow this at the children when they don't comply. "I. AM. QUEEN." They startle, their neck hairs standing on end, and then she winks, and they giggle and do as they are told. She has the majesty of hurricanes and explosions.

I try to sit up, and Gabriel fluffs the pillows behind my back. The oatmeal orphan sets the tray across my lap and then steps back, still staring at me. The jam jar orphan puts the jar beside the bowl on my tray. I can see now that the grass within it is full of ladybugs. "To keep you company," she says. Her voice is wispy, like Jenna's, and I feel for a moment like a little shard of my dead sister wife has fallen back to earth and exploded into these little candy-red bugs. They crawl around the blades and along the maze of my brain. I think I'd like to cry, but I can't; Claire has pressed the spoon into my hand and I have to eat now because—She. Is. Queen.

The oatmeal is full of raisins and slices of almond, and the residue grinds between my teeth like the abundant sugar in Cecily's tea. Cecily, whose breasts were always leaking, whose eyes were puffy and purpled from tears. Has she pulled herself together by now? Taken my place on Linden's arm at parties? Is he pouring her champagne and calling her sweetheart?

My mouth is losing its feeling. The flavors stop making sense. Gabriel dabs the oatmeal that's dripping down my chin, and he looks so frightened. "Do you need to lie back down?" he says, already preparing to help me.

"No," Claire says. "She needs to eat. And then a hot bath." This must be a cue for the orphans, because they hurry from the room. I watch them go, and their bare feet splash against the floorboards where the water from the ceiling has made puddles. The smell of damp wood

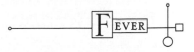

and the spring air through the open window make me think of the home I shared with my brother.

When the bowl is reasonably empty, Claire pulls back the blankets and helps me to my feet. My legs feel strange, though; my knees bend against my command, and I find it difficult just to step forward. Somehow I know this is not the flu. This is only the beginning of something much worse. This numbness will spread from my legs and travel up through my blood like a toxin. It will reach my heart, my brain, until everything is a continual fog and I'm unable to form a solid thought, just like I'm unable to form a solid step. And then? I don't know. Maybe I'll die. I can't help thinking Vaughn has something to do with this, but how is that possible? He can't poison me here. I'm finally out of his grasp.

Jenna's voice whispers hotly in my ear, *Are you?*

Distantly I'm aware that this is all cause to panic. But I'm just so tired. I think only about the bathwater as I ease into the tub. It's nice. Hot and steamy and smelling of soap. Actual soap, not a valley of marigolds or a sprig of jasmine. There's no strange foam crackling against my skin, no fluff, no illusion.

As I'm soaking, Claire lifts up my hair and pours a cup of water down the back of my neck. Then she massages shampoo into my hair and I start to drift off to sleep, but her voice pulls me back, saying, "Stay with me, baby."

"Claire?" I say, raising my eyebrows but keeping my eyes closed. "I think I'm dying."

"No, you're not," she says, tilting my chin up so that she can rinse my scalp with a cup of hot water. "Not on my watch."

I don't know why, but her words make me smile. Even if I don't believe them.

"Listen, I have a brother. His name is Rowan. You'll know him if you see him—his eyes are just like mine. If anything happens to me, please find him." I don't know what I'm saying. If I can't find him, how can I expect someone else to?

"You'll find him yourself," Claire says.

"Find him, and tell him—" I begin, but she pours the water over my face. It shoots up my nostrils when I breathe in, and I splutter and open my eyes. She douses me with water again. Her expression is unapologetic.

After my bath I'm left feeling groggy and chilled. I tie a bathrobe on over my pajamas and take my time coming down the steps, ignoring Silas's worried glances. There is something in his eyes that knows when the worst is true.

My next couple of nights are so fitful—a malaise of coughing, vomiting, and nightmares that have me muttering frantically in my sleep—that Silas begins sleeping on the couch. Gabriel quits sleeping entirely. When I resurface from nightmares, he is there, with cool cloths, glasses of water, and worry in his blue eyes. He helps me drag myself to the bathroom, and then he holds back my hair when I get sick, and rubs my back, and lets me curl up on the bathroom floor and lay my head on his knees.

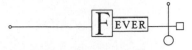

I press my shoulder against the cool tiles and I think: *This is how Jenna must have felt. This is the pain I saw in her eyes at the end.*

But I can't say this to Gabriel. It will only upset him, start him on a tangent about orphanages and the flu and my feeling better soon. So instead I say, "I don't think Jenna died of the virus."

"Me either," he whispers.

"I mean, it was the virus—it had all its symptoms—but there was something off about it."

Neither of us says the word we're thinking. Vaughn. We don't want it brought into this room. I close my eyes.

After I've been still for a while, Gabriel whispers, "Are you falling asleep? Do you want to go back to bed?"

"No. I don't want to move."

He sweeps the hair from my temple, and a light, contented sound escapes me. I just want to lie here like this, not sleeping, not talking, barely even thinking. The small window is open over the bathtub. It's very early, still dark, but outside there's the warm smell of springtime, like things rotting and blooming in one stagnant mist. I realize now that I've always craved the brutality of it. Shoots forcing their way up from the earth, petals popping open.

The start of life is always brutal, isn't it? We're born fighting.

I was born on January 30, a minute and a half before my brother. I wish I could remember it. I wish I had a memory of that first violent shove, the shock of cold air, the sting of oxygen into new lungs. Everyone should remember being born. It doesn't seem fair that we only remember dying.

If I am somehow dying, I refuse to accept it. I refuse to slip quietly, easily into death. This can't be it. The flower on the iron fence and on the cloth napkins, the river that has my name, the exploding labs, the Gathered girls—all of it moves through my mind, a puzzle flung from its box. All the pieces mean something. I know they do.

And then I remember something I haven't thought of for a long time. It was late, and I was very young. I remember liking how small I was in my bed; it made me feel safe. My brother was turned away from me, the blanket a canyon between our bodies. One of my parents opened the bedroom door, bringing in a rectangle of light. I closed my eyes. I hid in the dark, like I was playing a game of hide-and-seek. I heard the soft smack of a kiss being placed on my brother's forehead. Then a kiss for me, and a hand smoothing away my hair. Footsteps retreating. The light stayed on my eyelids, though.

"Perhaps we should have told them from the start," my father whispered.

"They're only children," my mother whispered back.

"Exceptionally bright children."

"In a few years." My mother's voice was almost pleading. I heard my father kiss her.

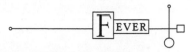

"All right, love," he said. Darkness, the click of the door. "All right."

I didn't question it. I was so warm and loved and happy. I had faith in the things I didn't yet understand. Everything would come together in time.

When my parents died, the memories became too painful to dredge up. I avoided them. But lately there's a purpose to them. An urgency. I let my parents back in, the way I did when they were alive, let their voices flutter through my head.

In my dream tonight the world dangles from my mother's neck as she kisses me good night, and I reach up to grab it.

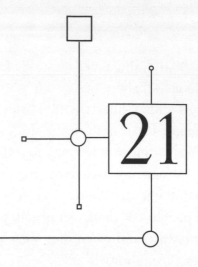

21

THE NEXT DAY I make an effort. I get out of bed. I go to the kitchen and force down a bowl of oatmeal and dry toast. And after, when I'm feeling nauseous, I sit very still until the feeling passes. I take the aspirin Claire gives me. I ignore the dizzying bits of light. I wash the dishes. I say nothing about the fistful of blond hair that came out this morning when I was tying my ponytail.

The effort is more exhausting than the ailment, though, and by noon I'm hiding in the shed, leaning against an old car covered by a tarp, to catch my breath. There is the stale, dusty smell of unused things. Pieces so rusted that I can't tell what they are line the shelves. Jars full of bolts, nails, safety pins. Things that are of no use to me.

All day I've been going through the motions of a well person. I don't know if anyone is truly convinced, but Claire didn't complain when I scrubbed the bathroom tiles and vacuumed dried cereal from the living room carpet. Right now I'm supposed to be taking inventory on what supplies are running low and writing up a shopping list.

I just need a few minutes to get my bearings. While I'm clearing the haze from my mind, I try to imagine where Rowan could have gone. We have no living relatives, and we always kept to ourselves.

What I know for certain is that if he believes I'm alive, he's searching for me. Otherwise he's avenging my supposed death. Nothing Rowan ever does is in vain. Nothing without purpose. There are so many places for Gatherers to dump an unwanted girl's body, and Rowan would have stayed long enough to search all of them before moving on. But a body dumped a year ago would be gone by now. If he's looking for me at all, it means he thinks I'm still alive.

Now the question is, how do I go about finding him? When I was little, I was taught that if I ever got lost, it was best to stay in one place so that I'd be easier to find. But now my brother and I are both in motion. He won't be back here to find me, that's for sure.

I make my way back to the house, still trying to reason out a plan. I take comfort in the chores, menial and repetitive. Gabriel helps me fold towels and tells me I don't look as pale anymore. I can't tell if he's only trying to be kind, because I still feel as lousy as ever. But I manage to keep my dinner down.

it is—stealing girls and making them obey. But people used to get married to spend their lives together. There's intimacy. It implies it was consensual. It's not just our freedom that was taken, it was our right to be unhappy, too."

At first I couldn't rationalize it. Being a bride was something I wanted to escape, but surely it was better than being a prostitute or a faceless baby machine. "We still have a right to be unhappy," I told her. "We just have to pretend with Linden, that's all."

She laughed bitterly. "Oh, Rhine," she said. She rolled on top of me and took my face in her hands and smiled so sadly. "None of us are pretending."

I think about that now, and Gabriel watches me with his head tilted. His eyes are so full of life and curiosity. He's been caged up too. And now, suddenly, I understand what Jenna was saying.

When I was married to Linden in the gazebo, my hand was limp in his. My eyes bored through him. I didn't hear the vows being spoken. And when he talked to me, much later, my smiles were lies. My kisses were for the higher purpose of escape.

"What are you thinking?" Gabriel asks. He demands nothing of me, and there's only one thing keeping me beside him:

"Choice," I say softly. "I'm thinking about choice." And I lean forward and kiss him.

He kisses back, readily. We're fast learning the ways of one another.

I've made the right choice, haven't I? A life outside of Linden's mansion isn't a pretty life, or an easy one. And the small annoyances of life on the wives' floor are the things I miss now: Cecily sneaking into my bed when she couldn't sleep. My sister wives shrieking with laughter as they played games when I craved silence. And Linden, who was present even when he was not. Every second of every day held the promise of him. Even when he was nowhere to be found, before the day was over he would come by to say good night.

I push the thought of him away as soon as it comes. I have no business missing Linden Ashby. He spent his days doing as he pleased while his wives were made to wait in their cage. I was right to run away. Even Cecily, ever content to be his prisoner, had enough sense to recognize that. Life without those safe little walls isn't easy, but it's mine.

I close my eyes, feel Gabriel's breath on my face as he repositions himself beside me. He whispers my name like it's the most important thing in the world. "Yes?" I reply, but our lips are already touching, spurring all my nerves and muscles and my bloodstream to a strange, wonderful upward motion. Everything alert, buzzing.

It's the first time we've kissed without the stigma of my marriage, my sister wives looming in the hall, or one of Madame's perverse displays. I make a noise, and then he does, faraway and unrecognizable.

This delirium is not to be confused with that brought

on by my fever. This is happiness, so sudden and unexpected. This is the world disappearing around us.

There is only a wisp of a memory of that man's hand on my thigh, erased in a second when Gabriel brushes his fingers over the spot, bringing flutters of warmth and light. Everything that happened before feels like a million years ago now. This is the freedom I craved throughout my marriage. To share a bed not because of a wedding ring or a one-sided promise that was made for me, but because of desire. Inexplicable yet undeniable. I have never craved closeness like this for anyone else.

His hand reaches under my shirt, palm flat against my stomach, and then his head draws back a little and he goes still.

"What's wrong?" I say.

"Your skin is burning up," he says.

"I'm all right."

"Can't you just be honest with me?" He sounds angry now, and I feel as though I'm shrinking under him. I open my mouth, but I can't think of anything to say that wouldn't make matters worse.

"Something is wrong, isn't it?" he says. "And you've been trying to keep it from me."

When I don't answer, he pushes himself upright, away from me.

"Gabriel . . ."

He turns on the light, looks at me, his hair a mess, eyes dark with worry and something else—affection? Pain?

"Don't try to take this on yourself," he says, with more force than I'm used to hearing from him.

That's fair. He has given up everything to follow me. I owe him the truth, seeing as it's the only thing I have left to give him.

"Okay," I say, pushing myself upright. "Okay, yes. I feel terrible all the time, and I don't know what's happening, and I'm scared. Okay?"

I fall back against the mattress, gather up the blankets, and turn away from him.

"Rhine . . ." He touches my shoulder, but the way I tense up makes him withdraw. He's so quiet that I think he must have left the room, so frustrated with my secrecy and lack of answers that he had to be away from me.

Then I hear him say, very softly, "Vaughn."

"Maybe," I admit. "But I can't imagine how."

Gabriel touches my shoulder again, settles behind me on the mattress. "I won't let him hurt you," he says.

"How will you stop him?" I say, more wryly than I mean to.

He kisses the back of my neck, and a surge of electricity runs up my spine.

"You let me worry about that," he says. He reaches overhead and turns off the light again.

As I lie there, trying to fall asleep, I think of Gabriel's words after he fought Greg off me.

I won't let anyone touch you like that ever again.

But if he's right, and Vaughn is somehow the cause

of this, what can be done? How can he protect me from something that is already deep within my tissues and blood, ruining me from the inside?

Still, as exhaustion clouds my reason, I begin to feel something bizarrely like peace.

I won't, he promised, enveloping me in his warmth, much like he does now. *Not ever again.*

The following morning I'm awoken by a thud. I open my eyes, grumbling unkind things as the stack of books comes into focus. My head feels full of shattered glass, and all I can manage to get out is "What?"

"Medical journals," Gabriel says, sitting on the edge of my mattress.

"We found them in a box in the shed," Silas says. He's leaning against the door frame, holding a pancake like it's a sandwich and taking a bite that reduces it by half. "Claire used to be a nurse."

With effort I sit upright, my hair spilling into my face. Gabriel hands me the glass of water that's gone warm sitting beside me all night. I take a painful sip and ask, "What are we going to do with them?"

"We're going to figure this out," Gabriel says.

"Well, have fun, kids," Silas says around the last mouthful of pancake. He stretches his arms over his head, hitting the top of the door frame as he goes. "Some of us have real chores to do."

Gabriel and I spend a good hour going through the

books, looking up everything from influenza to scurvy. There are so many ailments. Things I never could have imagined. Tumors that can more than double a person's bodyweight. Diseases that cause gums to bleed, and toe-nails to turn yellow. Nervous disorders that can produce auditory hallucinations.

As for my symptoms, every source seems to agree that what I have is the flu. Coughing, fever, light-headedness. There's no category for the feeling of dread, the sense that something is amiss. There are no chapters about sinister fathers-in-law or what types of things might be done in a labyrinthine basement.

The pages are spread out between us on the blanket, and I can feel Gabriel's desperation the further we get from finding an answer. His eyes are still on the page when he speaks, and at first I think he's going to read a passage aloud, but he says, "We have to confront him. We have to go back to the mansion."

"I'm sorry," I say. "Have you lost your mind?"

"He followed you to Madame's, didn't he? Maybe there was some truth to the things he was saying. Maybe he wanted to tell you about what's happening to you."

"Or maybe he was trying to lure me back to him so that he could split me in half and devote a chapter of his sick experiments to the vital organs of a subject with two different-color eyes and a defiance toward his son," I snap. "I'm not going back there, and neither are you. He'll kill us both."

Gabriel looks up from the page. The ferocity in his eyes startles me. "Take a look at yourself," he says. "He *is* killing you. I think that when he followed you to the scarlet district, he meant to undo whatever this is that's happening to you."

"That makes absolutely no sense," I say, ignoring the small bit of me that agrees.

"Who's to say?" Gabriel says. "Maybe when you ran away it interrupted an experiment."

"Well, I think that if I go back, he'll kill me for sure," I say.

Gabriel looks back into the book, muttering something about Jenna being right.

"What was that about my sister wife?" I say.

"She knew you so well. She was right—you don't get it. Vaughn doesn't want you dead. What use would you be to him dead? He wants to see what makes you breathe, and why your eyes are that way. There's something in you that gives him hope."

I think of how eager Jenna was to help me escape. How she disappeared that one afternoon to the basement and slammed the door on me when I asked what it was all about. It wounds me that she would share these things with Gabriel. I held her head in my lap as she died, and she never trusted me with a word of her secrets, though it seems a lot of them had to do with me.

"Don't talk to me about Jenna," I spit back. "You're so sure she knew everything. Do you know where she

is now? Dead. Under a sheet on a gurney, just like Rose. And even if Vaughn's plans don't involve killing me, I won't go back to that place to find out what they are."

The page is shaking between my fingers, and I slam the book just in time to see it drown in the blur of fresh tears. "I won't go back," I repeat.

My head is pounding. I hear whispers in my blood, and I know—I *know*—that there is something lethal inside of me that cannot be explained by these books. When Gabriel crawls across the mattress to be next to me, I lean my head against his shoulder even though I'm furious with him. I crave the safety he provides, even if it's temporary.

"Okay," he says into my ear. "Okay. We'll find another way to fix this."

I don't believe it, but I nod. The nausea turns a tide, becoming something more profound. My nerves come alive, raising their heads like flowers come to bloom. I look at him, and his thumb is just swiping a tear from my cheek when I push forward and kiss him.

He kisses back, all the pages spread out around us like riddles waiting to be solved. Let them wait. Let my genes unravel, my hinges come loose. If my fate rests in the hands of a madman, let death come and bring its worst. I'll take the ruined craters of laboratories, the dead trees, this city with ashes in the oxygen, if it means freedom. I'd sooner die here than live a hundred years with wires in my veins.

I sink back against the mattress, and when he moves his mouth from mine, I find that I'm trembling, flushed, my hands going hot, cold, hot. But I pull him back down to me before the concern can overtake him.

A book slides down the mattress with my weight, tapping my ankle as though to remind me. I kick it away, see it hit the floor like a bug I've just squashed.

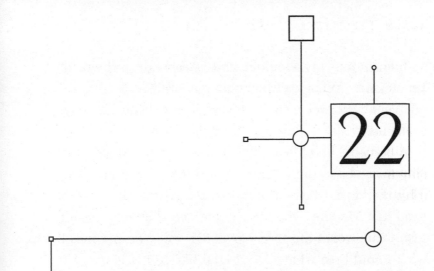

IN THE AFTERNOON I conjure the strength to perform menial tasks. I wipe sticky messes from the piano keys and countertops. Silas washes dishes, and I dry them to spotlessness.

"How're you feeling, princess?" he asks, handing me a plastic sippy cup.

"Great," I answer with authority. I used to find him irritatingly superior, but now I think we aren't so different.

He has meaningless trysts with young girls, little affairs that have nothing to do with love. The girls come willingly, even eagerly, and I've decided that they're nothing like those in the scarlet district, enduring men for profit. Rather, Silas and his adoring female cavalcade have decided that they will seize whatever thrills they can find in their short lives. And how can I fault them for that? Aren't I doing the same thing? Living with the promise of death, thinking only of today.

Silas bumps my shoulder, and I nearly drop the plate I'm drying. "What are you smiling about?"

"What do you mean?" I say. "It's a beautiful day; that's all."

Silas cants his chin at the window, beyond which gray clouds are hovering. "Right." He thinks I've gone mad. Maybe I have. Maybe I'm lost in the realms of my own head like Maddie, who is so immersed that she doesn't grant this world the privilege of her voice. Sometimes I wish I could see what she sees. I'd like to try it.

"Hey," Silas calls. Water is sloshing between his fingers. "Where are you going?"

"The heart of the song," I say, leaving him behind as I head for the sound of piano chords in the next room.

Nina plays like an angel. Her left arm, bearing only the shriveled idea of a hand, rests at her side, while her right flies over the keys, evoking a fluttery sound like gasps or bullets.

Maddie is under the piano on all fours, her hair in her face, her shoulders hunched, eyes wild. She's a beast without its herd, as brave as she is small. I lie on the rug, and we watch each other, blinking curiously.

"Do you know what my father used to say?" I ask her. "He used to say that songs had a heart. A crescendo that can make all your blood rush from your head to your toes."

She crawls toward me and then rests on her haunches. She seems like a small thing looking into a deep pool of water, and I'm sinking far below. My eyelids feel heavy.

I watch her blur and then disappear, taking with her the song and its heart.

"—ine? Rhine!"

Something acidic bubbles up in my throat, and I feel sick. An arm reaches behind my shoulders and pulls me up from the depths just in time for me to vomit into my lap, gasping and choking on the burn of it.

"There it is," Claire coos, mopping my face with a wet cloth. "Let it all out."

This is what I get for forcing down breakfast, I suppose. When I open my eyes, it's as though someone has smeared ointment across them. I splutter again, and when it finally stops, I'm laid on my side. Claire is saying, "Let the girl breathe. Give her room."

Silas and Gabriel are talking, but I can't understand the words. Small, cold fingers trace my forehead. Maddie. How could Madame show violence to this harmless little creature?

Nina leans close. "You scared her," she whispers, giving Maddie a voice. "She thinks she broke you."

"She didn't," I murmur. My voice is small, and I worry it won't come through. "She didn't. Someone else did."

I can't hang on to what happens next. Someone carries me up the stairs, and then there's the vague knowledge of soaking in a cool tub, and then a soft towel, and a firm mattress. Something cold covers my forehead. An icepack; I can hear the ice moving like rocks. The frozen smell of it is a shock to my nostrils, but a relief overall. "Rest now," someone whispers, and I do.

When I wake up, the window shows me a night sky. I hear children murmuring in the house, and Claire telling them, "Shh, shh."

I'm in Silas's bed. My head feels stuffed with cotton. I stare at the numbers on the bedside clock but can't comprehend them.

"Are you awake?" Gabriel asks. He looks up from a sea of papers.

With effort I prop myself on my elbow. Something buzzes angrily in my skull. "What happened?"

"Claire said it must have been a kind of seizure," he answers, all gentleness. "But she was only guessing. You were lying on the floor, bright red with a fever; nothing we did could wake you." He holds up a medical journal, his face unreadable. "I guess it would interest you to know that it not only doesn't sound like a seizure, but it doesn't compare to anything I can find."

I lie back down and rub my eyes with the heels of my hands, trying to quell the buzzing. *Think*, I tell myself. Surely the daughter of two scientists cannot be bested by this. But I was never as brilliant as my mother and father. All that comes to me are my brother's notes, scribbled amid the burned and crumpled pages. He was making a list, trying to figure something out. We're fighting different battles, my brother and I. If only we could be together, maybe we'd have an answer between us.

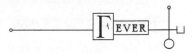

"We have to go," I say, and try to clear the hoarseness from my voice.

Gabriel looks hopeful. "Back to the mansion?"

"To find my brother."

Gabriel shakes his head. "That's not a priority right now."

"How could you say that?"

"Because you're dying!" he snaps. The room falls silent. He looks at the open book, penitent. Clearly he didn't mean to say this, but he's been thinking it. After a few seconds he repeats it, softly. "You're dying, and I'm not going to sit here and watch you without doing a thing about it."

I sit up. It's as though my blood has turned to sand. I am an hourglass. All the sand goes rushing from my head, and I can hear it whooshing. "Rowan might be able to help," I say.

"He might," Gabriel says. "But you're here, and we don't know where he is, and we can't afford the time to search the country over."

I have no way to argue this. I open my mouth, but the words don't leave my lips. *More time. I just need a little more time.* I know that he's right. I know that the answer to all of this might be in the very place I left behind. I know that my madman father-in-law can work miracles just like he can murder an infant—or his son's defiant bride.

How did I come to be at the mercy of such a man? What horror did I commit in a past life to warrant his interest?

"A doctor, then," I insist. "Or a shaman. A clairvoyant! Anything else." The bed lurches, and I grip the edges. Gabriel sees this and eases me back down. He tucks the blankets to my chin, like I am a child.

I pretend that I'm back in the mansion. Not as Vaughn's prisoner but as Linden's wife. I am sandwiched between silk sheets, amid down pillows. My sister wives are sleeping across the hall. Be still. Listen. I can hear them breathe. And Gabriel has just brought breakfast for me, before the sun is up, while the empty hallways are filled with ticking clocks and plumes of smoke from incense sticks that have just extinguished themselves after burning through the night. Later there will be trampolines and orange blossoms and bright orange koi flicking their tails to delight me. There's nothing to fear. Everybody's safe.

Gabriel presses the back of his hand to my forehead. His mouth tightens into a frown. "Tomorrow we'll find a hospital," he says.

"Okay," I whisper.

Exhausted, I close my eyes. "Are you coming to bed?" I ask him.

"Not yet," he says. I feel his weight leave the mattress. I fall asleep to the sound of him flipping through pages.

When I wake, it's still dark outside. Gabriel sleeps with his arm across my waist, his chin on my shoulder.

Every muscle in my body hurts, and in my mouth there's the coppery, bitter taste that tells me I am going to

be sick. But the pain is progress; it means my limbs are no longer numb. I can move, just so slightly, out of Gabriel's arms. His fingers are gripping my shirt, and as I touch them, one by one, they uncurl. He mumbles something and then turns onto his stomach, hugging the pillow.

I'm careful not to wake him as I climb out of the blankets and make my way to the bathroom. I take some aspirin from the cabinet over the sink, hoping it will somehow curb this nausea. I swallow them with a handful of water.

Then I close the cabinet door, and a blond corpse meets me in the mirror. She is a zombie from the film at the Florida cinema, a sickly shade of gray, with hollow eyes, pale lips, and thinning hair.

I look away, too horrified to let that girl be more than a stranger. In the morning I will have to wash up before anyone sees me.

As I walk down the hall, I am comforted by all the different bodies breathing around me. Some of the children have their own beds, while others huddle together like sardines.

I pass through the living room. Silas, an amorphous mountain of blankets on the couch, says, "You are a ghost, the way you haunt this place at night."

"Boo," I whisper.

He chuckles, the sound fading as he returns to his dreams. I cross the room and make my way to the kitchen, and there I make a cup of tea for myself.

I can hear the gentle wind sighing outside. I tiptoe past Silas, who is now snoring, and I open the door to breathe in the spring air. There is something eerily welcoming about nighttime in this small borough. I close the door behind me and sit on the top step. Not too far. I stay close to the house, away from the street, ready to hurry back inside if there's anything dangerous.

But it's calm. I look out at the bleary sepia-toned houses on this street. The malnourished, skeletal trees. The wilting brown grass. And I know I'm where I was meant to be. I was born into a world that was already dying; I belong to it. I will take it over holographic oceans and spinning diagrams of beautiful houses. Because even if the lie is beautiful, the truth is what you face in the end.

There is something else here too, so jarring against the rest because it does not belong. In the darkness I can just see it approaching—a black limousine pulling up to the curb. I wonder what the occasion is. I suppose a child has been purchased; I think there are other orphanages on this block. Surely nobody is being picked up for a party. There's no wealth in this area.

The engine idles for a bit and then dies.

Then I'm filled with a sick feeling of dread. That limousine looks very familiar.

The front passenger door opens, and I watch the shadowy figure of a man step out. He tightens a scarf around his neck and then steps onto the sidewalk, tilts his head toward me.

"Beautiful night for stargazing, isn't it?" he says.

My skin swells with goose bumps at that voice.

Run, run, run! Maddie's old warning flashes at me, but for some reason I'm frozen to the spot, clinging to my cup of tea with both hands. "How did you find me?" I say.

"That's no way to greet your father-in-law," Vaughn says. "I know you can muster a warmer welcome than that."

There's a clicking noise, and then a flame appears in Vaughn's cupped hand. It takes a moment for me to realize that he is not holding fire itself, but rather a small candle. He moves toward me, and I inch for the door, but he stops a couple of yards away.

"Fire is such a clever little thing," he says. "Especially for clever girls who can think of a good use for it. Setting fire to some curtains to create a diversion, perhaps?"

The light shows me all the hundred creases in his smile.

How is it possible that my worst nightmare has arrived and I am unable to move from this spot, holding my cup of tea?

Slowly I get to my feet, avoiding sudden movements as though he were a venomous snake. He takes a quick step closer, and I flinch.

He only laughs. "Relax, darling. I wasn't going to set fire to the place, if that's what you were thinking. Not with all those helpless orphans and your true love inside."

He comes closer, until he's on the bottom step, and he holds the candle to my face. Its heat in this chilly air immediately causes my nose to run.

"You aren't looking too well." Vaughn tsk-tsks. "Look at those bags under your eyes. That haystack you

call hair. You've let yourself go, darling."

"Circumstances beyond my control," I say bitterly.

Vaughn goes on as if I haven't spoken. "You've always had such ravishing beauty. Untamed, but lovely. That's the sort of thing my son prefers, you know."

He tucks a wisp of hair over my shoulder. His eyes hold that kindness again; I first saw it one afternoon when he walked me through the golf course. It startled me then like it startles me now, the way my sole enemy can at once transform into a version of his mild-mannered son.

A pang of longing moves through me, sharp and unexpected. If someone had to come to drag me back to that prison, I wish it had been Linden. Linden, whose eyes were always filled with love for me, even if I never quite believed that love to be real.

Vaughn traces his finger from my scalp and down the line of my hair, and to my shoulder, which he grabs so hard I can feel his fingertips on the bone. "Let's you and me have a talk," he says.

I could scream. In an instant Gabriel, Silas, and Claire would be in the doorway, several pairs of blinking eyes behind them. But my gaze is trained on the flame and all that it implies. It's a very small warning of a very large destruction. He would think nothing of burning this place to the ground and killing everyone inside if that's what it would take to recapture me. And I know that he is only here for me, not them.

Those bright pieces of light are back, flurrying in

the night air like the snow on my last night in the mansion. Linden and I watched it on the verandah, letting it stick to our hair.

I don't move, and Vaughn doesn't try to pull me. I know he won't shove me kicking and screaming into the back of that limo. It's not his way. But I also know he is confident that, one way or another, I will wind up there. His smile is full of teeth and triumph.

"How have you been feeling?" he asks me. "Any unexplained symptoms? Fevers?" He strokes my hair away again, holding up the thin blond pieces that have fallen out between his fingers.

My breath catches. That lone pang of longing for Linden to be here instead of his father has doubled, tripled, transformed into something ugly. My ears buzz with the electricity of it.

"Just the flu," I say coldly, unbelieving.

"Your immune system is shutting down," he says. "Right now your antibodies are moving through your bloodstream, trying to combat a foreign bacteria that isn't there. Perhaps you've tried medication. That will have the same effect, which is to say none at all. Your nerves are losing sensation. Extremities inexplicably numb, especially upon waking."

I twist my shoulder from his grip. "What did you do to me?" I say.

"Darling." He chuckles. "You did this to yourself. You're in withdrawal."

Withdrawal? No, that's not possible. The angel's blood was weeks ago. Surely there's nothing left of it in my system. And Gabriel went through much worse withdrawal, and he's fine.

Vaughn searches my eyes for understanding as I stare at him, uncomprehending.

"Really?" he says. "A girl as smart as you?"

He's enjoying this.

"The June Beans," he says.

This starts him off on a tangent I am having a hard time following because my mind, already reeling, has started to go numb. I think he is being deliberately convoluted. Something about blue June Beans—specifically the blue ones—the candies that somehow always made it to my meal trays, even after Gabriel was no longer able to sneak them to me. An experiment to test chemical dependency and bacteria resistance.

"It's revolutionary," Vaughn raves. "The only way to break your dependency would be to gradually reduce the doses. But to cut it off all at once? A fascinating thing happens. The body begins to shut down much the way it would in the latest stages of the virus. It's uncomfortable at first—nausea, headache—but then the body begins to lose sensation, the pain receptors in the brain are deadened. It's a bit like dying of hypothermia."

Jenna. The word creeps up my throat, but I don't say it aloud. He's telling me that this is how he killed Jenna. That flame in his hand is nothing compared to

"I'm proud of it," Vaughn says. "The concept is quite primitive. To prevent contraction of the flu, one would receive a flu shot, which is, in fact, a small dose of the flu itself. And so my thinking was simple: Replicate the symptoms of the virus and administer them slowly, over several years, until the body works up an immunity."

I feel sick. The pavement lilts and buckles under my feet. He killed my sister wife. I always believed it, but to receive confirmation is more pain than I ever anticipated.

"You were the perfect candidate," Vaughn says. "I'd thought Cecily at first, being young as she is, but her body chemistry would already be changing with the pregnancy. I thought it best to leave her alone. You, however—" He laughs. "Linden told me you were uncooperative about consummating your marriage. He asked for my advice on the matter, and I told him he should let you be. He agreed much more easily than even I expected. He was content just to stare at you, let his daydreams run wild at the mention of your name. And I knew you wouldn't be getting pregnant anytime soon."

Just knowing that this conversation took place makes me feel sure I'll vomit. To think that all those nights with Linden, when we held fast to each other to quell our separate pains of loneliness, were shared with my scheming father-in-law. To think our kisses were analyzed, our touches and glances just notes for Vaughn's mad experiments. I feel invaded.

Distantly, I'm aware that I'm walking. Vaughn steers me toward the limousine and opens the back door for me. "Don't be foolish, Rhine," he says. It's so rare for him to speak my name that it jars me. "We can have this mess straightened out once we get you home. Or you can die here, and I'll see to it that everyone in that house joins you."

I know he means it. I stare into the car, at the wraparound leather seat that held my sister wives and me before we knew one another's names, when we were three frightened girls spared a gruesome death but sentenced to lifelong imprisonment. And there, beneath the sunroof, is where Linden and I sipped champagne and sagged against each other, warm and drunk and hiccupping with laughter after his first expo.

"Go on in, darling," Vaughn says. "Let's go home."

And I do, knowing all the while that it will be the last ride I ever take. That something much worse than marriage awaits me this time.

"You're still wearing your ring," Vaughn remarks as he settles in beside me. I barely feel the pressure from the syringe he jabs into my forearm.

In what I can only describe as dumb luck and good timing, I vomit on his lapels before I lose consciousness.

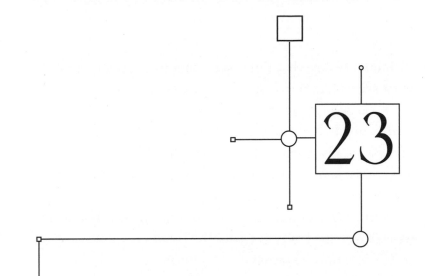

23

I AM A CORPSE on a rolling cart.

I am weaving through the labyrinth of hallways, warmth in my veins, vision smeared.

All at once I'm aware of how loud everything is. Attendants talking—no, shouting—one of them holding a bag of fluid over my head. I have some faraway notion that all of this fuss is for me. But I am nothing. I cannot speak. I wouldn't think I was breathing if not for the mist I see on this plastic dome held over my mouth.

I don't know where I am. Other than the attendants' uniforms, there is nothing familiar.

But then suddenly there is.

A blur of her red hair. A fist held to a gaping mouth, my name on its lips. Her baby screaming in her arms. Footsteps running. "Wait!" her voice cries, but they don't, and she is swallowed up by the distance between us.

I close my eyes. Cease to exist.

I don't realize that I'm resurfacing from the darkness, what seems like years later, until I hear a voice.

"I warned you not to run," Vaughn says. He is a black bird in my dream. His talons break skin. Blood rolls out of my arm. I lie very still so he will think that I am dead. There's no sport in carrion, and I will not let him enjoy my defeat any more than he already is.

"With my son you had love. You had safety. But you were determined, weren't you?"

His breath is a hot wind.

"Determined to leave, and so I let you go," he sighs. "You've done me a favor, really. Linden has denounced you."

Awareness creeps up on me, but I refuse to let it win. Just before I swim back into unconsciousness, I hear Vaughn say, "Now you belong to me."

You belong to me.

No matter how deep the dreams bury me, there are those words. On street signs. Sung from the lips of Madame's weary girls. Murmured in the rustle of October leaves. They bloom from lilies that shoot open their starfish petals.

I open my eyes, sometimes, and am met with attendants I've never seen before, who avert their eyes as they scrub my skin with sponges, insert and remove IV needles from my forearm, change bedpans, take notes on clipboards, and leave without a word. I wait for Vaughn,

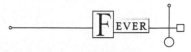

but he only visits me in nightmares. I dream that he's standing on the threshold with a scalpel or a syringe, and I wake in a cold sweat. And so it goes for what could be eternity. It's impossible to measure time; there is a fake window on the wall, the only thing in the room besides the machines, and it is always glowing with a fake sun, illuminating a field of fake lilies.

When the attendants go, there's the soft sound of a door closing, and I'm alone. There's no Jenna to devise my escape plan; no Gabriel to sneak in and talk to me; no Deirdre to draw a chamomile bath. And no Linden sketching dismal, elegant pictures for me, or coming into my bed and holding me until I fall asleep.

This is worse than death, the rest of my days ticking away in a malaise of needles and loneliness. That's the worst of it, I think—the loneliness. The attendants won't speak to me, even on the rare occasion when I'm lucid enough to watch them work. Sometimes, phasing in and out of consciousness, I dream of them bringing me June Beans (any color but blue) or the champagne Linden and I would drink at his parties. But I never dream of anyone important, and maybe that's my mind's way of letting go of everyone I've ever loved.

I begin to envy the dead girls the Gatherers couldn't sell. It would be easier for my brother to find my body, to mourn but carry on knowing what happened. But I will not think of him again. I've banished him from even my darkest dreams. Along with Gabriel and sunlight, and even Maddie.

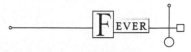

Until one time I open my eyes, and there's a little girl standing on the threshold to my room. She's wearing a flimsy hospital gown, like mine. Her eyes are like Jenna's after she died. Hollow and gray. There's no semblance of youth in her face. Her skin is yellowed, her arms bruised from the injections. She sways like she's going to fall. I want to think she is just a bad dream in this place of nightmares. Or an apparition. But I blink several times, and she's still there.

"Deirdre," I whisper. The first word I've spoken in a thousand years. "Not you, too."

"Your room is so bright," she says, and I can hear my faithful little domestic in that weary voice. "He keeps the other rooms dimmed."

I fight against my restraints. I don't know why. Even if I could get out of this bed, what could I do to save her? She shuffles barefoot to a pitcher of water that rests on one of the machines. She pours a cup of water, and she brings it to me, holding my head up as she tips the contents into my mouth. I'm not surprised by how greedily I drink; when the attendants give me water, it's only teaspoons at a time. Dehydration must be a part of the experiment.

"Your lips are chapped." She frowns. "I wish I had something to fix them."

"What's happened to you?" I say. "What has he done?"

She shakes her head, strokes my cheek. Her little hand, at least, feels soft and familiar. I can't help taking comfort in it, and I hate myself for it. Something awful

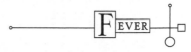
has happened to her, and it's my fault because I left her behind. I should have known Vaughn would have something horrible planned for her.

"I'm so sorry," I whisper.

"Shh. I can hear him coming. Pretend you're somewhere nice and go to sleep."

Footsteps are coming down the hall; worry shadows her face. "Shh." She sweeps her hand over my eyelids, lowering them, and hurries away. She runs on quiet feet. She doesn't burst into blood or disappear. I am sure she was real. I hear a door closing down the hall.

Pretend I'm somewhere nice, she said.

I dream I'm wearing the sweater she made me. She is in the distance, cupping starfish in her hands, moving like shutter clicks through a camera lens. The ocean laps at her feet and mine, wanting to drown us.

She visits me again. I'm not sure how long it's been. Minutes? Weeks? I feel her loosening my restraints. "There's a trick to these," she says when she realizes I'm awake and watching her. "You can move them up to the next notch, and they'll still look tight enough, but you'll be able to wriggle your hands and feet through. The attendants come on a rotation, so we know to be in our beds in time. Your schedule is erratic, though. It's hard to know when they're coming for you."

"Where am I?" My voice comes out hoarse. My throat is raw, and I have some distant memory of a tube being down it.

Deirdre frowns. Her soft hair is rumpled and matted, her neat braids gone. There are so many bruises on her.

"We're in the basement," she says. "The Housemaster brought you in a month ago. You were so ill." Her eyes swell with tears. Gently she eases my hands out of the restraints, and I'm able to sit up. But after lying on my back for so long, this causes a head rush, and more of those bright lights. I rub my forehead and blink several times until the lights are gone.

Deirdre, I think. *What has he done to you?* She's only a child—nine, ten years old, but she's as haggard as a first generation in the worst shape, her skin yellowed and pruning at the elbows and fingertips, the bones in her face sharp and too defined.

But I don't ask the question right away. Whatever horrible fate has befallen her is my doing. When I ran away, I took away her purpose at this mansion. Vaughn could lie to his son and say that, in my absence, Deirdre would be better employed elsewhere. Linden wouldn't even question it. He trusts his father.

Still the question comes, almost against my will. "What did he do to you?"

She shakes her head. "Early treatments, I think," she says. "Soon he'll try artificial insemination," she adds timidly. "From what I understand, the Housemaster thinks he's found a way to speed up fertility and gestation, so girls can bear children before natural puberty."

The words are so unreal coming from her warm voice

that I'm sure I'm dreaming. But seconds pass, and nothing strange happens, like the ceiling caving in or the floor trying to swallow me.

"It hasn't worked yet," she says, still avoiding my gaze. She is behaving like a domestic suddenly, tucking the blanket at my waist, rubbing the circulation back into my wrists. "Lydia has been here much longer than I have. She almost carried to term, one time, but . . ." Her voice trails off.

Lydia. Why is that name so familiar? While the fog is still clearing from my mind, along with any suspicion that this is a dream, I remember. Lydia was Rose's domestic, sent away after Rose became so distraught over losing her newborn daughter that she couldn't stand the sight of the young girl who'd tended to her affairs.

"Deirdre." I reach for her, to gather her in my arms, to comfort her. But she is beyond comfort, and she inches away.

"I think I heard the elevator," she says, staring at her hands as they knot around each other. "I'll be back when I can." She hurriedly helps me back into my restraints, and then she skitters from the room.

When the attendants come, I feign unconsciousness, but my heart is pounding. One of them takes my blood pressure—I feel the band tightening around my arm and releasing with a gasp. Too high. This is cause for great concern. It sets them muttering about side effects and palpitations.

The nightmare is throbbing all around me. The squeal of carts, the rattle of tools they're using to monitor, prod, and inject me. I feel something on my forearm, and I wait for the sting of a needle, but all I feel is a light pressure, hear a series of mechanical beeps.

The top buttons of my nightgown are undone by cold dry hands. Something cold splatters onto my chest— some kind of gel, I think. Something moves along my breastbone. I know it's a piece of machinery, not a human hand. They're running some kind of test. I feel like something less than human. An experiment. A cadaver.

It's okay. I won't let anyone touch you like that ever again.

But there is no one to save me.

Eventually the attendants clean me up, scribble their notes, and leave. I hear one of them saying, from very far away, "What do you suppose he'll do with her eyes after he's done with her?"

Something new is swimming in my veins after that. And that's when the real nightmares begin. Faces, mutated and decomposing as they lean over me. Ghosts hurrying in the hall, whispering my name. A tide of blood splashing across the tiles. Linden, standing in my doorway.

His sad green eyes are trained on me.

"I thought you didn't love me anymore," I whisper, and he turns into dust.

Since there are no clocks, and the holographic window is always showing me the same degree of fake sun-

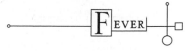

light, I have no concept of mornings and evenings. I suspect it's morning when Deirdre visits me, because she is
always disheveled as though she just awoke. There are
so many tubes and wires springing from my arms that it
doesn't even matter if she frees me from my restraints,
because I can hardly move. She whispers nice things to
me, describing her father's paintings, admiring aloud the
many shades of my blond hair.

I am almost never lucid enough to respond. I suppose
she gets used to this, because eventually her sweet stories take a dark turn. "I'm sorry I haven't been to see
you," she whispers. "I lost another pregnancy."

I cannot even find the strength to open my eyes, but I
think if she knew I could hear her, she wouldn't be saying this.

"Lydia died this morning. I watched her bleed out.
And the Housemaster was there when they wheeled her
away." Her voice cracks. I feel the pressure of her soft
fingers weaving through mine.

"She knew things, though," Deirdre says, her voice
heavy with impending tears. "Rose's baby? I told you I'd
heard it cry, before the Housemaster announced it was a
stillbirth. Lydia told me she saw it. She saw the baby, and
there was something wrong with it. Its ears were shriveled, and its face was—wrong somehow. Malformed."

My heart starts pounding again, in that helpless, futile
way. It's the only thing left in me that seems able to move.

Rose. Linden's first wife, perhaps the only one he ever

truly loved, was forced to give birth alone at the hands of a monster. She knew what he was capable of. She warned me not to cross him, and I didn't listen.

Deirdre is still talking, but I can't hang on to consciousness long enough to hear what other horrors she tells me.

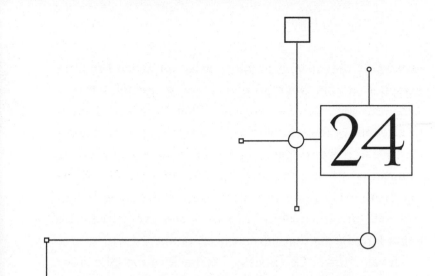

THE DREAMS break like water against rocks.

When I open my eyes, my first thought is that my little sister wife has gotten taller. And prettier.

A strip of light from the fake window hugs her cheek, then darts to her shoulder as she turns. For an instant her red hair is entirely ablaze.

She doesn't realize yet that I'm watching her. She moves candidly, humming a little, dancing as she pours pitcher water into a paper cup. Her hair is wrapped around her head haphazardly, rivers of it coming down her neck, which has also grown to be slender and more elegant. I think of the winged bride with her hair in a beehive skipping the way to her wedding—that little girl was already growing up when I left the mansion, weathered by childbirth and grief, but she's grown much more in my absence. There's a vague hourglass shape to her.

I ignore the fat black bees that swirl around her, and

eventually they disappear. She stays, even when I remind myself that this can't be real. I am so grateful to see her—this soft, familiar presence, that I am sure I must be dreaming. I welcome this dream, though. Perhaps I can live in it for the next four—no, three—years. While Vaughn is turning my body into his playground, while my brother is roving the earth to no avail, I can live in this safe imagined place. Maybe I can even dream up some June Beans that haven't been tampered with.

"Awake now?" Cecily asks, her back to me. She spins around and carries the paper cup of water to me. "The air is dry down here. I thought you might be thirsty."

Not a dream. She's really here. Testing my abilities, I move my arms and legs, find that they're still weighted by tubes. Cecily lays her hand on mine and says, "No, no, don't try to move. You'll hurt yourself. Here." She holds the cup to my lips, watching me drink it, with not quite a smile or a frown on her lips. She looks like she wants to say something, but for a long time nothing comes.

There's a soft light radiating from the ceiling tiles, making all the edges appear fuzzy and soft like the camera filter in Jenna's soap operas.

"I hid in the hallway and heard them talking. They said your heart rate was through the roof. They thought it was going to be a heart attack," Cecily says, and there's sympathy in her voice. There's something else, too. Remorse? Shame? She won't quite meet my eyes. I must look pretty terrible, because she traces her index finger

along the curve of my face and chokes on a sob.

For better or worse, Cecily will always be my sister wife. Nothing can undo what we've endured together. We will always be connected. And at the sight of her tears, mine come immediately. I turn my head to stare at the wall, trying to will them away before they roll to my cheeks.

"Oh, Rhine," Cecily says. "Don't you realize what you've done by coming back? You'll never get out now. Not ever."

I close my eyes. My chest shudders with a sob. What she says is true. I'll never see my brother or Gabriel again. The way things are going, I'll never even see daylight again. I had my chance, and I failed.

She leans forward and kisses my forehead, and all I can register is that she smells like Jenna. That assured, womanly blend of pretty scents and pastel lotions.

"I have to go before Housemaster Vaughn catches me down here," Cecily says. "I blackmailed an attendant I caught sleeping in the library, and he let me use his key card. I just—" She sniffles. "I had to come. I never thought I'd see you again."

I don't answer her or open my eyes. As long as I stay perfectly still, the tears won't fall.

She doesn't go right away. She runs fingers through my hair and whimpers and apologizes, muttering about things so long ago they don't matter anymore. Or they aren't her fault.

And despite my best attempts to stay awake, I begin weaving through nightmares of still infants with malformed faces, hallways that carry a baby's cry, houses that hold unspeakable horrors drawn in black ink, spinning in holograms before me as Linden beams with pride.

I finally manage to say words out loud. "Did Linden really denounce me?"

But Cecily is long gone by then.

Hushed, angry voices. A whinnying baby noise.

"But you'll kill her," Cecily says.

"We know what we're doing," a voice says. Not Vaughn. An attendant, maybe.

"Let me see her. Let me see her or I'll scream." Cecily's tone is pleading but fierce.

"Scream all you want," the voice says. "You'll only be hurting yourself."

She screams anyway, over and over in my nightmares. I follow her through uncertain depths, down long hallways, stepping over bits and bones and shivering bodies. Her red hair is full of sun; her footsteps are piano keys pounding out a nonsense song. And then, just when I'm sure I've reached her, she's gone.

I call for her, but my voice is only a moan as I regain consciousness. Fingers move through my hair like spiders.

"I'm here," she answers. "I can't stay long. Listen to me. Are you listening?"

The blurry room doubles. Two Cecilys come together into one solid girl. I move my lips and discover I have a voice. "Yes."

"I'm going to find a way to get you out," she tells me. "Trust me."

Trust. The concept is too perplexing in my muddled state. She has tears in her eyes. She's wearing a green bikini top, and her wet hair is dripping onto my arm. Several of my syringes have been unplugged. Did Cecily do this, to wake me up? She must have, because the numbness in my body is giving way to pain. Still, I cling to consciousness.

I try to focus on her face, but her eyes are as black as stab wounds. The room jolts and blurs behind her. "I'm having a nightmare," I say.

"No," she says. "You're awake now."

"Prove it," I say. I have been taunted by her too many times, only to wake and find myself alone.

"When I was pregnant and not feeling well, you used to tell me stories," she says. "About twins. They didn't fight crime or save the world or anything, but they had each other. Until one day they were separated."

"Those weren't just stories," I say. "They were about me and my brother."

"I know that now," she says. "I guess I always knew. And I was being selfish. I wanted you here with me. You, me, Jenna, and Linden." She brushes the hair from my forehead. She smells like pool water and suntan lotion, prompting a memory of bright holographic guppies swimming through me. "If you stay here, you'll die," she says. "You don't belong to me or Linden. You belong out there."

"Linden doesn't want me anyway," I say. "He told his father that."

Something like pain flashes in Cecily's eyes. Or maybe it's surprise. She can't believe Linden would be so callous.

"You came here even though he told you not to," I say. "Didn't you?"

Cecily bristles. "Well, of course he doesn't know I'm seeing you. He thought it would only upset me. He's very protective, you know. He thinks it's better if we just forget you existed, and . . ." She trails off, busying herself with straightening out my gown.

"I have to go now," she says. She kisses my forehead, ever the aspiring mother figure, and plugs all the syringes back into their right places. "Linden thinks I'm swimming."

I watch her back away from me, dripping wet, a towel knotted around her little waist. "We're going to have another baby," she says, not quite achieving the smile she's trying for. "If it's a girl, Linden says we can name her Jenna."

She turns to leave.

"Wait," I try to say, but my voice is drowned out as the drugs reenter my veins.

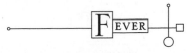

For what feels like days I live in a state of nonexistence, emerging only for moments at a time. When I do, the same thoughts are there to greet me:

It's true that Linden gave me to his father.

Vaughn still has his talons in my sister wife. She's giving him another grandchild to experiment with.

I will not be able to protect her this time.

Rose's baby was malformed. Vaughn killed it. Linden will never know.

My brother will never know what happened to me.

Somewhere very far away, Gabriel woke up and realized I was gone. He will never know what happened to me either.

I will exist in this basement for as long as Vaughn lives, in limbs and pieces and genes.

I start trying to stay unconscious. The problem with this is that no amount of willpower can change the reality. I can't control when I awaken, or what will greet me when I do.

I see Deirdre standing a few feet away from my bed. She doubles over, making retching sounds for a few awful seconds before the bile comes up, strange and odiferous and green. Her gown is slipping off one shoulder; I can see the notches in her spine. Her knuckles are white, her fists clenched. And when it's over, she's quiet for a very long time, taking deep breaths.

She looks at me, eyes all pupil, and says, "He's planning far worse things for you. You shouldn't have come back."

"Deirdre," I say, my voice full of longing. I want to pull her into my arms and keep her safe. My sweet, loyal domestic who devoted her days to making sure I was cared for, who once upon a time never could have imagined such awful things as are happening to both of us now. And it's all because of me.

I struggle against my restraints as she takes a towel to the puddle of vomit and then disposes of it in the biohazard container where the attendants dispose of my needles. She throws her hands into her lap, and she looks so hopeless, but she won't cry, maybe because she still has some fight left. I remember this about her. She's a small thing, but she was always resilient. "It helps if you think of someplace nice." Her sallow face is lit up by the fake sunlight over holographic lilies that are animated on a loop. I've memorized the way they sway: left, left, left, waver for a bit, right.

Think of someplace nice. Claire's house at night, little lungs breathing in every room. My head in Gabriel's lap. He said he wouldn't let anyone hurt me, and I knew that this was beyond anyone's control, even his, but I closed my eyes and pretended to believe it.

I force the thought away. I won't think of someplace nice; it makes it that much harder to open my eyes and remember that I'm here.

"I should have taken you with me," I say. "Hidden you someplace he couldn't find you."

"He would have found me when he found you," Deirdre

says. She makes her way to my bed, and when she touches my thigh, I flinch. As Linden's bride I grew used to the fussing and pampering of Deirdre and the attendants. Grew used to the hair braiding and makeup and the deep-tissue massages when I was too tense. But a few rounds of needles has reversed that. At my flinching, my once-domestic frowns apologetically and then hikes my gown up to my waist. "There," she whispers. "You probably can't see it, but this is where he put it." She indicates the fleshy part of my thigh, where I see nothing but sickly pale skin and veins.

"What am I looking at?" I say.

"Before your wedding a doctor inspected you," Deirdre says. "For fertility, among other things. And you were implanted with a tracker so that the Housemaster could always know where you are." Her wispy voice is being drowned out by the pulsing in my ears. "You and your sister wives are his property. You'll always belong to him."

This honestly never occurred to me. While I lived in the mansion, Vaughn tricked Cecily into spying on me. I'd entertained the thought of surveillance cameras, recording devices, attendants who might do his bidding. But I thought I would be safe out in the real world. *My* world.

And then I laugh, for the first time in I don't know how long. Of course Vaughn was tracking me. How could I think I'd ever be rid of him? The laugh is broken

and weak, and maybe it's a bit hysterical too, because Deirdre looks concerned. She claps her hand over my mouth and shushes me. "Please be quiet," she whispers. "They'll hear."

"I don't care," I mumble into her palm, but for her I lower my voice. "What more can they do to me?" I say. "Or to you, or to anyone else who's down here?"

Deirdre smoothes the hair from my face. Her eyes are pleading. "You shouldn't ask questions like that," she says.

We both know it's dangerous for her to visit me, but she still comes often. She removes one of the IVs from the needle that's in my arm, and she must know what she's doing, because I slowly come back to awareness.

I always knew Deirdre was brave. She's small, but she maintains a steely resolve in the face of all this atrocity. She's still trying to care for me. Maybe it comforts her. Like a ghost that doesn't know it's dead, repeating the same last action over and over.

For the first time, today she allows herself to receive my affection. I ease my wrist out of the restraint and let her climb onto the mattress beside me. I tell her the stories I used to tell Cecily, about the twins and the kites. I leave out the laboratory explosion and instead make up new stories about ferry rides and mermaids swimming below the waters of Liberty Island.

The sound of elevator doors startles her. In one motion she is off the bed and reinserting my IV as I move my wrist back into its restraint.

"I'll be back soon," she whispers, and hurries off.

I close my eyes, feign unconsciousness while I wait for the drug to overtake me. But it never does. I hear footsteps in my room, and feel the pressure of something being taken out of my forearm.

"I know you're awake," Vaughn says. "That's good. You'll need to be conscious for this one."

He pries my eyelid open, shines a flashlight at me. "Your pupils aren't dilating the way they should. Somehow I suspect you've been tampering with your dosages." He laughs. "You always were difficult, weren't you?"

I squeeze my eyes shut. I wish for him to be a nightmare. But I can still hear him milling about, preparing my next dose of hell.

"I much prefer you when you're unconscious," he says. "It's just easier to keep track of you. But now I need you on a more normal sleep regimen. You might experience some vivid dreams. They're nothing to be alarmed about."

Just before he leaves, he taps my nose. It's the same condescending affection he usually reserves for Cecily.

"I'll be back to check on you soon, darling," he says.

I don't have the vivid dreams Vaughn promised me. Rather, I lose the distinction between dreams and reality entirely. There are times when I'm sure that I'm awake, but the sterile walls start to become black, as though an invisible brush is painting them. I begin to feel a painful throb in my thigh, where Deirdre told me the tracker was. I hear voices whispering to me. I see my father, pale and lifeless, standing in the doorway watching me. He never says anything, and eventually he leaves. Sometimes Rowan comes to loosen my restraints. He is always in a hurry, always trying to push me from the bed, but I'm never able to move fast enough before he disappears.

There is a man in the holograph window. He stalks through the lilies, shrouded in dark clothes, and I know he's coming for me.

Sounds become twice as loud. I can hear the rolling carts in the hallway as though they are moving inside my skull. The hushed voices of the attendants get trapped in my head and beat against my brain like moths.

I hear every footfall within this mansion, every creaking floorboard, every trill of laughter from the kitchen, every murmur and sigh from my sister wife's bedroom when Linden visits her. There is no escaping these magnified commotions, no way to cover my ears. And even when it's quiet, my own heart beats like gunfire.

Vaughn comes in frequently. The first few times, I keep my eyes closed and try to lie still despite my pounding heart. But then one time, while he's fiddling with my IV bag, he says, "The orange blossoms look especially lovely today."

I open my eyes. There are white petals on his shoulders, spilling off him when he moves and dissolving before they reach the ground. His eyes are very green

today. They're Linden's eyes, I think. How did they find their way onto his father's face?

Vaughn smiles at me with none of his son's kindness. "You're looking flushed," he says. "Don't worry. The fevers are normal."

I watch as an orange tree sprouts up behind him. A flock of starlings rushes across the ceiling, and I say, "Wherever I go, you'll find me, won't you?"

"That's neither here nor there," he says as he taps the barrel of the syringe. "You're not going anyplace."

I stare at the ceiling tiles, knowing what he says is true. Cecily promises an escape, but this, like everything, is out of her hands. That is best, I think. She would only endanger herself by coming down here. Better for her to live upstairs. She is always trying to take charge of things much too big for her; but how can I hold that against her? I'm the same way. Jenna was right to worry. Perhaps she was the only bride who knew what she was dealing with; she accepted her fate with grace and serenity.

I can hear the rush of air through the vents; the temperature in the basement is probably regulated. Sometimes I think I hear Rose crawling through the air ducts, but none of them lead her outside. She'll never be free either.

"Have you noticed anything unusual?" Vaughn asks me. "Chest pains? Headaches? Heartburn?"

"Just the orange blossoms," I say, as though he'll know

that I can see them now. I turn my head and blow at the few that have settled on my shoulder.

He adjusts a bag of fluid and finds a vein, and I watch as the blood gets drawn from my arm. "Rose said you wanted me for my eyes," I say.

"Rose was not a stupid girl," Vaughn says. "I made suggestions that day, but my son picked you out on his own. If he hadn't, maybe things would have been easier."

"Because I'd be dead," I say.

He extracts the needle from my arm, dabs alcohol on the spot. "Of course not, darling," he says. "You'd have been here helping me find the antidote much sooner. Do you know much about heterochromia? Picture your genes like a mosaic," he says. "All different pieces that don't seem to blend together, but step back and you'll find that those mismatched pieces make a coherent picture. They just take a more creative approach to making it."

He's losing me. But lately I have a hard time understanding even simple things. "I suspect that what you have is genetic mosaicism. Two different populations of cells, where the average person only has one. One blue eye; one brown eye."

He leans forward and strokes the hair from my face, as if I'm a small child unable to comprehend his bedtime story.

If Rowan were here, he'd understand this. Maybe he has already figured it out on his own. But it doesn't mat-

ter. I'll never see him again. And I will never tell Vaughn
about my brother; if Vaughn is fascinated with me, he'd
be downright giddy to know I'm a twin.

"I could never have anticipated how much my son
would love you," Vaughn goes on. "I knew I couldn't take
you away from him."

"He doesn't love me now," I say.

"He absolutely loves you," Vaughn says. "Love unre-
quited is violent. He loves you so much that he's turned
it into hate."

Hate. I try to picture it in Linden's sullen face, but I
can't. Maybe it's for the best that I don't.

"How have you been sleeping?" Vaughn asks.

I laugh. The sound explodes into echoes. His concern
for me is just that absurd.

When he leaves me, I hear Rose in the ceiling start to
scream.

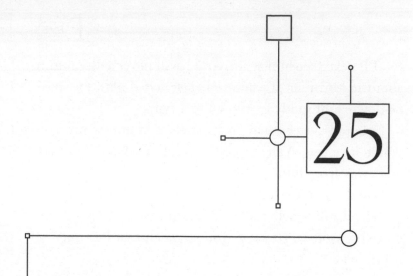

IN MY DREAM the windmill in the golf course is spinning, its bolts loosening in the hurricane winds. Gabriel is calling for me to come back inside.

"Rhine?"

The windmill is still grating. "Cecily?" My voice is less than a whisper. "Get back inside." Her red hair whips up over her head; she reaches for me, but I'm too far away. I watch her lips move.

"Wake up," she says.

I open my eyes, and she's leaning over me, breathless, flushed, lights speeding over her head. This isn't a hurricane, though, and after a moment I realize I'm being pushed through the basement on a rolling cart. Like Rose's corpse. Cecily is pacing to keep up. She's surrounded by attendants in white. One of them is yelling at her to get out of the way, but she hops up onto the cart and sits beside me.

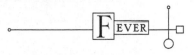

"What's happening?" I say. Deep within me is the dull sense of panic, but my body won't react. I can hardly feel my hand in Cecily's grasp.

"The Housemaster would have your head if he saw you down here, child," one of the attendants tells her, and she scowls.

"I'm no child. And my father-in-law will do no such thing," she says pertly. "Because he won't know."

"Who keeps letting her down here?" the attendant says.

"Can't very well tell House Governor Linden's bride how to behave," another says.

Cecily winks at me, smug. "Housemaster Vaughn isn't here," she whispers to me. I can just make out her voice over the grating of the wheels. "He's in Seattle giving a presentation on antibodies."

The cart stops moving. "Off," a voice commands, and Cecily lets go of my hand. My arm drops to my side, as heavy and useless as a board. I'm transferred from the gurney to a bed that leaves me propped at an incline. An IV is hooked into my arm, and I wait for the familiar fade of unconsciousness, but it doesn't come. My eyelids are taped open, but I wouldn't be able to blink them now if I tried. Before the numbness overtakes me, I can just move my lips enough to get out my sister wife's name one last time, and she's there.

Cecily climbs onto the bed and inches behind me so that her knees straddle my body, my back against her stomach. She puts her chin on my shoulder, and suddenly

I can feel the heat of her cheeks, can imagine them turning red the way they do when she's about to cry. It takes me a while to realize that the words she's whispering over and over are "Be brave."

The attendants are all gone, except for one who is fiddling with a piece of machinery I am having a hard time seeing. Everything is starting to blur.

A voice booms through the speakers, annoyed and firm. "Off the bed, please, Lady Cecily."

"Go to hell," she says.

There's a whirring noise. Through the blur I see the attendant adjusting a large mechanical arm that comes down from the ceiling. Some sort of needle protrudes from it, as long as my leg.

"Rhine," Cecily whispers into my ear. "Remember the stories you told me, about the kites?"

The voice in the speaker starts prattling off commands for the attendant with the needle. Adjustments. Fluid levels. Something about video recording and monitors.

"Well, I tried making some out of paper, but they wouldn't fly. So I was thinking maybe I would ask Linden about ordering some plastic sheets. So the air wouldn't move straight through them, and maybe they'd fly then."

She pets my hair, and the voice in the ceiling says, "Keep the subject's head still." So she does. She holds my temples in her palms. The attendant reaches over me and draws down some sort of helmet device that will prevent

my head from moving—not that I can move anyway. He secures it over my head and locks my chin in with a strap. "Move her back three quarters of an inch," the voice says. The attendant obliges.

"Is it going to hurt?" Cecily asks. I want to tell her that I can't feel my body at all, so I doubt it, but I can't move my tongue to form the words. The attendant doesn't answer.

"Lady Cecily, if she's moved during this procedure, she could be blinded. Do you want that?"

She listens this time. She climbs off the bed. "I'm right here with you," she says while the attendant repositions me as the voice in the ceiling directs.

I try to answer, but I can't. I try to blink, but I can't.

Maybe this numbness is an act of mercy. I've almost convinced myself that this experiment will be no worse than the others. Until the attendant brings the needle closer to my eye and I realize what's about to happen.

Whatever they're using to numb my body is no longer effective at keeping my heart still. It's pounding in my ears. It's hard to breathe. Cecily starts up a desperate tangent about kite tails and spring breezes.

I want to scream. I've never wanted to scream so badly in my life. I am thousands of wings flapping in a tiny cage. But the sound I make is less than a whimper. My body is useless, miles away, though my mind is still very much awake.

The needle breaks into my pupil. I think I hear the impact.

Count. When I dislocated my shoulder, my brother told me to count the seconds as he prepared to snap it back into place. *Count, and it won't be so bad.* So I do.

I count forty-five seconds before the needle leaves my eye.

That's five seconds less than the next needle.

When it's over, the helmet is removed, the tape pulled from my eyelids. My head drops lifelessly to Cecily's waiting palm. She is still telling me about what would make a kite fly, as the IV is removed from my arm and I'm transferred to the gurney and wheeled out into the hallway.

"I figured it out eventually," she says. She's sitting on the edge of the gurney again; her features slowly materialize as my vision clears. "It's momentum."

"What?" I whisper. The feeling is returning to my lips, spreading out to my fingertips and toes.

"Momentum," she repeats. "You can't just stand there if you want something to fly. You have to run."

Vaughn returns, smelling of fresh spring air and the leather interior of the limo—all the places he's been. I can tell he has stopped to visit me even before changing after his trip from Seattle.

"They tell me you didn't make a sound during the retinal procedure," he says, stroking my cheek like I'm some sort of pet. His hand is cool. I don't tell him that I would have screamed during his procedure if only I'd been able.

Count. It takes him four seconds to trace my jaw and retract his finger.

"I told them, of course you didn't. You have always been the epitome of grace." An IV has been removed from my arm, and it dangles from a bag of fluid by my bed.

Vaughn arranges needles and tools, and I focus on the ceiling tiles. They are much clearer today than most days. I can see the punctures on them like pinholes. Nothing crawls behind them. A pop in the air duct makes me flinch.

"Grace," he repeats, "and class. You're steely. Has anyone ever told you that?"

"That's a new one," I say. My brother always called me too soft.

"Well, there shouldn't be any more procedures as gruesome as that," Vaughn assures me. "What that did was record the inside of each eye. Like a scope. The footage should be all I need."

The memory makes my skin swell with goose bumps. My fists clench against the restraints.

"How have you been feeling?" Vaughn asks. "I thought we might try solid foods next week, since you've been so cooperative."

I remember Claire's pancakes, dripping with butter and syrup. But I was so depressed, they were only like paste in my mouth. Or was it really depression? Was it just the start of this illness taking over? If I could sit at

Claire's breakfast table again, I'd savor every last precious bite. I'd take longer walks through Manhattan. I'd
kiss Gabriel until I lost my sense of gravity. How could I
have squandered that freedom? The illness I felt during
that time, the listlessness—all of that was Vaughn's hold
on me, and I didn't even know it.

"No?" Vaughn says when I don't answer him. "Perhaps later, then." He holds out my arm, presses his fingers to my wrist, and goes silent, nodding slightly in
time to the throbbing in my vein.

"Heart rate is down today," he says. "Beautiful. I was worried you were going to go into cardiac arrest for a while."

"One of the perks of dying young," I say dryly, "should
be that my heart won't have a chance to go bad."

He laughs, sterilizes my forearm, and draws a vial of
blood. "I couldn't have anticipated your reaction to any of
your treatments, darling. You are something of an enigma."

I don't tell him that Cecily has been botching his
experiments behind his back. When she comes to see
me, she unplugs my IVs. After the retinal procedure she
kept bedside vigil until dinnertime, when she was told
Linden had been looking for her. Before she left me, she
whispered, "We have to get you well enough to get out
of here, don't we?" And when nobody was looking, she
slid the needle from my wrist. Without the contents of
that IV, I finally slept without nightmares until Vaughn
returned and she had to replace it.

Now Vaughn is reading through notes the attendants

left for him. His expression is deadpan. His green eyes are bright, though, like Linden's reveling in his latest sketch at the very end, when everything comes together even better than he'd hoped. My husband is a prodigy, and Vaughn knows it. That's why he keeps him so blind.

"Did you dissect your son?" I ask. "The dead one, I mean." Now that Vaughn has seen the insides of my pupils, we've moved past rigid formalities. Several months ago he told me of a son who had lived and died before Linden was born; I'd been too horrified to ask for more details back then, but it takes a lot more to frighten me now.

"'Dissection' is a cruel term," Vaughn says simply. "But yes. And do you know what I found?" He looks at me over the edge of the notebook. "Nothing. Absolutely no indication that anything was amiss. A vital, young heart. Excellent body mass index—he was a swimmer and quite the runner. Healthiest kidneys I'd ever seen."

"You just cut him open," I say. "Like he was nothing?"

Vaughn closes the notebook, sets it on one of the humming machines. "If he were nothing, I wouldn't have bothered, would I?" he says. "It just so happens he was everything. And I'd failed him. As a father, as a doctor. I owe it to Linden to do better."

"Do you experiment on him, too?" I ask. "Behind his back?"

"You're full of questions this evening," Vaughn says, giving me a smile I can't read.

"All you need to know is this: You are helping me save lives. It's best not to wonder at what cost."

Vaughn tells me with delight that he's trying a new drug on me. He says it won't cause nightmares.

I suppose he expects me to be grateful. But without the nightmares there's silence. I can no longer hear Rose in the air ducts, or the footsteps upstairs, or Cecily and Linden and the creaky mattress coils. The original drugs brought me to a state of madness, a murky twilight in which my fear took other forms. Now all I see is a sterile room. Fake lilies in the window. I feel the cool spot on the mattress where Gabriel would sleep beside me when we were at Claire's. And before him it had been Linden climbing into my bed, or Cecily, or Jenna. And before them, my brother and the shotgun keeping watch while I slept.

I had thought Vaughn was feeding me these drugs to torment me, but maybe he had only meant for them to keep me company.

You have a different kind of strength, love, my mother had said. But what would she say now? Her daughter, exhausted, bound, buried deeper than the dead in a madman's labyrinth. A twin without her brother. One half of a whole.

I'm helping to save lives, Vaughn says, and don't wonder at what cost. He talks about solid foods like they're some sort of luxury. He tells me I have grace, but he

straps me to a mattress. Wasn't it only a few days ago that I felt the Manhattan breeze in my hair?

Or maybe it's been weeks.

Or months.

And maybe I was kidding myself to think my brother could still be looking for me. He thinks I'm dead. He dug up the small treasures our parents had left us. He burned down our home.

It doesn't even matter that I'm still alive. I am a root in the earth that will never grow. I am so far down that the footsteps of the living world don't even rattle me.

I stare at the ceiling for a long time, until the pinholes in the tiles begin to look like constellations. Then I look at the IV line lying on the mattress where Cecily pulled it from my forearm. She's stalling for time. She thinks that if she can keep me lucid, she can find a way for me to be free. She doesn't understand how impossible freedom is.

After a while I wriggle one of my hands from the restraints using the trick Deirdre taught me, and I fit the IV back into place.

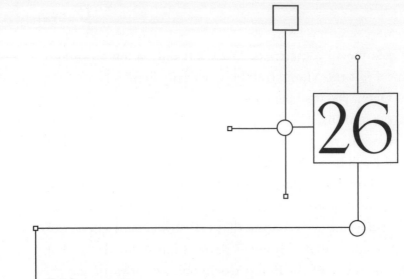

IT'S BEST *not to wonder at what cost.*

Freedom is the only price to pay for anything in this place.

The tracker in my leg is throbbing; and as long as it's there, I will never be free. I have nightmares that my leg has been sawed off, and when I finally, finally tear myself awake, I know what I have to do.

Freeing my wrists from the restraints is easy, but freeing my ankles is more difficult because my feet have swollen to twice their normal size. I unplug the needles, one by one, and stagger out of the bed. It's the first time I've used my legs in I don't know how long, and they fail me.

I have to crawl across the cold tiles and hoist myself up on one of the machines until I can reach the water pitcher. It's the only pretty thing in this room, light blue with a diamond texture that reminds me of the pool water breaking in the sunlight.

I'll never leave the mansion. I'll never find my brother or see Gabriel again. I've accepted that. But I cannot take another minute as one of Vaughn's experiments. Cannot bear the thought of him finding me no matter where I go. If I can cut this tracker out of my leg, I know I can find a hiding place. There is a man thrashing through the lilies in the hologram; I could let him kill me. Or I could wander the hallways until I've found a dark place to die quietly. If I'm lucky, I'll decompose before Vaughn finds me, and I'll be too far gone for him to dissect what's left.

I throw the pitcher to the ground, and it shatters. I crawl among the pieces until I find one that's sharp enough, and I cut into my thigh.

On some distant level there is pain. I hear a scream. But I ignore these things because something much more important is at the forefront. This invasive thing is keeping me tethered to my father-in-law, and it must be removed.

Hands try to stop me. My name is being shouted. At first I think Rose has finally found an opening in the air ducts and made her way to me, but then those hands grab my cheeks, and it's Cecily's brown eyes I'm staring into. Blood on her shirt. Hysteria all over her face. "Rhine, please!" she shrieks.

All of my nightmares come screaming to the forefront. The cacophony of sounds. The man stomping through the lilies. The dead sister wife crawling through the vent. And Cecily, right in the line of danger. "You have to go upstairs," I tell her. "It's not safe for you here."

"Stop!" She's trying to take the glass from my fist, and then she's trying to stop the bleeding with her open fingers, and she won't listen to a word I'm saying about it not being safe for her here and the tracker needing to be bled out.

Finally she runs off, and I hear the chime of the elevator.

She comes back moments later, Linden gasping and pushing past her in the doorway, saying words I don't understand. I know he can't be real. He let me go, abandoned me like I abandoned him. But still he runs toward me, shouting something that sounds like my name.

Cecily lingers in the doorway, cloaked in an impossibly bright light. In her arms she's hugging a bag of writhing snakes, and the snakes have a baby's cry. The cry is bright red; it washes over everything.

"Get Bowen out of here," Linden says, in a voice that's too calm. "He doesn't need to see this." He's wrapping something white around my leg, and the white is becoming red because of the crying and the blood.

"Yes," another voice says. It's Vaughn, coming to finish me off. "Show some common sense, darling. You are his mother, after all."

"Linden," Cecily cries over the wailing snakes. Her voice is shrill. "Do something—she's bleeding to death!" The snakes are slithering out of the bag, coiling around her throat, disappearing under her clothes. The word echoes. *Death. Death. Death.*

"What have you done to her?" Linden says to his

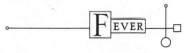

father. I close my eyes so I don't have to see what's happening to Linden. The flesh is melting off his skull; his too-green eyes are bulging from their sockets. "How long has she been here?" he demands. "Why wasn't I told?"

"It's an experimental drug I was working on. It boosts the immune system. Like vitamin C, really. There's just some mild hallucination involved." Too close. Vaughn's voice is too close to me. No matter where I go, he's always moving closer. He can track me using whatever he's planted in my leg. He can lure me to his laboratory like a fish caught on a hook.

"She must have gotten out of her restraints somehow," Vaughn says, pondering, his tone trailing.

"*Restraints?*" Linden splutters, with more vitriol than I've ever heard in him. The earth booms like thunder, and for a second I think the mansion is going to finally collapse in on itself, the way I used to wish it would. But then Linden brushes the hair from my face, and his touch is so soft. "What's happened to you?" he whispers.

I feel Cecily pacing. Her voice is squeaky and panicked. She is saying to Vaughn, "You said you wouldn't hurt her! You said she'd be safe!"

"You knew about this?" Linden growls at her. The color in my eyelids becomes angry orange.

Cecily is in hysterics. All she can manage is, "I—I . . ."

Vaughn is clucking his tongue. "Both of you are overreacting. A mild sedative, and she'll be fine."

"Get it out," I try to say, but my voice won't form

words. I can't even scream; my tongue has gone numb, and only heavy, horrible moans come out.

"You had no right, Father," Linden snaps. "She isn't your guinea pig. Under this roof she is still my wife!" I feel my body being cradled in his arms.

"Now, Son, be reasonable."

"She needs a hospital!" Pain breaks through his voice.

"They won't know how to care for her," Vaughn says. "Just set her back on the bed, Son. We'll have her fixed in no time. And then, once you've calmed down, I can explain how this drug is benefiting her. Benefiting all of us."

Linden is whimpering, begging me to open my eyes.

"Don't just stand there like a pair of idiots; you heard my husband," Cecily says over the baby's screams. "Get the car. Now! Move!" Footsteps respond, pounding down like rain, attendants muttering "Yes, Lady Cecily" and "Right away" and "West entrance door—one minute."

"Oh, God, Linden. Is she breathing?"

"For heaven's sake, Cecily, get that screaming child out of here," Vaughn says. His voice is the last thing I hear. I feel his papery hand touching my forehead, and it's more than I can stand. My limbs give way. My mind dissolves.

The breeze moves through my hair. I take a deep breath, smell the air of the Florida coastline. Things baked and deep-fried mingling with salt water and new concrete.

No illusion could replicate it. The real world is speeding all around me.

"You're going to be okay," Linden says. "The hospital is just another two blocks."

"Don't let him follow," I whisper. My voice is feeble, but at least I can form words now. I open my eyes, and I see the city through an opening in the tinted window of the limo. I thought I'd never see the world again. I want to reach for it, but my arms won't move. I know this view will be short-lived, and I try to home in on a memory to take with me, but the moon won't hold still. It darts behind buildings, gets tangled in trees.

Linden is holding me, my blood smearing his delicate cheeks and caking in his dark curls. He brushes the hair from my face. It's been so long since I was this close to him, but I never forgot his frailty, his skin like a paper lantern ensconcing a warm light. He says, "Nobody is following you."

"Yes," I insist, but he doesn't believe me. His piteous stare says he thinks I've lost my mind, and maybe I have. So I say the only thing I know will keep me safe. "Don't leave me."

He presses my head against his chest, where I can hear the blood gurgling around his tissue and bones. I can feel his warmth in my ears and in my ribs. "I won't," he says. "I promise."

By the time the car has stopped, the sheet around my leg is dripping with red. I'm being swept up, pushed

forward, rolled away. I struggle to stay afloat, but the world is blurring around me. I can feel the blood spilling from my skin, taking with it my ability to comprehend or to speak or to focus. I become something less than human—wild and primal. I fight against the new faces and new hands that try to pin me down, but this only makes them more forceful. They're shouting angry things at me, and I can't understand them. I can't hang on to what they're saying. The only voice I can make out is Linden's, a thousand miles away, saying, "She doesn't know what's happening. She doesn't mean to fight you."

I'm on a metal table, writhing under a bright light. My legs no longer seem to work, but I'm able to land a few punches without seeing who takes them. Vaughn is coming; they don't understand. I try to tell them about the tracker in my leg, but my words are shrill and non-sensical. "Shh," Linden is saying. "It's okay. You're in a hospital. They're going to help you." That's no comfort; Vaughn owns every hospital in the area.

Linden catches my fist midair and then holds it, strokes the length of my arm. All the fight leaves me. I'm a whimpering mess. I can't even open my eyes. Some sort of mask covers my mouth and nose, and I think it means to suffocate me, but all it does is make it that much harder to stay awake.

Linden doesn't know the depths of his father's maddening drugs. Doesn't know this dark looming canyon that surely awaits me. Death has never felt so certain,

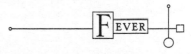

so close. It was always a distant reality, and Gabriel was right, I don't like to think about it. But now it's unavoidable. It's here. It's pulling me under.

The darkness swallows me a moment before the words can reach my lips:

I don't want to die.

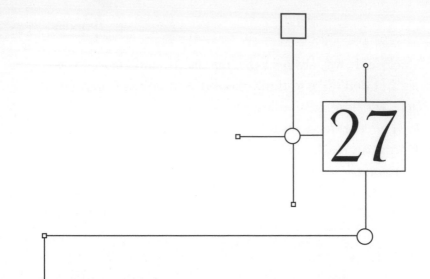

THE SOUND of rain, traffic, and thunder.

I open my eyes to a steady rhythm of beeps and realize there are once again wires in my forearm. But this isn't the basement. I'm sure that window isn't a hologram.

Linden isn't looking at me. His bleary eyes are on the television bolted high up on the wall near the foot of my bed. The soft oval of his chin is flecked with stubble; his skin is pale. I don't know how much time I've spent in this bed, but I doubt he's slept for any of it.

Not looking at me, he says, "Do you know where you are?"

"One of your father's hospitals," I guess.

"How about the month?" he asks tiredly. "Do you know what month it is?"

"No."

He looks at me, and I keep waiting for his face to mutate into something nightmarish, but it doesn't. There

is only a wilted, sleepy look, and the distance in his eyes.

"They thought you were mad," he says. "The way you were screaming. The things you were saying. Do you still think there are bodies in the ceiling tiles?"

"I said that?" I ask him.

"Among other things."

I look at the ceiling tiles. Ordinary and white. I wait for the sound of Rose crawling through the air ducts, but there's nothing. "No," I say.

"You said something else," Linden tells me. "You said there was something in your leg that you needed to get out."

"A tracker," I say. I know that much was real. Wasn't it? I'm still trying to make sense of this newfound lucidity. I grew used to a world wherein everything became a nightmare. I'm still expecting Linden's flesh to drip from his skull. He frowns at the way I keep blinking. "Your father put a tracker in my leg, so he'd know where to find me if I ever got away."

Linden nods, looks at his lap. "So you said." I can't tell if he's angry with me, or hurt. I can't read him at all. But the usual softness is gone from his face, and I know, whatever he's feeling, he's not happy with me. Gone are the days of his blind affections. I threw those back at him the night I ran away. I'm not even sure why he's here, but I'm afraid of saying anything that would cause him to go.

"I thought you were delirious when you said that," he says. "Your fever was . . . dangerously high. I thought for sure you were imagining . . ." He trails off.

"I don't know how much of it was real," I admit. "But I'm sure that was."

"They found it," he says, watching as his finger traces shapes on his thigh. He's wearing pajamas, and when I search back to my memory of him standing in the doorway in the basement, he was wearing them then, too. And Cecily was in her nightgown. My bloody fit with the smashed pitcher must have gotten everyone out of bed. "It was the size of a pea," he says. "I'd never seen anything like it."

"Your father found me all the way in Manhattan with it," I say.

Linden raises his eyes to me. The brighter, kinder version of his father's eyes.

"So that's where you went," he says, and looks away. There's a long pause before he asks, "Why?"

"That's my home," I say. Or, it was my home. There's nothing left for me in that charred house now.

Linden stands, paces to the window, and watches the torrential rain. I can just make out his reflection in the glass, and I know he's watching my reflection too. Maybe because he can't stand to look right at me. I don't blame him. He should hate me for my betrayal, and I can see him struggling with this, because hate has never been a part of who he is. When we were first married, I thought he must have been the most heartless, hateful man I'd ever known, but he was just as much a prisoner

as I was. Where Vaughn imprisoned me with walls, he imprisoned his son with ignorance.

"Linden . . ."

He raises his head.

I open my mouth to speak, but nothing comes. And when I struggle to sit up, he turns and watches me, not helping, not cooing words of encouragement. Gone are my days of taking his love for granted. There is emptiness where that love once thrived. I was wrong about Linden's abandoning me; he wouldn't have given me to his father to be a guinea pig. But that's because he's kind, and compassionate, and not at all because he has any love left for me.

"You should rest more," he says. "You're not a hundred percent."

I manage to prop myself up against the headboard, and my vision doubles. It helps when I focus on the television screen. Bright, moving images start to make sense again. The sound is down, but I can tell this is a news broadcast about the wind levels rising close to the shore. Maybe there will be another hurricane.

"I can't stay here. I need to get home."

"My father isn't coming for you," Linden says with a hint of impatience. "I won't let him, all right? You need to rest."

"You don't understand. People will miss me. They'll think I'm dead."

"Oh, yes," Linden says. "That attendant."

And all at once I can see this tentative civility turning ugly. Linden has a right to be unhappy, but so do I. He deserved better than to be abandoned, but I never asked to be his bride.

"Oh, yes." I mimic his tone. "That attendant. Among others."

"What are you going to do?" He falls into the chair beside me. "Walk all the way up the East Coast?"

"Don't be so smug, Linden," I say. "You have no idea what I can or cannot do."

He laughs humorlessly, studying the floor tiles. "You're right about that." He's hurt. And he doesn't know what to do with himself. I watch his hands fidgeting in his lap. How awful it must be for him to try to reconcile this new image of his father. This new image of me.

"Do you even know what it feels like to lose someone you loved?" he asks.

"I lost everyone I loved," I tell him. I wait for him to look at me, and then I add, "The day I met you."

As soon as I've said the words out loud, I regret them. Linden shifts his weight in the chair, averts his eyes, and asks no more questions.

The next time I awaken, Linden is asleep in the chair by my bed. There's an open notebook in his lap, and from where I lie I can just see the outline of a building he has started to draw. Music notes stream from the windows, along with road map lines and telephone wires.

I wonder how long he's been here. I wonder why he stays.

My head is full of drought, and I don't bother trying to sit up this time. Instead I lie in the hospital bed and stare at the muted television. They're running some story about infants. The caption reads: *Doctor believes he has duplicated virus symptoms.*

That brings me out of my haze. This story is about Vaughn. The newscaster, with her cheerful young face and windswept blond hair, can't imagine the horrible extremes the doctor has taken, the holocaust of brides and domestics and infants. All of those things had moved to the back of my subconscious when I first awoke in this hospital; there was a dull sense that something was not right. But I was too overwhelmed, too busy trying to sort out what was real, to deal with them.

"Cecily," I blurt.

Linden's eyebrows wrinkle as my voice reaches him.

"Linden. Wake up."

He draws a sharp breath, immediately alert. "What? What's the matter?"

I'm struggling to sit up, and he helps me this time, propping the pillows behind me.

I blurt out everything I can remember, not pausing to separate what I know to be real from what might be fiction. Deirdre, aged and fragile, the victim of Vaughn's ventures. Lydia dead. Rose crawling through the pipes. Cecily sneaking down to see me, and nightmares of her screaming. By the time I've recounted everything, my pulse is going rapid on the monitor and Linden is telling me to take deep breaths. Then he's looking at me like I've lost my mind again.

"Cecily will tell you," I insist. "She was there. I'm sure she was there. She probably knows a lot more than I do."

"Yes, and she should have told me," Linden says. "She didn't until it was almost too late. And I will deal with her when the time comes, but for now you need to calm down before you make yourself sick again."

I shake my head. "It can't wait." I'm pleading. "You need to get Cecily out of that house. She can't be left alone with your father."

Linden speaks slowly, deliberately. He's trying to soothe me. "I won't justify my father's actions. He nearly killed you. He didn't tell me that you'd come back, probably because he knew I would never allow testing on someone against their will." So that's it. Cecily lied to me. She never told Linden that I was in the basement. I would have expected as much from Vaughn, but maybe I overestimated my sister wife. It wouldn't be her first deception. And it's proof that Vaughn still has his hooks in her.

"He took things too far," Linden goes on. "Sometimes he doesn't realize how dangerous his treatments can be. If he'd told me, I wouldn't have agreed—"

"You don't know the half of what your father isn't telling you, Linden." I press my hands together in

frustration, and Linden opens his mouth to speak but then pauses to look at my wedding band. "No one is safe in that house!"

"You're still delirious," he says.

"Your father is a *monster*," I spit, and Linden actually winces. He gets up, steps back.

"I'm getting a doctor," he says. "You're getting hysterical." He's walking for the door, his frightened eyes trained on me as though I'll attack him. He's never seen my anger, not really. I always kept it to myself so I could earn his trust. But now I have nothing to lose, and all those months of silence come bursting out.

"He killed Jenna," I cry. "He almost killed me. You think Cecily is safe? He keeps Rose's body in the basement. I saw it! He lied about her ashes—"

"Enough!" Linden bellows, and it's so frightening coming from him that I shut my mouth. "Do not," he growls. "Do *not* bring Rose into this. Not ever. You know nothing about her. Or my father. What right do you have to say these things to me?"

He's trembling, and I'm trembling, and tears are welling in his eyes. He's looking at me with such anger, such heartbreak, that I hate myself for what I say next. "Linden, he killed your child."

Linden's face immediately changes, goes white. His expression becomes guarded and distant. His voice catches when he says, "Impossible. Bowen is perfectly fine."

"Not Bowen," I say. "Your other child. Your daughter."

I'm sorry, Deirdre; this was your secret, and I swore I'd keep it. But telling may be the only way to save any of us.

"I know Rose had a baby." I keep talking, propelled by some awful momentum. Linden's face keeps changing into all kinds of surprise and pain. "The baby died. Your father took it away, said it was a stillborn. But it had cried. It was born alive."

"Did Rose tell you this?" Linden's voice is breathless. "She was delirious with pain. She couldn't accept what had happened."

"Rose never said a word to me about it. I swear. I didn't know until after she was gone."

Linden paces the room, hyperventilating, clenching and unclenching his fists. I've never seen him like this.

"Please, Linden," I say softly. "I know you have every reason not to trust me, but this is the truth. Your father is dangerous."

"Why?" he says.

"Your father killed your daughter because she was malformed," I say.

"No—I mean. Why are you saying these things? I—" He shakes his head, disgusted with me. "Why are you being so—" He grits his teeth and can't bring himself to look at me. His voice fades when he adds, "So awful. You're awful."

When he paces toward my bed, I reach out to touch him but think better of it and withdraw.

"Every word out of your mouth," he pants, "has been a lie, hasn't it?"

"No," I say softly. "Not everything."

"What about your name?" he says. "Is your name even Rhine?"

I know I've earned his mistrust, and even still I can see him working through it, fighting the year of instinct that led him to believe me. "Yes," I say.

"How can I believe you?" he says. "How can you expect me to? I have no way of knowing what's real when it comes to you."

"Linden," I say, "my name is Rhine." Then I add, deliberately, "Ellery. I was forced to marry you against my will. I spent our marriage trying to break free so I could go home. Jenna was trying to help me, and your father knew that when he killed her. He killed your daughter and told you it was a stillborn. Cecily is in danger if she's alone with him. I'm telling you the truth."

My voice is calm, reasonable, and Linden holds his breath as he listens. Then he stares at me, his eyes suddenly bleary and colorless. He's pale and haggard. And the way his mouth twists—like he wants to sob or shout something horrible at me—makes my body ache with longing. It's an old instinct from all our nights together, so many of which were spent grieving our separate losses. I want to hold him. But I don't dare try.

And after a few moments of hair pulling and heavy breathing, my once-husband takes the horrible news I've given him and turns to leave.

"Don't you care about Cecily?" I ask. "If it were Rose, you know you'd go back."

Once I've said it, I fear it's going to make him angry. But his face goes distant, his tone practical. "I love Cecily," Linden says, "whether or not you believe it. Not in the same way I loved Rose, or you. But what should that matter? I've loved all of my wives differently."

"Not Jenna," I amend.

"Don't presume to know my relationship with Jenna," he says. "There are things you don't know about her. About us."

That's true. Jenna kept a lot of secrets, knew how to dodge questions, smile when she was filled with hatred. I'll never know the whole truth about her, but I was certain there was nothing between her and Linden. She never quite forgave him for selecting her to live when her sisters were killed.

"We had an understanding," Linden goes on. His voice is softer, maybe because he knows the pain of losing my oldest sister wife is still fresh.

I keep my voice measured, and I straighten my back. "What do you mean?"

"I watched Rose die. There was so much life in her, and then one morning her skin was bruised, she could scarcely breathe. She would cry out if I touched her."

"What—" My voice cracks. "What does that have to do with Jenna?"

"Jenna knew that she was going to die," he says. "She

didn't believe she'd ever see an antidote. And deep down I didn't believe it either. Not after what I'd seen. So we came to an understanding: When we were together, we wouldn't feel or think anything at all. In a way, it rid us of loneliness for a while."

That was what Jenna did best, wasn't it? Doing away with a man's loneliness for however long he paid for her company. There are thousands of girls like that; I've seen them spilling from Madame's tents, their faces painted like dripping China dolls. I've heard the clink of coins in glass jars as the men come and go. But there was only one Jenna, wild and kind, beautiful and deceptive. The girl Linden knew is not the girl I knew. I still feel her absence, as strong as her presence was. I still dream of her shape in the clouds, daylight burning through.

I clear my throat and look at my lap. "If you know her so well, you know she'd agree with me. Your father shouldn't be left alone with the brides you claim to love so much."

"Yes, well," Linden says, walking for the door, "she was always a cynic. You need your rest; I'll check on you in a bit."

He doesn't slam the door behind him, but it somehow feels that way.

I slump against the pillows, heartsick with guilt. In all our months of marriage, I kept Linden from getting to know me. I lied, I manipulated. But I got to know him very well. A year after Rose's death, he can hardly bring himself to say her name, much less hear that her body is still a part of his father's experiments. And I never intended to tell him about Vaughn murdering the only child Rose ever gave him. The child that could still be here, malformed but alive.

It's true that Linden has no reason to believe me. But I saw the belief in his eyes. Now he can't even look at me. But that doesn't change the fact that Deirdre and who knows how many others are trapped in that basement, dying, maybe dead. And Cecily, who tries so hard to play the grown-up, has no idea of the danger she's in. Linden is shocked by all this, and really, why wouldn't he be? I think of the moment when I learned of Rose's baby, how stunned and sickened I was. I wanted a more compassionate way to tell Linden, but it's the sort of thing that has to be blurted. There's no kind way to tell it.

I'm pinned to this bed by the wires in my arm, and there's nothing I can do but wait. Even if I could get up and find Linden, he's in no state to listen to me. If he didn't hate me for running away, he certainly hates me for what I've just said. But at least I am sure that no amount of hatred would cause him to allow his father near me. He'll come back, or he'll tell the doctors to release me.

Images move without sound on the screen. Dreary side roads, cratered buildings that vaguely resemble houses. The air is ashen from a recent explosion. The cheery young newscaster walks backward, chattering into a microphone. I recognize her as the nationwide correspondent; this particular segment airs in every state. The caption reads: *Pro-naturalist rebels disagree with antidote efforts.*

The newscaster stoops down. She's too clean and prim for such an ugly place. There's a run in her stockings, and her red heels are starting to be overtaken with mud. She's holding the microphone out to a group of young men and women who sit on the curb, looking filthy and exhausted but eager to speak.

One of them takes the microphone from her hand, and he's speaking so angrily that she leans back. The camera pans in on him, the matted hair, bloodied cheek. His eyes, though, are bright and eager. And if not for them, I wouldn't recognize him at all. Because those eyes are exactly like mine. I open my mouth to speak, and only a cry escapes. I cover my mouth, wait for the joy and fear and shock to become manageable, then try again.

"Rowan."